CLAMOUR
OF CROWS

CLAMOUR OF CROWS

RAY MERRITT

THE PERMANENT PRESS
Sag Harbor, NY 11963

For information, address:
The Permanent Press
4170 Noyac Road
Sag Harbor, NY 11963
www.thepermanentpress.com

Library of Congress Cataloging-in-Publication Data

Merritt, Raymond W., author.
    Clamour of crows / Ray Merritt.
    Sag Harbor, NY : Permanent Press, [2016]
    ISBN 978-1-57962-442-2
        1. Private investigators—New York (State)—Fiction.
    2. Murder—Investigation—Fiction. 3. Humorous fiction.
    4. Mystery fiction. I. Title.

PS3613.E77657 C58 2016
813'.6—dc23   2016010106

Printed in the United States of America

for cm&kc

MOST MEN DIE FORGOTTEN
HEROES AND VILLAINS LIVE ON
THE BEST THE WORST
AND A FEW WHO WERE BOTH

RWM

I

I awoke as the sun was gaining height. It was resplendent in its pumpkin orange, enjoying its solitary place in the sky.

Moments later, she stirred. I reached down and touched her. I heard a faint moan as she lay on her back and parted her legs. It has been eight years since the first night I brought her to my bed and she has never left.

"Good morning, love. Time to get up!"

Without hesitation, she rolled over and wagged her tail.

Nip, as she came to be called, is my constant companion. We eat, sleep, think, laugh, and mourn together. Her given name is Junipero, her namesake a Franciscan friar who was credited with settling California, at least for civilized (read white) folks.

It was a bit of a family joke.

When I was twelve, I was confirmed and, as is the tradition in the Church, I got to select my confirmation name. It was, perhaps, the first independent decision I would make in my young life. I wanted Junipero since I had the romantic but misperceived view that Father Serra was a bold adventurer who conquered the West—dashing, daring, and dedicated, attributes I wished to emulate.

Unfortunately, Jonathan Hanson Junipero Tucker just didn't wash with my mother. "Too ethnic" was her retort, in keeping with her insular bias and insecurity.

I later tried to use it with my firstborn, but my wife scotched it, insisting that he be named after his father and his father's father.

No issue, no discussion.

So when Nip came into our lives, I knew the rooster would not crow that day. I would not be thrice denied.

"Up, up, we're outta here."

While I relieved myself, Nip went through her morning scratches and stretches. Once outside, our roles reversed. The mornings were growing cooler and it seemed to be taking longer for each of us to get our joints lubricated.

The seashore was already alive with the din of its inhabitants. The October sky had lost its luster and its exclusivity and was now relegated to a pale blue backdrop for passing clouds.

Life below, however, went on without much notice.

A flock of hapless gulls trolled the water's edge for edibles as a gulp of cormorants continuously fished. The crows were busily cawing while a solitary heron stood disdainfully by. A crow's song mingled with the gentle lapping of waves, like a duet, as one sound gave way to the other.

Nip and I were accepted denizens.

"Do you know why seagulls fly over the sea? Because if they only flew over the bay, they would be called bagels!"

Nip perked up. She seemed to enjoy my jokes, at least this one, judging from her energetic tail. Quickly, however, her attention was diverted as she ran off to chase a skein of geese back to their bay haven.

I should note that we are not talking here about trekking in the San Juan Islands or the Barrier Islands of Georgia, but rather a twenty-acre tract of land on the southeast end of Long Island, just a few hours from New York City.

Fortune comes in many wrappings. A few years after I graduated from law school, I assembled an assortment of parcels using a goodly portion of my family inheritance at a point fifteen years ago when real estate in the Hamptons was considered neither a luxury nor a necessity.

Just a place to live.

This parcel did not boast of ocean beaches and dunes but rather a placid bay, a shallow inlet, some wetlands, and an abundance of woods that had probably not suffered human intrusion for a century and a half.

After I left the law firm, it was here, in what I dubbed my "Twenty Acre Wood," that I set down my roots while keeping a toehold in Manhattan. It is here I lick my wounds, pound the sand, and attempt to banish the demons that assail me.

Nip and I, as is our wont, left the seashore to traverse the back eighteen. As we progressed, the sun that assuaged me earlier became filtered and, as the sounds of the seaside receded, I became pensive, watching a crowd of crows foraging nearby.

"Nip, let me tell you the raven's tale." She didn't seem to pay attention, but I continued anyway. "The world originally was inhabited only by spirits and birds—no dogs yet. One day, a raven, perhaps out of boredom, flew high in the sky carrying a stone in her beak. You know ravens—they're the ones you like to chase. They're just big crows."

Well, almost. A raven's wings are a deeper color—more purple than black—and when it comes to feathers, they have one more. So you could say the difference is just a matter of a pinion.

Nip was not amused. She cannot abide birds. Labs are birders. It's in their blood.

"Back to the story. The raven became so tired carrying the stone, she dropped it into the ocean and it then expanded to create a land that humans and dogs could live on."

Nip was now listening intently. She wagged enthusiastically. The mention of any food does that and I sensed she was still thinking about the bagels.

Costner was onto something. Perhaps dancing with wolves is going too far, but talking to dogs is clearly an acceptable pastime, especially for lawyers. For us, talking is an occupational necessity—an acquired habit we can't seem to break. Additionally, lawyers really don't like to be interrupted. So it is no coincidence that this man's best friend cannot talk. She does, however, listen.

Back to crows. The truth is I'm drawn to them. Crows—and ravens—are complex, mythological creatures, and they deserve our attention. Last night I dreamt about crows and it was again unsettling. For the last three years, I haven't slept much, and when I do, I always dream. I think that dreams are important—not that I view them as messages from a higher being or psychic premonitions. At the risk of sounding Freudian, I do believe that they can act like photographs—mirrors to the past and windows to the future. On the other hand, perhaps they might well be nothing more than stories we tell ourselves in our sleep when the mind has nothing else to do. Nevertheless, I think it foolish to dismiss dreams.

Especially when they involve crows.

Some view crows as nothing more than menacing magpies. Hitchcock and Poe did a job on them, branding them as annoying and deceitful. That's not quite fair. They're extremely intelligent survivors.

One corvine trait seems undisputed—they never forget.

2

I was only halfway through our morning trek when my other less lovable but equally indispensable companion vibrated. The inbox read: Evan Trombley . . . 7:45 A.M. . . . Bad news.

With one touch, my Pandora's box slid open to his message— "ben baum died yesterday london. family n firm would like u to attend funeral. pls call."

Sad news delivered by e-mail most often comes unwrapped and unvarnished.

Ben Baum dead.

Bad news? More aptly, sad news. And, for me, it caused an instant eruption of emotions that were lying dormant just beneath the surface—memories replete with smiles, sadness, nostalgia, anxieties, anger, and regrets.

Dr. Seuss was right. There are indeed troubles of all kinds. Some come from ahead; some come from behind.

Mine were the latter.

"Thanks for calling back, Jonathan."

I smiled. Evan Trombley is the senior corporate partner at Winston Barr & Trombley, my former firm. He was my mentor and the only person other than my late mother who called me by my given name. To the rest of the world—human and animal—I am simply Tuck.

Evan was my "rabbi." In large-firm legalese, that is the partner who takes you on as his primary assistant. It had been on Evan's coattails that I was dragged up the ladder of success. I quickly became his straw boss—chief honcho, team leader, his thane.

He came from a mold that almost assured success: prestigious background, prodigious work ethic, independent wealth. He was in the office before the associates and left only for a client engagement. He was very smart—and great to work for. He was a somewhat respectful listener, a willing delegator, and an aggressive partisan. He was, however, aloof.

I always wondered if he had a dark side. He was at times petulant and even devious. His ambition, however, was transparent. He had a big book of business and as a result was often resented by the worker-bee partners. Apparently he was not keen on sharing the partnership pie. It took his kind of obsessiveness, however, to shepherd a client like Ben Baum and Ozone Industries—an enterprise that had grown into the Firm's largest client.

Evan never married, had no relatives, close or distant, and no known significant other. His social life seemed satisfied by serving as a decorative walker for New York's power dowagers, his emotional desires satiated by corporate deals.

If Evan had any fault, it was his singular vision. He cared only about his practice. He had no hobbies or addictions. He abhorred sports; he seemed to indulge in spirits only at client dinners.

He was the quintessential type-A corporate partner and a career cardiac candidate. His immersion in the affairs of Ozone

was almost religious. To many—both at the Firm and at Ozone—
Evan and Ben were one.

"Oh, I'm so sorry. What happened, Evan?"

Matter-of-factly he responded, "Heart attack here in
London. Poor bastard! He was alone in his room at the
Lyceum Hotel. We called the house doctor and he went in
the room and shortly thereafter advised us that he was dead."

"How is Kati taking it?" I asked. Evan was dismissive. To
him, Kati wasn't important; mistresses never were.

"His widow, Tremaine, insists on holding the service here
in London. She is already into the arrangements. Seems Kati
panicked when the doctor told us and promptly fled. Tremaine feared that the mention of Kati's presence might bring
unwelcome attention to the family—tarnish her image. She
thought that the best way to keep the top on the teapot is
to have the funeral immediately. The house doctor took care
of the removal of the body before anyone arrived. Tremaine
made the financial arrangements. His daughter, Dorothy,
asked specifically if I could have you here. Hope you don't
mind. Dorothy was most insistent."

He already knew the answer. My professional life—and,
as a consequence, my personal life—had become enmeshed in
Ozone and the Baum family. Not only was I Evan's principal
assistant on the Ozone account but I had insinuated myself
into the confidence of Ben's daughter, Dorothy, and not only
for business benefit.

I felt particularly bad for her. Being Big Ben's oldest child
must have come with heavy baggage.

It is not easy when your father's entire energy is devoted
to his business. I had faced down that demon myself with
an uneasy compromise—my wife, Alice, and I parceled out
parental duties as best we could. She was very understanding
and did a yeoman's job in covering for me.

Baum and his first wife, Maude, I understand, made no such effort when their children were young.

"I'm at the hotel suite. Funeral's on Tuesday at Trinity Church in Chelsea. Service is at ten. After the burial, there will be a reception back at the hotel. If you need anything, call my assistant, Claire."

No mention of paying my way.

Evan rang off. No thanks, no small talk, not even a good-bye. I hadn't expected more. It had been more than three years since I tendered him my resignation from the Firm. That was when we had our last conversation and it wasn't that pleasant.

Again, I felt that flare-up of emotions—some bad, some sad, some mad. For me, there had been a long hiatus from positive emotions. Instead, I just hurt. If it weren't for Nip, I would have been consumed by emptiness. So to try to manage my melancholy, I turned to her. She was—and still is—good at diverting me.

"Nip, bad news! We're going to the city and you are going to have to stay in our apartment for a few days with Ethel."

The furrow in her brow indicated her disgust. She tried the eye thing to no avail—that mock look of despair and disbelief at my impending abandonment, made ever more incanine by delivering her into the meaty clutches of smelly Mrs. Grady. Dear Ethel was originally our nanny and housekeeper, and even when her services in that regard were no longer needed I kept her on.

Unfortunately, as much as she was devoted to the kids, she was disdainful of animals, particularly as pets. She was more at home braising them than raising them. As a consequence, Ethel and Nip barely tolerated each other. They had, however, evolved a fragile truce. Ethel for her job; Nip for her food. I made it crystal clear that when Nip goes, she goes.

I could live without Mrs. Grady.

3

The flight to London was as anticipated—discomfort and boredom in the lap of luxury. I had elected to fly in the morning—for a number of reasons. First, I wanted to avoid the ceaseless inane personal queries from the Firm's leadership contingent that would attend the funeral. That delegation, I would soon discover, consisted of all six members of the Executive Committee, augmented by Charlotte Williams, the Firm's youngest estate partner. She had handled Ben Baum's estate planning. Next to Evan and me, she probably knew the Wizard, as Ben was dubbed within the Firm, best. Ben was obsessed with his legacy. He wanted to orchestrate his affairs even after he died. That necessitated long hours with Charlotte.

Flying during the day was a luxury available to the less employed. One arrived in London just in time to eat a late dinner and did not need to subsist on peanuts alone. You could get a good sleep and start the next day alert.

The Firm's lawyers would be on night flights. They were too important to spend a whole day without iPhone access and would never give up seven hours of billable time. Another and not the least important reason for day flights was personal. I was a chronic "white knuckler." I preferred to see what was out there and when necessary it was better to cringe among strangers.

"Can I take your breakfast order?" whispered a surprisingly young, succulent-looking, and sweet-sounding flight attendant. Dash the momentary urge—this was not the time or the place.

I, of course, ordered the most extravagant and least health-sensitive item—Cinnamon French Toast with Smoked Summer Sausage. The menu boasted that the toast was enhanced by cinnamon-flavored yogurt and blueberry-infused virgin maple syrup and topped with a candied-apple compote.

You should expect nothing less for 180,000 "anywhere, anytime frequent flyer miles," which for the uninitiated means doubling the number of miles required if you don't want to fly from New York to Dallas with a four-hour layover to pick up your one-stop flight to Heathrow. That was underscored when my breakfast arrived in a form that suggested that our pilot, Mike, as he was introduced, had brought it on board in his back pocket.

Pushing the panini-style pancake aside, I satiated my appetite with the contents of the little plastic containers of Land O'Lakes butter and Knott's Berry Farm red raspberry preserves. At least I knew I could trust them. They helped me pace myself until my universal favorite—the mixed nuts medley—arrived.

My mind wandered. One of the pastimes I had embraced in the past three years to take the edge off loneliness was venery, or as it is more properly called, the "venereal game." In the fifteenth century, a time less hectic, English gentlemen—not my ancestors—spent much of their leisure coining fanciful or descriptive terms for groups of animals that inhabited their land: a gaggle of geese; a herd of horses; a waddle of ducks. Published lists of such terms had the status of social primers and had to be memorized and adhered to by members of the upper class. They got much more imaginative as time went on. An army of ants; a bale of turtles; a brace of bucks; a skulk of foxes.

I learned the collective noun for every creature that called Twenty Acres home.

Lately I had moved away from collective animal nouns, having exhausted the search for those I might come in contact with, and decided to create a compendium of collectives for the human species. There were already many well known—a coven of witches, a bevy of girls, a gang of thieves, a jam of tarts. And others less known—a blush of boys, a giggle of beauties. But I wanted to coin some myself, only to find that others had beaten me. A bore of classmates, a trial of associates—perhaps tribulation would be better—a ponder of philosophers. So I turned my attention to the medical field—a brace of orthopedists; a joint of osteopaths; a rash of dermatologists; a stream of urologists; a vise of gynecologists. Then I turned back on my own confreres. An augmentation of attorneys; a balance of accountants; a fraud of auditors: a collection of clients.

No hint of condescension there.

Any good lawyer knows to whom to pay deference and I was coming to pay respect to one of the best of them. A jolt of turbulence brought me out of my reverie and back to the matter at hand.

I was a bit flattered, but not surprised, by the invite. Ben was a decent man. I had not known his first wife, Maude. She died shortly after their twin boys perished in a boating accident at their family's summer retreat in Michigan. Ben was left to care for his remaining son and daughter. As I understood it, he stanched the pain of his losses by devoting all of his energy to creating his empire. Starting with a small electronics operation, he parlayed the company through a string of astute acquisitions into a national electronics chain with more than 1,800 outlets.

It was when he took that enterprise public that I joined the Firm and it was that transaction that propelled him into client dominance and me into Evan's fold. Even though I was only on the third-tier team, I became within weeks the "oil canner," the one who made sure that the disparate teams—tax, securities, corporate, estate planning, and due diligence—were in sync and that the deal was moving smoothly. Thirty lawyers from within the Firm and a swarm of outside consultants who brought patent, trademark, and intellectual property expertise were needed to complete the transaction. With a small dose of manners, a large amount of moxie, and some considerable sucking up, I was able to survive until the deal closed.

After that there was no stopping Baum. Using stock instead of cash, Ozone became a rapacious acquirer and a darling of the market. Within a few years, the company amassed an asset base of over four billion dollars and its success accelerated my rise to partnership, for I was Evan's boy.

The rest was a short and painful history—climaxed by my self-imposed exile to Twenty Acres. All those memories were beginning to gurgle up like bad wine and no digestive was going to quell them.

At the edge of my eyes, I noticed that the video screens on the plane registered "Estimated Flying Time 1:38 hours, altitude 37,000 feet." The little airplane icon was aimed at London with Grindavik and Reykjavik in the upper corner.

I was having second thoughts.

Maybe I should be going to Iceland.

Often the unknown is better than the known.

In London I was staying at the Sloan Club, a small residential club nestled in Chelsea. Formerly a service officers' facility catering to women in the armed forces during World War II, it later morphed into the Helena Club for Ladies under the tutelage of Princess Marie Louise. By the late seventies, it was liberated—men were admitted—and it became simply the Sloan Club.

It was one of the few places where I could be sure of not having to bump into, or bunk with, any of my former partners. The rooms were not Wi-Fied; there were no minibars.

Unacceptable for the twenty-first-century law practitioner.

The club consisted of a four-story red brick building with facades festooned with gables and gargoyles. Behind its centuries-old exterior, extensive refurbishing had spawned a number of modestly appointed rooms, suites, and apartments.

The management was proud of its atmosphere, which belonged to an earlier, more charming era. The most endearing member of the club's staff was General Dogsbody, better known as Badger the Beagle. Badger came from a long line of soldiers. Beagles were bred originally as desert scouts and performed admirably in the Boer Wars, providing early alerts to Zulu attacks. For that, they were awarded the right to smoke—the only breed (of dogs) to gain that distinction.

Fortunately for them, they keep dropping the pipe.

Having Badger to myself was yet another reason I liked day flights. You arrived during the dinner hour when almost all the other guests were out of the hotel, so you had the beagle all to yourself.

Badger's domain was the club's public rooms. His favorite pastime when he wasn't officially greeting new guests at the front door was policing the sitting room during afternoon tea, where he brazenly helped himself to tea cakes. It was

represented that he did so with no thought of his own pleasure, but to fulfill his canine duties of ensuring that only the
best remained to be served.

I was jolted as soon as I entered and came face-to-face
with an elegantly framed copy of Badger's obituary.

His death hung in the air, fitting for this trip.

4

Ambien helped me get to sleep.

It did not, however, prevent me from dreaming.

Crows again, gathering with a purpose known only to them. Two of the more fascinating animal encounters I've had at Twenty Acres involve crows. One was a mating ritual in early spring. It had snowed the evening before we came upon them as they were making their match. The male, I presume— there is apparently no way to tell other than by close physical examination—strutted and fluttered and then slid down a small embankment; the female dispensed with her preening and followed suit. They then did it together repeatedly, very much in sync. Having tired of that, they flew together again in paired formation for what seemed like an hour, finally flying off for what would be a lifetime together.

Forevermore.

They soon became almost our house pets—expecting and often demanding alms, in the form of food bits. We named them Heckle and Jeckle—not original but apt.

The other encounter was more somber. Several years ago, about this time of year, I went for a long solo walk. Alice, the kids, and Nip were off on errands. It was a bleak day. A muster of crows had gathered in a clearing and cawed raucously for a long time. I stopped to watch. When the cacophony ceased, silence took over except for the cawing of one crow. Then, as if on cue, they all took off—leaving a corpse to nature. I assumed it was the soloist's mate.

Together nevermore.

Huntsmen coined many collective nouns for a muster of crows or ravens—a conspiracy, a hover, a mob, a clamour, a murder, and an unkindness. They have a gravitas about them that you don't find in the more flighty and decorative members of their species.

My dream did not seem to have a point, or perhaps I awoke prematurely. The clock read 9:05. I bolted up. Funeral at ten. Holy Trinity! Holy shit! It would be criminal to be late, and with lightning speed, I wasn't.

The parish church of the Holy Trinity is a Chelsea landmark—an imposing, if not inspiring, edifice. The architect who designed it for the Earl of Cadogan at the close of the nineteenth century seemed to freely incorporate French, Gothic, and Renaissance influences.

At least that is what the bronze plaque on the wall indicated.

I read it intently, as a way to catch my breath.

Entering the vestibule, I came upon a receiving line, which consisted of Evan, then Dorothy, and finally the grieving wife, Tremaine. Peter Abelard, the executive director of the Baum Foundation, and a close confidant of Tremaine's, stood a few feet away, ever watchful of his patroness. Dorothy's eyes were weary and raw but welcoming. Tremaine's were hidden behind her designer sunglasses.

Strategic for her; she was never a good actress.

Lady Tremaine, as she was maliciously nicknamed by those who had to do her bidding, was clearly the event coordinator. It was abundantly evident that she was going to wrap her dearly departed in enough pomp, piety, and pretense to dissipate the sordid stench surrounding his demise.

A fortune of flowers brought life to the century-old entrance. A profusion of candles softened the somber interior. The line of mourners moved steadily along, with the greeters giving rote thanks for each person's presence.

I took the most inconspicuous seat I could find. It turned out to be a good one for viewing those assembled to pay their respects and fealty.

I was surprised at the size of the crowd. The Firm's attendees, led by Evan, consisted of all of the Executive Committee plus four lawyers from the London office and Charlotte. Across the aisle was a large contingent from the Ozone board, as well as a sprinkling of company executives whose faces were familiar, led by Luc Grogaman, Ozone's second-in-command and heir apparent to Ben's throne. One person missing was Ben's son, Leo. Perhaps it was thought too much for him.

The rest of the audience appeared from their sartorial elegance to be Tremaine's London support group. She was born here and in fact met Ben here at a charity event that Ozone had underwritten.

All the women were in traditional ceremonial garb—black dresses adorned with diamonds and furs. The gems struggled to glitter in the muted light but the furs worked well to take the chill out of the church. Their escorts sat in uncomfortable silence. It clearly wasn't their thing.

Kati Krkavec, I was later told, was not there.

In the back of the church, anonymous onlookers filled the seats. Funerals always seem to attract strangers. In a way, modern-day death rituals are the original reality show—a spectacle played out with pomp where the participants often manifest openly emotions normally submerged. Positioned attentively, kneeling on needlepointed cushions, these voyeurs seemed wrapped in collective relief.

Perhaps here but for the grace of God they might well have lain.

A solemn choir and a sonorous organ attempted to project over the collected beats of heavy hearts. They easily succeeded.

The minister rose and spoke:

> *Death is nothing at all.*
> *I have only slipped away into the next room.*
> *I am I and you are you.*
>
> *Whatever we were to each other, we still are.*
> *Wear no forced air of solemnity or sorrow.*
> *Smile, work, think of me.*
>
> *Let my name be the household word*
> *that it always was.*
>
> *Let it be spoken without affect,*
> *without the trace of a dark shadow on it.*
>
> *Life means all that it ever meant.*
> *There must be an unbroken continuity.*
> *I am with you, somewhere very near,*
> *just around the corner.*
>
> *All is well. I will bask in the grasp of my friends*
> *and the lovingness of my children.*

That sermon, he advised, was penned by the canon of Saint Paul's Cathedral well over one hundred years ago.

Intentionally generic; unwittingly on target.

Tremaine did not seem to appreciate it.

Ministers often get it right. If religion is the human response to inevitable death, then it's understandable that funerals are the mainspring of the church's activity.

All of this was getting me edgy.

Perhaps death brought closure for the deceased, but not for those left behind. For them it often left a festering wound.

I could attest to that.

Evan then mounted the podium and delivered a well-crafted eulogy, gamely touching on all the proper politic points. Those of us who knew Ben felt it was a belated plea for his defense delivered after the verdict was in.

Following the minister's somber closing prayer, the cortege of mourners began their exit. As they passed by, it only underscored my implacable abhorrence of this death ritual. Clearly this event was more for the vanity of the living than for the honor of the dead.

I was right three years ago in forgoing the funerals.

After a few perfunctory salutations to those who lingered on the steps outside the church, I invited Charlotte back to my place for tea. She quickly accepted. Both of us were apparently looking to avoid Tremaine's reception.

Charlotte Williams was one of the few partners whose company I missed. She was my contemporary and had served all my clients' trust and estate needs. And she did it very well.

Trust and estate lawyers, however, are a breed apart. While the rest of us turn to the sports page or the business section with our morning java, they scour the obits, looking for opportunities.

They are, however, a relatively kindly lot. The one practice group that makes house calls. They ooze tact and diplomacy. Since, as a rule, estate planning is a loss leader, they rarely work their way into the Firm's power ranks, especially if they are female. They simply make too little rain, and rainmaking—fee generation—is essential for a power position. As a result, they often have less agenda and more transparency. You know where you stand with them. And, since the corporate lawyers are in a true sense their clients, they are invariably accommodating and pleasant to us.

Charlotte was no exception; she exuded empathy.

Additionally she was good at contemplating life's fragility. She understood powerful clients' need for validation after death, if only through the carefully constructed distribution of their wealth.

For moguls like the Wiz, wealth transfer was often their greatest gift to their progeny, friends, and retainers. Correctly done, it would wash away the sins of the deceased or at least deter those left behind from despoiling their grave.

Clients love to create testamentary plans so complex that it secures their progeny in a tightly woven family web—all to create a more perfect life for those they leave behind.

Charlotte spun their webs.

I remember spending many hours after work with her and some of our cohorts contemplating life with the aid of some liquid spirits. Charlotte was always amused by men's preoccupation with death. It seemed to appeal to her slightly arachnid side, especially when mellowed by merlot.

She would start those conversations with a challenge. There was for her only one question: "Are you afraid to die?" The men in the group would muster enough false bravado to proclaim not.

"If not," she retorted, with irrefutable logic, "then death is sad but acceptable. If you are," she warned with the subtle dramatics of a darker voice, "it is unimaginable and unacceptable."

She would then take another sip from her glass as she wryly observed our individual discomfort. She would not let us squirm too long.

"That leads us to the ultimate question. What implications does that have for the meaning of life?"

At that point, things got too heavy for her male audience and we would force a change of subject and trade Firm gossip.

I thought back to the time Charlotte reviewed Ben's estate planning with me. She confirmed after hours upon hours of planning sessions with Ben that he was no exception. He viewed death as nothing more than an insidiously dirty trick. Ben had told her that, for him, death was not a segue to a better place—for life was the end, not a means; death was an atrocity.

5

Charlotte and I settled into a corner of the Sloan Club's public rooms. Plush couches of paisley framed a well-worn table that comfortably held a classic afternoon tea setting, complete with cakes. It still exuded warmth, but it was missing Badger.

A subtle unease settled between us.

I took the initiative. "What did you think of the service?"

She took the lure, and from there on, things went better.

"Well, it was the Lady T show, for sure!"

I could sense the feline in her taking over.

"You were probably oblivious to the high priestess's garb. That dress that covered her very expensive breasts was Narciso Rodriguez. And the jacket Chanel. The shoes Manolo Blahnik. Gucci sunglasses and a Hermès Kelly handbag. Just the right touch, right down to the diamonds, probably borrowed from Winston. They set off her Cartier watch to a T. She always feels more secure when she's properly architected. This was her coming-out party for membership in the Sisterhood of Gilded Widows."

She kept going.

"No Hindu suttee for her to throw herself on. She had enough flowers, music, bells, and candles to placate any spirits that might be nosing around. She is no 'Monaco Maiden,' but in all fairness Ben was no prince. Before the Wiz, she was at best D-list—all attitude and implants. Now she has bankability!"

"Smart lady!" I interjected.

"And she had the comfort of her friends. They came in enough mink to deplete the whole farm. Their men seemed ill at ease. I'll bet many of them knew Tremaine quite well. Before snaring Ben, she was known as the 'London Open.'"

Her claws were now fully extended. No sweet purrs here. I half expected her to cough up a hair ball on the couch.

"What got your tail, girl?"

"I'm sorry. That woman really gets to me. When she got news of Ben's death, she had her lawyer, Jasper de Vil, call me. You remember him?"

"He repped her when you did the prenup. I remember him as particularly obnoxious."

"One and the same. He called shortly after Ben died to inform me that Tremaine would prefer for his firm to handle the administration of the estate. When I advised him that it wasn't her call—that Ben had named Evan the executor—he all but accused me of being conflicted. The conversation did not end well."

Charlotte sensed that she had gotten a bit too spiky so she crossed her legs, smoothed her hem, and delicately picked off a few errant balls of wool, buying just enough time to gain her composure.

"Poor Dorothy," she volunteered, changing the subject. "She seems to be in so much pain, but she is handling herself, as you would expect, with dignity. She adored her father. Must be gruesome to share the cortege with that grass widow. By the way, Dorothy is quite anxious to talk to you. She called me twice to confirm you were coming. What's up?"

I answered honestly. "No idea."

"Tuck, let's get back to you."

I knew I couldn't avoid the subject for long, especially with her.

"It's really good to see you. I've missed you. Can't tell you the number of times I've thought of calling you, but I was afraid of intruding on your mourning."

"I'm all right. I'm not so much grieving as I am healing." That was my preferred stock response, even though it sounded a bit canned.

"What are you up to?" she inquired.

"Not much. I work around my property. I really have little to do and no time to accomplish it."

A feeble attempt at humor on my part.

"I'm glad you're here, Tuck. As you can imagine, this is a big to-do at the Firm. Evan is in full battle gear. He's assembled a transition task force. Put me on exclusive duty until the Will is probated. I'm surprised he let me come over here for the service."

"I am too. Evan likes to be center stage and in control. I'm impressed that he's letting you share confidences with the bereaved."

"Well, it's a big deal for him. His best friend who runs the Firm's biggest client dies! The king is dead; long live the new king—except no one knows for sure who that will be. Did you hear that Luc Grogaman is interim CEO? Evan is working him hard. He's a smart guy but he's no Wizard. Those are mighty big red slippers to fill!"

"Silver, don't you mean?"

She smiled.

I didn't have to explain.

Charlotte's mood then got a bit pensive.

"Tuck, what do you think the Ozone board will do? Some of the corporate partners think they might go outside the company and bring in a seasoned veteran to fill Ben's shoes. They have to be worried about the market's reaction to Ben's death. The hedgehogs are snorting. Their funds have large positions in Ozone. They may be more interested in a quick profit than the long haul."

"No idea," I responded, indifferently.

That, I had to admit, would be a blow to Evan. He had always assumed that Grogaman would be the successor and that, if anything, his influence would grow.

"Does the Will say anything about that?" I asked.

"Well, yes, in a way, but it is complicated. Can't really go into it. You understand."

That brought me up a bit short. I had sort of presumed that I could still climb under the tent of client confidences. But in reality, I could not. I had resigned my partnership. If anything, I was now only a client and Charlotte was my lawyer. After the accident, she handled all the necessary details. She arranged for my family's bodies to be returned, probated my wife's estate, and changed all the account names. She even worked out the settlement with the insurance company. She handled everything but the funerals.

There were none.

Sensing that I was slipping back into sad memories, she intervened.

"Tuck, how are you REALLY? I must say you're looking quite studly," she uttered without the slightest blush. "Time off is wearing well on you."

I reddened, perhaps for the first time in years.

"Reports have it you're spending your time as Dr. Doo-little with your dog Lucky."

"Not quite," I smiled.

"More like Dr. Snooze Little and my dog is indeed lucky, but her name is Nip and I do spend most of my time with her. She's the only living being who truly knew Alice and the kids.

"Really, I'm OK. Still can't emotionally process the accident. I should know by now that it wasn't my fault, but I haven't been able to convince myself of that. I'm just not a good advocate when it matters. Guess that's why I never wanted to be a litigator."

"Tuck, you're being evasive. You should talk about it, at least to me—we were tight and remember, I *am* your lawyer!"

She had me there.

"You want the short version of my life story. Well, here it is. Like all of us, I was born bald with no control over my bladder and that is how I'll die. But in between it's been rocky. Truthfully, I also think I was born scared, which I par-layed into a touch of hypochondria, a delicate constitution, a hefty dose of insecurity, recurring bouts of self-doubt and a constant yearning for significance. I think that's what drove me to succeed in the marines and the Firm—both of which I rather quickly exited."

"You're not being fair to yourself," Charlotte protested. "After the accident, who could blame you for taking time off?"

"I didn't take time off. I quit. The revulsion that was fes-tering in me about the concessions one makes in the practice came to a head. I wanted out—and Twenty Acres called me home. The truth is I love nature. In some ways I worship it. I find more in the natural than in the spiritual. It's the only place where life and death exist in harmony. Leaves are born green. They quickly mature into a flourish of colors and return when they fade to feed the earth that nourished them. It all fits. Twenty Acres is my place of worship. I'm the high priest and Nip is my acolyte. I didn't know peace until I heard the dirge of crickets at the end of summer mingle with the sounds of evening and the morning serenade of sparrows followed by the rap of mockingbirds. They are the pipers at the gates of my new dawn.

"Yes, it has made me more than a little mad. And I'm haunted by the shadows of my old self. Jung would have a field day with me. Like Thoreau, I've become celibate, abstinent, obstinate, and increasingly distrustful of people. I remember something I once read. Tolkien, I think. 'Little by little one travels far.' I may be slow, but I am on my way. In truth, it's not working out as well as I hoped. I fill the time with just existing. Nip and I are fully occupied during the day with the necessities and niceties of living. At night, though, Nip abandons me to sleep. I don't have that luxury. I'm then solo. So I fill the night with books. I keep company with Conrad, Kipling, Salinger, and Hemingway. I've reread *Moby Dick* three times. I'm fixated on Ahab's quest for revenge. In some respect, those stories soothe the canker of my loss, but recently I have become restive. I fear they are no longer enough."

Charlotte sat upright, for once speechless. Our tea was finished and she sensed that our conversation was over. Hugging me—perhaps a little too long—she gently kissed my cheek.

I hadn't felt a woman's touch in three years. I longed for it, yet I was repelled by it. I must admit, though, she was easy on the eyes. I had forgotten how attractive she could be.

"Got to go back," she said. "Maybe I can catch the end of the reception."

I was beginning to sense that this trip was a mistake.

As I walked her to the door, the concierge handed me an envelope. It was a note from Dorothy.

Dearest Tuck, I so want to talk to you about a very personal issue. Unfortunately, as you might expect, my brother, Leo, is a wreck. His agitation level is very high. I'm taking him back to Paris immediately after the service. We're not going to the reception. Please come to Paris. It's an easy trip. We could dine tomorrow. It's very important to me and Dad.

It was signed simply "*Dorothy.*"

6

So here I was hurtling—literally and figuratively—on the Eurostar under the English Channel to Paris. I had blown off the reception. I'm sure I wasn't missed. Having left Saint Pancras Station in London less than two hours before, I was about to arrive at Gare du Nord in the center of Paris.

It seemed the gait of my life was picking up.

Maybe it was time.

I was being drawn back into a world I had walked away from and I put up no resistance. When a client calls, I still come running. Dorothy's note spoke softly with desperation. Somehow she knew I wouldn't refuse.

Luckily the concierge at the Sloan Club was able to get me room 4A at the Hôtel de Seine, although he could hardly disguise his disdain. It wasn't the Ritz or the Plaza Athénée.

For me, it was much better.

That was where Alice and I had stayed on our first trip to Paris. We had gotten to know that room very well. The bed small enough to invite contact; the tub big enough to bathe a small pony. We didn't need much more. We got a lot of use out of both.

It felt good to be back. I awoke early, even though I was still on New York time. Having twelve hours until dinner proved an unexpected dividend.

I could take my time. The little patisserie was still there. *Pave d'Alsace, palmiers, croissants aux amandes.* Those also were still there. I tried them all. From there the route I took was lined with old friends.

The street sweepers were out in their kelly-green garb, armed with the traditional branch and twig brooms, except now they were crafted from plastic. The French will only go so far to accommodate progress.

The one constant in Paris is the pigeons—often a child's first playmate and an octogenarian's last. They have always been well regarded and well fed by young and old. I sat and watched a parcel of them. If you take the time, you'll notice how luminous they are in their silky shades of gray, black, and white, with a touch of emerald green on their backs.

It didn't take long before I crossed the river and came upon the Jardin des Tuileries. That was where I most wanted to be. The gardens have their own dark history. The palace seemed hexed. Catherine de' Medici abandoned it, Louis XVI was imprisoned there, and during the Revolution, the people of Paris burned it.

I sat there and took it all in.

Lovers meeting and tourists basking in its ether. Parisians short-cutting through the park, indifferent to its treasures. It was the children, however, that interested me the most, particularly a group of boys who were chasing a kit of pigeons they would never catch. When that lost its allure, they turned and chased each other.

It was here in this ancient park, among the bronze goddesses, that I proposed—just twenty steps from the Porte des Lions, where a lion protected the entrance while a lioness guarded his back.

A fitting allusion for a young lawyer's wife.

I remember Alice's amusing response to my marriage invitation. It was a perfect acceptance.

"If you want someone to make you a soufflé, marry a cook's daughter. If you want someone to enhance your career, marry an heiress. If you want someone to light your candle every night, marry the candlemaker's daughter. But if you want someone who will love you and be your best friend and protect your pride—then I'm the one."

Case closed.

Verdict: lifelong enchantment.

Promises made but never fulfilled.

7

Paris is a city for all kinds of lovers, book lovers included. And Alice and I would qualify for that group too. I meandered down Saint-Germain-des-Prés, where Sartre, de Beauvoir, and Camus once lived. I had my croissant and coffee at Café de Flore, where James Baldwin once held court. From there I went west on Rue Saint-Benoît where Marguerite Duras had her flings.

I remember she once wrote, "The best way to fill time is to waste it."

I was good at that.

I slowly wandered back past Notre Dame, dallying at the art stalls, watching the strollers. It was good for me to be anonymous among people. Without design, I found myself at the Café Palette for a late lunch.

It was Alice's favorite.

Nothing had changed. The black-vested waiters had not lost their swagger nor the roses their bloom. Yellow-and-black rattan wove perfect mosaics into the chairs, which circled the age-worn tobacco-stained tables like petals on a sunflower. Together they cascaded onto the sidewalks, under the watchful cover of expansive green umbrellas. Life here seemed in order—unchanged, unrushed. One had only to sit and watch.

Flounces of skirts decorated legs that were made for more than walking and women's eyes seemed to do so much more than look. These women were no slaves to fashion; they seemed rather to dominate it. Almost all wore scarves. No one does scarves like the French women do. At that time of year, they are worn defiantly to fend off *le mistral.*

Americans have only one name for wind. In France, there are many: *l'autan, la bise, la tramontane,* and *le zephyr.* And these various winds are often blamed for all sorts of maladies— *la grippe,* the common cold, flu, menstrual cramps, and bad sex.

Hence, the scarf. It serves like a cross in front of a vampire.

Hours passed uncounted. Fortunately, my rendezvous with Dorothy was close by. As I approached the restaurant, I saw her striding with a determined gait—striking in her gray suit and signature silver shoes. Her sunglasses were the only telltale sign of mourning.

We exchanged sincere greetings, each expressing sorrow for our respective losses. Dorothy had obviously preordered our dinner. The pinot noir was decanted long before we got there; an iced tea was set at my side. She had remembered that I was addicted. Dorothy was classy in every sense of the word.

She had traditional features—fine cheekbones, a perfectly chiseled nose—was of medium height and had what appeared to be a well-proportioned physique. Her clothes made a quiet statement. It was her style never to wear any jewelry, except I noticed a new adornment—a silver friendship ring, which she twisted in perpetual circles as we talked. She might not be trophy material, but she would never tarnish. We had not been close friends, but were in many ways kindred spirits.

I admired Dorothy's sense of place within Ben's kingdom. She was his oldest child. I remembered that she and her family grew up in Schenectady, New York, and summered in Macatawa Park in Michigan. It was there that her twin brothers, Woody and Wally, had died. A rafting accident. Her mother shortly thereafter took her own life, leaving Dorothy as Leo's surrogate mother. Leo, I came to understand, was autistic and, throughout his life, had serious developmental challenges. Dorothy had to learn to cope and compensate very early. I understood better why she seemed to crave order in her life.

I wondered if she'd ever had a childhood.

"Tuck, I can't tell you how much I appreciate your coming here. I had intended to speak with you in London, but Leo was very distressed. You know he was in London when his father died."

"I'm so sorry for him. Where is he now?"

"He's with my partner, Eloise. She is wonderful with him. We have him heavily medicated right now. He is still quite agitated."

This conversation was difficult for me. Just a month before the car accident, we were advised by our pediatrician that JJ, our son, was an "Aspie." We were surprised to learn that this form of autism was not that uncommon. I remember Alice's mantra. "He's not disabled! He is just differently abled!" Fortunately, JJ was on the high end of the spectrum, meaning he could function moderately well socially.

"He's destined for great things," my lioness roared. She was fierce when it came to her pride.

Dorothy saw I was drifting and she reinserted herself. Dispensing with Parisian etiquette not to discuss matters of substance before dessert, she rushed into why she had reached out to me.

"The last three months have been very difficult. Few people know what I'm about to tell you. Ben was dying. He was battling an assortment of ills, including cancer. The doctors thought he might have no more than three, perhaps four, years before it would take him. He understood that and wanted to get his affairs in order while he could still be effective. I don't know all the things that were weighing him down, but he hinted at what he called 'dark stains' that had to be removed. He was not worried about me. He knew I was secure personally and financially. He had several years ago introduced me to his Swiss banker, Andreas Amaroso. He had established an account at UBS and he said it was more than enough to care for our needs—Leo's and mine. On the day Dad died, he told me he would give me access to another Zurich bank where he had a safe-deposit box. I would need to have the account number and a key. We subsequently got into a rather heated family discussion. I never got the number or the key. I expect they are in his Will papers. It all seems rather overcomplicated so I wanted your advice. I know nothing about numbered accounts and safe-deposit boxes and would not be comfortable dealing with those bankers. Dad's main concern was who would take my place in protecting Leo if something should happen to me. He did not want it to be my partner, Eloise, for a host of reasons I'd rather not go into."

She took a deep breath, squirreling up an additional dash of nerve.

"I would like to exercise my power of appointment under any trusts or accounts that Dad set up and name you as my successor should I be unable to serve at any time," she blurted out.

"I'm flattered."

An awkward response but it bought me time.

A dysfunctional widower and a career griever seemed an odd choice for a guardian. Who was I kidding? An unattached attorney who knew her family and their fortune very well and who had become an empathetic student of autism. A perfect choice.

"Hopefully, you'll never have to act. I intend to live a long life, but I won't be at ease until I know that Leo will be cared for should Eloise and I not be around."

I immediately agreed and punctuated it with a smile. With that, the stiffness between us dissolved, and we both seemed to relax as our emotional muscles eased. Perhaps the wine helped too.

The meal arrived without cue. I only picked at the first course—*dodine de lapin en gelée*. Thumper burgers made me queasy. Twenty Acres boasted only a small wrack of rabbits. Seems foxes were keeping the rabbit population in check. I couldn't possibly eat one. I did not want, however, to embarrass her, so I nibbled at the pickled vegetables that surrounded the fallen hare.

The *entrecôte béarnaise* was more inviting. I didn't know any cows. I devoured it and even finished the cauliflower.

"Tuck, it's not my business, but I can sense your pain. I know how hard it is to lose family from an accident. When my brothers drowned, I blamed myself. I should have gone with them, but I was in the midst of *Alice in Wonderland* and couldn't be bothered with earthly things. It took me a long time before I understood that blame is just a hair shirt you wear to deflect the pain. You come to realize when it's time to take it off. Maybe your time is here."

After a pause to run her hand through her hair, she continued.

"You know my mother took her own life. For the longest time I blamed her for doing so. She left me and crushed Dad.

But with time, I came to see that sometimes life is too hard and I forgave her. You will come to terms and forgive too."

"It should only be that easy," I murmured to myself, although I had never thought of it quite that way. There might be something to it.

Alice and I had bickered at Disney World. She complained that I had one ear permanently affixed to my cell phone. A common complaint but this time with good reason. This was supposed to be our family vacation—clients not invited. Yet I resented the accusation. This was how I made our living. I was working on the biggest deal of my career.

JJ's diagnosis had made both of us particularly prickly. We spat venom at each other.

By the end of the trip, we were just going through the motions. I was becoming anxious about the car trek back to New York—three days and two nights with the four of us in our van and little opportunity to conduct business with two overly excited and very tired kids overdue for major meltdowns.

When a crisis call came from Evan, just as we bade good-bye to Mickey and Minnie, I convinced myself I had to bolt and fly back solo. Alice's response was brittle, but a relief.

"Fine! You're not good company right now. Even the kids are starting to call you Grumpy! Besides, I'm a better driver."

That final dig was intended to hurt.

Two hours later, Alice, JJ, and Lilli were dead, crushed against a concrete pillar in an underpass on I-95 North. An SUV had slid into their lane, according to eyewitnesses. It never bothered to stop.

"Dorothy," I responded with more than a trace of resignation, "I know what you're saying. I tell myself that all the time. But if I were driving, their fate might have been different. Perhaps we would not have been at that underpass as the SUV came through. I'm a much slower driver. It was my place in the order of things to protect my family and I didn't."

What I declined to add was that my ambition and insecurity had deflected me.

Dorothy reached across and put her hands over mine.

It was more comforting than any words she could have uttered.

It was the first time that I had verbalized the core of my grief. I had been far too possessive about my loss to share it with anyone. I'd always felt that to do so would bring to anyone who touched it a bit of my darkness.

From that point on, I was sure Dorothy and I were indeed kindred spirits. At least kindred in our grief. She was the first being other than Nip with whom I was not on guard. It felt good.

"Are you seeing anyone?" she queried, to my surprise.

"No."

That was my stock response—a Pavlovian one, intended to cut off any further inquiry in that direction. In fact, it was also an accurate one. People think that there is a shelf life to grief.

"Well, there will be someone someday, Tuck. Trust me, I know," Dorothy proclaimed.

I nodded a polite assent.

I had no desire to release myself from melancholy. Solitude was my penance and also my balm for what I sensed was a chronic condition, and having Nip helped the past, the present, and the future all meld together. Nip was all the comfort I needed for now.

In truth, it was inconceivable that there was someone else for me. I sabotage every budding relationship that threatens to make Alice and the kids part of an older version of me—a footnote in my biography.

Finally the conversation evolved into mellow chatter about her job as Ozone's president of European operations, the company's recent successes, her partner, Eloise, and other equally safe subjects. Ben was not discussed at all.

Our meal ended and we promised to keep in touch.

8

The return from Paris proved painless. A perfect flight. Mrs. Grady met me at the airport with Nip in the car. She gave me the keys; I gave her the laundry. Within two hours, Nip and I were home, fed, and in bed.

Things felt good again.

That night I dreamt of the white deer, the most prized and respected inhabitant of Twenty Acres. She was a delicate creature, having been born without body pigment. For an animal, whether it's a predator or prey, this condition is a handicap. Unpigmented irises make strikingly beautiful white-pink eyes, but result in very poor vision. She was, nevertheless, beautiful, enigmatic, and elusive. She rarely ventured close by.

Perhaps nature warned her that she was not inconspicuous.

Our little Lilli had christened the albino doe Snowdrop. Whenever we took family walks, we were always alert for Snowdrop and the first one to see her got to select dinner that night.

That meant pizza, three out of four times.

This was not a good way to start the day, for the tale of Snowdrop is not a happy story. One day our family went out to gather acorns, chestnuts, and fallen leaves for the Thanksgiving table. I remember it was a picture-perfect autumn day. JJ was the first to spot her, proclaiming delightedly, "Snowdrop! She's sleeping."

Nip sensed her too, but her reaction was much more guarded.

The fur on her back rose, accompanied by a low growling murmur. She raced off toward Snowdrop, with JJ and Lilli in close pursuit. Nip then did something very unusual. She ran with manic energy around in circles three times and then lowered herself in a suppliant position.

It was then I saw the arrow in Snowdrop's haunches. She had been decapitated—her head a hunter's trophy. Alice gathered JJ and Lilli in her arms. I covered Snowdrop's bleeding neck with my sweater. It was the only thing I could think of. I knelt down and touched her. She was still warm. I remained still until I felt a rattle in her stomach. I would later learn she was pregnant and the last of her twins had just expired.

That was the children's first exposure to the death of somebody they loved. It would be their last. Three weeks later they too would be dead, also at the hands of an unknown killer.

I could not bring myself to walk the woods that morning after dreaming of Snowdrop.

I wanted no part of Twenty Acres that day.

Nip is best at licking wounds and that's what I needed most. Whenever my mood turns down, a wag of her tail or a stutter-step dance can turn up the edges of my lips.

"Nip," I said, "I'm not trying to change my lot in life; I'm just trying to understand it. I know there's a life out there. I glimpsed it between the cracks when I was away. I saw a bit of the world I left behind, but I am still drawn back to this place and my time here with them. I would rather live here with their memories than live elsewhere without them. You are all I have left."

9

The phone rang as I was preparing breakfast. I still don't have the kind of land line that identifies the caller, so I was taken aback when the friendly voice on the other end was Lutwidge Dodgson Barr, known to his friends as Wiggie. To the rest of us he is known simply as "sir." He is the Firm's reigning WASP and the chairman of the Executive Committee, a position he has held since well before I joined the Firm.

I have never quite understood the deference mongrels bestow on thoroughbreds, but I'm observant and he clearly fit the template. Wiggie traced his ancestors all the way back to England and had the gilded portraits on his stair walls to prove it. His manor in Bronxville seemed imported from another time. He welcomed all Firm lawyers there every Christmas season. Attendance was mandatory.

"Good morning. Sorry to disturb you, but a matter of significance to the Firm and Ozone has cropped up. The Executive Committee would like to discuss it with you. We need to impose on you and have you join us at your earliest convenience."

"Well," I began, rather awkwardly, "what is the nature of the matter?"

"It's exceedingly delicate. Best we not go into it on the phone. I must apologize, but could you accommodate us by coming in?"

I was somewhat annoyed, even though I can't deny I'd found the London trip quite exhilarating. I had put myself out for the Firm in attending Ben's funeral. Now they wanted me again.

"I suppose I could do a round-tripper today and meet you at one. If I leave in an hour, I should make it. Traffic might not be too bad this morning. Would that work?"

"Yes," he responded with a hint of relief.

I really did not know Barr well and had not thought about him in years. I had only glanced at him from afar at the funeral. He was as I remembered him—tall, a touch portly, with white hair and blue eyes that matched his blood. He was aloof, yet not condescending. He was hard of hearing and had a bit of a stutter he'd developed, I understand, from a childhood disease. That made him somewhat less patrician and a bit more avuncular.

All in all, he was to the office born.

The Executive Committee of a Wall Street law firm is more than a knight's roundtable. It's the College of Cardinals, the Duma, and the Guardian Council wrapped into one, and Wiggie was its Supreme Leader.

To those not on it, an invitation to attend was greeted with trepidation. Those summoned to the nest were often devoured career-wise. Even though that really wasn't any longer a concern of mine, I still didn't take the invitation lightly.

Nip was still out of sorts. I then realized I had forgotten to feed her. I quickly corrected that oversight. I then arranged for my caretaker to take her for the day and I took off.

I was bemused by my submissiveness to Barr's request. Old neuroses never die. Barr would always be "sir" and I would always be accommodating. In my working years, I tried my best to avoid him. He was a rabbi to no one but himself and therefore could only hurt you, not help you.

What possible problem could they need my help on? If this was a pretext to lure me back to service the Ozone account, they were wasting their time and mine. I might someday rejoin the legal community, but not in my old suits and not yet.

There had to be something more to this summons.

10

I arrived precisely on time. I was never late—an acquired trait of all good associates. Partners and clients do not like to be kept waiting. I was quickly escorted into the conference room. It was clear that they did not want me responding to inquiries from old friends and acquaintances.

I couldn't help feeling like the knave being called before the Court of the King of Hearts. And no, I did not know who stole the tarts. Barr's request—although polished and polite—was in fact a command. I had been heralded to attend and I, like a good subject, obeyed.

It took me only a few seconds to size up the room's occupants. The Firm had more than twenty conference rooms of various sizes and configurations. This was its special one—super-modern, yet classy. It was reserved for very important clients and Executive Committee meetings.

Barr was at the head of the table, Evan was to his right, and Gordon Brady, the Firm's senior litigator, was next to Evan. The vacant chair was for me. That put Dan Finn, the

Firm's other senior corporate partner and Evan's nemesis, to my right. The last three seats were taken by Caden Caufield, the senior investment-banking partner; by Reed Sawyer, the very proper senior estate partner, and by Charlotte.

She wore a black blazer. Her hair was constrained in a tight bun. She looked much more vulnerable in this pond of power partners than she had in London. She was clearly nervous. I couldn't stop watching her long fingers caressing a chain that dangled from her neck as her wrist brushed the swell of her undeniably alluring cleavage. Her presence signaled that this had to do with Ben's estate. That, however, did not advance my speculation very far.

"Jonathan—or would you prefer Tuck?"

"Tuck's fine, sir," I responded.

Wiggie was his baronial self, nattily turned out, even though his Brooks Brothers suit was well into its second decade. His Sulka tie drew your attention, as it rested casually on the Egyptian cotton of his starched white shirt. Although his hair had lost its luster and faded to gray, his face radiated character that only age can bring. It was lined by the tumult of a thousand deals and creased by years of partnership politics. Notwithstanding, he seemed relaxed and at ease. You could not say the same for the others. Evan seemed drained and tense. Charlotte, in turn, looked meek and penitent. She deflected my stares. The rest simply looked as if they would have preferred to be elsewhere.

"Ah . . . well, Tuck, I'm sure you know that all of us here appreciate your extending yourself to accommodate us and I'm sure you will understand why we needed to see you when we explain the situation. I will let Reed do that."

"A situation has arisen that requires immediate attention. It has to do with Ben Baum's Will," Reed intoned archly. He was Charlotte's boss. He was, like Wiggie, an aristocratic

WASP and he did his best to emulate the chairman's polished grace.

"It seems that Mr. Baum left a Precatory Letter attached to his Will, with instructions that it not be opened until after his funeral. The letter presents the Firm with some exceedingly difficult issues. He dictated it two weeks before his demise and, in part, it seems to suggest that if he should die in the near future, it might be the result of foul play and that the perpetrator was someone close to him."

He paused as if to gather his thoughts.

Evan seized the moment.

"Tuck, Ben was quite conflicted in his last few months and this letter may well be nothing more than a release of his pent-up frustration. You know how melodramatic Ben could be."

Barr interrupted him with more than a trace of annoyance. "Evan! I think it best that we don't color the introduction of this matter with personal opinions."

To spare Evan any further awkwardness, I preemptively said, "Perhaps it would be helpful if I read this letter before we discuss it further."

Gordon Brady quickly concurred.

"Yes, I think that would be appropriate, but there is a matter of professional ethics, or perhaps etiquette, that must be resolved. Since you are no longer associated with the Firm, we are reticent to share too much information with you from a privilege standpoint. So we would like to propose that you accept an appointment as special counsel to the Firm to make us all more comfortable in giving this information to you."

He had me.

I had no choice but to crawl back under the Firm's tent.

"I accept for this limited role. I should, however, advise you that recently I agreed to serve as the successor trustee and personal guardian for Ben's son, Leo, at the request of his daughter, Dorothy."

Charlotte's frozen trance cracked a bit with my pronouncement.

"I don't see that undertaking to be a conflict. Does anyone else?" Reed rejoined.

The assembled all swayed their chins in agreement.

"Fine. If you'll give me a few minutes, I'll read the letter in the caucus room."

"Good idea," said Wiggie, as he handed me the folder.

"You might want to take a cup of coffee with you. Wish we had something stronger."

11

ᚻᛖ ᛚᛗᚷᚠᛚᛗ

Dear Evan,

I am dictating this from my office. At the outset, let me profess: I am not lonely. I am not unloved. I am not tired of living. And I am not ready for the hereafter. I quite enjoy the now and here.

I own the building below me and a large share of the company it houses. My assets exceed two billion, if you trust my financial advisers. My corporate reach extends from Kansas to New York, Boston to Washington, London to Paris, Spain to Nigeria. We produce products every one of us uses, provide technology that every one of us needs, and create entertainment and fantasy that every one of us should enjoy.

I have had all the spoils of that success. I've tired of them all.

Perhaps fate has tired of me. As you know, I have the black menace and I fear its shadow is spreading. They say

I may have but a few years left so it's not too early to right some wrongs, settle some scores, make some amends, and profess my love—in a way not found in wills. You lawyers don't want any emotion to melt your frozen prose.

I do not fear death. It cannot take away my memories. If one has the courage to live, one has the courage to die. I lived as I wished and am doing so now. I laugh. I love. I cry. I hurt. I know it's all part of the circle of life.

I left the comforts of Glend End a long time ago. There, I was the daydream believer and Maude the homecoming queen. I was blessed with a little wisdom and a lot of luck and I needed to spread my wings. In doing so, I have been beset by trolls and goblins. Yet I am no hobbit. I still prefer excitement to comfort. That is where Maude and I parted.

Now let me tell you a little about what I believe. Imagination trumps knowledge; myths are more potent than history; dreams are more powerful than reality; hope triumphs over despair; love is stronger than hate; questions are more engaging than answers.

I have little faith in religion as we know it today. I find my gods in books and in nature. Who then are my gods and angels, you might ask. I found in children's stories the Alice and Dorothy and Bilbo and Frodo in all of us. I loathe the Wicked Witches and, yes, even the Tinker Bells we always find lurking about. But the hobgoblins have not prevailed over me, at least not yet. I've had Roäc on my shoulder.

The one spirit who affects me the most is my own Duende. That force empowers me to public success while torturing me in private. It alone understands why I did the things I did.

So I am off down the road again. And I'm late, I'm late, I'm late. This may be my last adventure. Kerberos will not stop me. If I don't succeed, there could be dire consequences for all those I love. I will continue my quest until my body gives out. I may just end it there, if someone else doesn't do it before me. Either way, I will have given everything to life itself.

Now let me get back to the matters at hand. To build a lasting kingdom on earth, one should take the right paths even if they are not easy. If I had done so more often, I would not be faced with the problems I am now encountering. Those problems are my private purgatory.

I will solve them before I go.

I have among me people who have no shame and who will go silent to their graves. I will not. I will right my ship before I die but I sense an unkindness—a murder most foul. So I warn you, if I should die from other than my curse, look carefully at the cause. And look at those who would benefit, particularly those who have the most to gain if I die and the most to lose if I live long enough to finish my tasks. I can taste their disappointments at my impending actions. Evil may be coming my way and even the Dark Lady cannot protect me.

Please do not take any of this as the ravings of a demented soul. My mind is very sound, even though my body is failing. Tereza and Viggie can attest to that.

As imperfect as I have been, I revel in small morals, my family, my friends, and the company of animals. Yet I have done things, ignored things, and excused things that were wrong. I want to do my best to erase them.

A number of those around me fervently wish me to leave this stage now. Tremaine communicates only through her advisers and her consort. She is rapt in emotion with her Abelard and she claims it's all for the love of art. Kati has tired of me too, but for a different reason. I would not give her what she wants. At least she is honest about it.

Luc is champing for his chance in the sun. I would have thought he was smart enough to stay on the dark side. And there are others too close, too despicable, to mention in this letter. What some of them may not know is that I have been marked and measured by the mortician, so fate or I might just save them the effort.

When I started my journey, I had no prevision of where it might end. I know now at least my love will last beyond the grave, especially for Dorothy and Leo. That will not be buried with me.

ᛁᛏ ᛁᛋ ᚾᛒ ᛚᛈᚾᛗ ᚥᛈᚱ ᛒᛗᛚᛚᚩᛗᛈᛁᛚᚠ ᛏᚺᚠᛏ ᛈᛁᚺᛏᚠᛁᛈ ᚾᛗ

ᚾᛒ ᛁᛁᚷᚺᛏᛈᚺᚠᛈᛗ ᛈᚠᚾᛗᛈ ᚾᛗ ᚾᚥᚱᛗ ᛏᚺᚠᛁ ᚥᛁᛈᛗ

I am not an innocent. I sometimes wish I had more Frodo than Holden in me, more Tom than Huck, more Woodman than Wizard. There is little I can do about it now.

So please proceed with caution as you attend to my affairs.

Obviously, much of this is intended for limited ears only— you, Charlotte, those who have to know, and those few you know I would trust.

I have made provision for all those I love. Viggie and Tereza are provided for in my Will. Argos has just passed away and I will soon join him on endless walks in Elysium. I'm counting on him to use his charm to get me in.

As for my earthly possessions not otherwise allocated in my Will, I request my executor to give Leo my clothes and jewelry, such that he may want, and Dorothy all my diaries as soon as possible after I die, along with any of the books, furnishings, and other things she desires. Whatever remains is for Tereza. My car is to go to Viggie. He understands why. Both have been loving, faithful, and loyal—attributes not dispensed easily to someone as insensitive and petulant as I can be.

Maude and I planned a large family, but fate frustrated us. After the miracle of Dorothy, Leo, and the twins, we lost the twins, and then Maude passed.

All that's left of the Baums now is Dorothy and Leo and I would not barter them for immortality. I feel confident that they will honor and perpetuate the good that I have done. I expect great things from Dorothy. And for Leo, my wounded lion, I pray for inner peace and great happiness. His heart is bigger than mine could ever be.

Dorothy knows how much I love her and Leo senses my love for him. They have made me very proud. And Dorothy, I need to say to you over and over that I am sorry. Your pain was the lifetime mortgage I took out to maintain our love. I will spend eternity paying it back.

There are many powers in the world for good and for evil. Many are greater than I am. Against some I have not yet been measured. My tests are coming. The road goes ever on.

Perhaps I have said enough. The hour of departure may soon be upon me and we must go our separate ways.

Namárië.

L. Benjamin Baum

Tereza Toboso   Marco Viggiano

12

I returned to the conference room. Before I took my seat, I leaned over and cranked the chair up a notch. I'm not sure if it was an act of independence or petulance. It was an old trick often employed by an insecure host. Lower the level of your guests' seats. It was thought to put them at a subtle disadvantage, permitting the host to loom larger. I smiled as I cranked it up, then slowly took my seat.

"It seems there is more to Ben Baum than I'd imagined," I uttered, somewhat inanely. Those were just word-fillers, for I was at a loss to say anything more meaningful.

Barr mercifully took over.

"I am sure you have not had time to consider the full potential import of the letter . . . for Ben's estate, Ben's heirs, the Firm, Ozone, and ultimately the Baum legacy. If Ben's death appears likely to be neither natural nor accidental, then we have to determine what course of action to take. If he killed himself, we would have to examine his mental capacity to determine whether or not to probate his current Will. If it reasonably appears possible that he might have died at the hands of others, then we must consider notifying the authorities. The permutations and the consequences are myriad."

Dan Finn picked up on that and reframed the issues in the vernacular.

"If we're convinced that Ben killed himself, we'll have a hard time keeping the lid on it. While suicide does not necessarily imply incapacity, it and other factors may give rise to a Will contest. If his wife was directly or indirectly involved, she will likely lose her inheritance, her prenuptial perks, and her place on the foundation's board."

I had forgotten that Tremaine was the chairman of the Baum Foundation, which I inferred was a major beneficiary under the Will.

"If his lady friend Ms. Krkavec did it," Dan continued, "she'll be frozen out. In either case, the press will have a frenzy. If someone at Ozone ordered it, all hell will break loose."

He paused, perhaps for effect, then resumed.

"If Luc Grogaman or one of his minions appears to be implicated, then it isn't so much a Will issue as a client issue. The Firm would have to assess the potential conflicts. We have to be careful not to jump to conclusions. A mistaken or premature accusation would clearly damage our reputation and likely cost us our largest client. Grogaman would fire us in a nanosecond. To sweep any of this under attorney-client privilege, however, could prove even more damaging—perhaps fatal—to the Firm's reputation. Its viability."

This was heady stuff.

I was processing the information as quickly as possible. I watched Evan grimace at Finn's words. He was potentially the big loser here. Charlotte looked very uncomfortable. I presumed that she was the first one to read the letter, not expecting it to be anything unusual. In doing so, she'd let the genie out and Evan couldn't put it back.

Barr reclaimed the stage.

"It is for all these possibilities that we need your help, Tuck. After much discussion, we have concluded that we need to retain special counsel—not so much to advise us, but to discreetly ferret out additional information to aid us in making a more informed judgment. After considering many candidates, we decided on you as our first choice. You bring an invaluable knowledge of the deceased and his family, Ozone, and the Firm. You have the shortest learning curve."

"What exactly are you proposing?" I asked, with a bit more resolve in my voice.

Gordon Brady, I gathered, was assigned to deal with that for he responded to my inquiry without prompting.

"Here's our proposal. You would be engaged as special Firm counsel, compensated at the rate of $200,000 per month. We would assign two associates to you full time for the duration of this project. We would expect you and your team to operate in an off-premises space. We suggest you use Mr. Baum's downtown apartment. We would make his secretary and driver exclusively available to assist in your efforts. You would pay them as well as the associates and we would reimburse you for those costs and all other out-of-pocket expenses. This undertaking would last three months at the longest. We feel we cannot delay filing Ben's Will any longer than that. We fully understand that you may make little or no progress, but it seems a valuable and perhaps necessary undertaking for us to have someone look deeply—and discreetly—into this. We will, of course, hold you harmless, whatever transpires."

He took a deep breath.

"Tuck, we could really use you on this."

His presentation was over.

I accepted the engagement. I did not dare ask for deliberation time. I was afraid my rational self would talk me out of it.

This assignment was too tantalizing to turn down.

13

I did not know Ben as well as I thought I did. Although I was very immersed in his business, I rarely spent time with him alone. That was Evan's place and he guarded it tenaciously.

Ben's public persona cast him as a larger-than-life figure. He was physically imposing, his silver-highlighted hair setting off a seemingly muscular physique. Yet he was not known to engage in any active sport—other than his legendary sex life.

In business, he was thought to be hard-wired, verging on ruthless. Yet to those of us who worked with him, he was effective, often calculating but never callous. What made him special as a client was that he truly appreciated his lawyers' efforts and never complained about the bill.

Uncommon traits.

And he was not only about business. His generosity made him quite well known to the public. Working through his favorite charity, UNICEF, he supported the rescue of countless children from genocide and provided funding for food and medicine to children in need.

Above all, he was always dominant. No matter what arena he played in, his presence was pervasive. Somehow he usurped all the oxygen in any room he entered.

His Precatory Letter, at least on first reading, indicated that there was much more humanity than hubris to the man; more brain than bravado; more angst than arrogance. Precatory Letters, often referred to as Letters of Wishes, are not that uncommon. As nonbinding writings normally directed to one's executor, they often contain desires as to how the executor might exercise his or her discretionary powers, most often indicating which heir should get what watch, ring, or family heirloom. Once in a while, they are used to express the deceased's feelings or explain his actions to those left behind.

Wills, most people are surprised to learn, are quite accessible to the public. Anyone can obtain a copy of a person's Will from the Surrogate's Court once it is probated.

Precatory Letters, however, remain private.

Obviously, Ben did not want his inner feelings made public. They would be prime fodder for inquiring authorities, not to mention media gossipmongers. This more private form of testamentary desires suited him well.

I had quickly bid my good-byes and bolted from the conference room as the meeting ended. I did not want to speculate on the letter before I'd had a chance to absorb it in private.

I dialed Charlotte from the car and was put right through.

"Hi. What a turn of events! I've never read anything like that. Can't talk right now . . . in the car, but can you messenger out to my home a copy of Ben's Will? Oh, and also copies of his previous Will and his prenup agreement. They may help me put the prec letter into some context."

"Of course," she responded. "I'll check with Reed and Evan but I'm sure it won't be a problem. Oh, just heard.

Drew Benson and Frank Dixon are the associates who have been assigned to you for the duration. Drew works in my department. I know her very well. She's a major talent. Don't be put off by her mannerisms. She's a bit of a yenta, but there's a lot of substance behind her veneer. Frank I don't know. He's in the corporate securities department. Supposed to be a real comer and very well liked by the associates. What I understand is that they will take leaves of absence and work exclusively with you, using Ben's townhouse as their offices. This weekend Ben's secretary is supervising the move of his personal files from his office at Ozone. Word of caution: Be careful, Tuck. Everyone here is drum-tight."

"Thanks, Charlotte, and thanks for the warning. I'll be in touch as soon as I've read the papers and digested the letter."

I clicked off.

Tight? More like fright. The stakes for the Firm were very high. You could not miss the tension that radiated between Charlotte and Evan. I imagined that Evan was not happy about her sharing the letter with the power partners in the Firm. All this would undoubtedly entangle partners' alliances, forge new ones, and result in the lopping off of a few heads. And history tells us that they kill the messenger first.

Poor Charlotte.

Traffic slowed to a crawl. The Long Island Expressway is like that. No particular rhyme or reason for the patterns. For once, it did not bother me. I could relax. I smiled at the letter's constant allusions to children's literature. I did not realize Ben was so into that. Beneath the letter's florid and obscure prose, I suspect, lay a very serious message.

This was no matter for mirth.

Accusations of murder and suggestions of suicide never are.

Like Ben, I too am drawn to the pleasures of children's classics. Even before the kids were born, I found comfort in

Lewis Carroll, J. R. R. Tolkien, and L. Frank Baum. Saint-Exupéry and E. B. White were not far behind. The best tonic for legal and corporate miasmas is the occasional retreat into fantasy.

Ben must also have found it in kid-lit.

I could not suppress my glee when I saw the hobbit hieroglyphics. Tolkien created several languages for his middle-earth, an imaginary place in the earth's history. Runes are the letters he invented for one of them. As soon as I settled in for the night, I'd translate them. Tolkien's runes had always fascinated me.

Back to the matter at hand.

Would Tremaine or Kati commit or commission the unthinkable? Could Luc stab his mentor, like Brutus did? Who else was there? And how would they have done it? And what or who was Belladonna?

Could Ben have induced his own demise? Perhaps he did not want to endure the pain of a lingering death. It could have caused him to lose his senses. That's a separate issue.

Here was a man who lived life fully. He took care of himself and his friends. He may have been a bit eccentric, but he seemed to be cognizant of his mistakes and appeared to have set out to correct them.

He was not perfect, but he was a perfect example of being human.

My guess was that he loved life too much to quit it. Few people kill themselves by throwing themselves off the pinnacle of success. He was certainly more cultivated, perhaps more destructive, indeed madder, yet a lot more sane, than the average person.

I was jumping to my own conclusions—a fatal flaw for any lawyer. Wall Street Woolly's rule number one: Let the facts guide you, not the reverse.

I had been out of practice too long. If I were to do this assignment justice, I'd better reboot quickly.

I'd have to recognize that there was now a fresh element in my life. I had seized the Firm's offer without hesitation—and without negotiation—in large part, I suspect, to crowd out my grief.

Even I was getting tired of it.

The reality was that Alice and the kids were long gone. It was time I had the fortitude to declare it. Maybe taking this assignment was that declaration. Perhaps I had a personal *duende*, as Ben would have put it, who has other ideas for me. That was one of the references I did not get in Ben's letter. At the house that night, after Nip went down, I deciphered the hobbit runes and Googled *duende*. Seems *duende* is a mysterious power that one can't quite explain, often seductive and potentially destructive. I suspect it is like a psychic kick in the butt. Maybe that's exactly what I needed.

Tomorrow I start, I told myself.

I had Ms. Toboso, Ben's secretary—Terry as she preferred to be called—contact the two associates to have them at the West Village townhouse at one the next day and arrange for Ben's driver to pick me up at eleven so I could speak to Terry and set up shop before they arrived. I had quickly prepared folders for the associates containing copies of Ben's Will, the prenup and the Precatory Letter, along with a copy of Ozone's last annual report, although I presumed they had already immersed themselves in all the Ozone information they could get their hands on.

I had developed a plan of sorts.

We would use as our pretext that we were working as a team to help the Firm prepare the filings necessary to probate Ben's Will and to effectuate his testamentary wishes. That would give us an excuse to speak to those I wanted debriefed, while hopefully keeping their hackles down.

I decided to interview Luc Grogaman and Dorothy and her partner, Eloise, personally. I would have Drew, the estate associate, cover Tremaine and Kati, if she could be located, and Abelard, Tremaine's assistant. Frank could run down the corporate side, which included Luc Grogaman's key operatives. Also, he could deal with the forensic and police matters that were needed and work with the London office to get a copy of the police file and see if we could exhume the body if they hadn't done an autopsy.

I would also cover Evan. He wouldn't suffer questioning by an associate.

The chauffeur arrived precisely at eleven the next day. Nip and I had driven in early in the morning.

I was waiting outside my apartment when a gray Mercedes SUV pulled up. The driver, whom I correctly assumed was Marco Viggiano, quickly exited and opened the car door for me.

He was hard to size up on first encounter. Physically, he fit the mold—black-haired, muscular, with a chiseled dark face that was highlighted by frown lines. His eyes were deep-socketed and devoid of agenda. His physique suggested that he was more than a car jockey.

Instinctively I liked him, although my attempt at idle chatter evoked only monosyllabic rejoinders. He seemed to neither require nor expect conversation. The only breach of that was when I commented on the dog hairs in the back of the car. Seems he was very fond of Argos, Ben's recently deceased golden retriever.

After a long crawl in traffic, we finally pulled in front of a townhouse in the West Village, distinguished from the others by its yellow brick stairs, which led up to a green wooden door, domed at the top and with a brass knob in the middle. I smiled. I suspected it was fashioned after Tolkien's drawing of Bilbo's hobbit house.

Viggiano pointed to the buzzer and returned to the car, quickly pulling away.

I was greeted by Tereza Toboso, an affable, robust woman who appeared to be in her sixties. I remembered her—Ben's personal assistant and the gatekeeper to his kingdom. She promptly reintroduced herself and again directed me to call her Terry as she offered me coffee and homemade muffins.

I did not refuse and I let her keep talking.

Seems she had been in Ben's employ for a long time. She knew him in high school, where she was the secretary of their school's literary society, at the same time that Ben served as president. After graduation, she joined Ben in his fledgling electronics company—never to leave. Later, when the company moved its headquarters to New York, she eventually settled in Carroll Gardens, Brooklyn, although she confided she spent most of the week in the townhouse.

She then took me on a tour.

The downstairs consisted of a large living room adjacent to a modern eat-in kitchen. In the living room, she had installed two temporary desks with phones and Internet access, as well as a printer. The remainder of the first floor was separated by a hall and consisted of Ben's library and his bedroom. The second floor held two additional bedrooms. One was hers and the other was utilized most nights by Ben's driver. Terry advised that everyone referred to him as Viggie. The third floor, she noted, was Ben's son's domain. In the back there was a beautiful garden that separated the townhouse from a 200-year-old carriage house. That was where Terry and her assistants worked. It also housed Ben's personal files.

This would be our digs for the duration of this project. Decorated in a cozy English country style, the house exuded warmth. Dark mahogany-walled rooms populated by charming, compatible art and artifacts were made inviting by the presence of overstuffed chairs and couches.

It could not be more commodious. And fitting.

It was truly hobbit-like.

Ben's library was the centerpiece. It had floor-to-ceiling bookcases on two sides. There were hundreds of books carefully arranged on those shelves. A quick perusal showed they were mostly children's literature. Mark Twain's works, C. S. Lewis's *Narnia* series, Saint-Exupéry's books, and Collodi's *Pinocchio* were the ones I recognized.

A large Edwardian pedestaled partner's desk, with a well-scuffed green leather writing surface, occupied the center of the room.

It was there Terry suggested I work.

She guided me to the middle shelf behind the desk where Ben's rare books were housed behind glass. There, bound in its original green cloth with blue lettering, was a first edition of *The Hobbit*, along with a first edition of *Alice's Adventures in Wonderland*. The latter, she informed me proudly, was acquired by Ben at auction for $1.6 million. As if to justify this extravagance, she quickly pointed out that only twenty-two remained in existence and that this one was Lewis Carroll's own personal copy. The *Hobbit* original, she noted as an afterthought, cost only $35,000—a steal in view of the fact that another original-edition copy had recently sold in London at auction for $120,000. Pretty impressive for a book that went on to sell more than 100 million copies. The fourteen books in the *Wizard of Oz* series came from Ben's grandfather.

I made a mental note to tell Drew and Frank that these books were out of bounds. I had already ordered copies of annotated versions of each to be delivered here and Terry advised that they had in fact arrived.

They would be required reading.

Terry, in almost reverential tones, went on to explain that Ben's great-great-uncle was the creator of the *Oz* series. His parents were proud of the success of their paternal ancestor and made Oz a big part of Ben's life.

Terry excused herself as the phone rang.

I could visualize Big Ben indulging his hobby here, with a fire roaring and Argos at his feet. I had a feeling that being here would give us a better sense of Ben than anything we could glean from our upcoming interviews. This space I was sure was his safe harbor from the storms that were besetting him and perhaps it was here that he hid the secrets and mysteries he spoke of in his letter.

From the history that Terry gave me, I surmised that Ben, as an only child, had endured a cloistered youth, spending much time at home. He found his excitement and inventiveness in the imagined company of Alice, Dorothy, Bilbo, and Frodo.

Terry returned to advise that Viggie had just called and he would be here soon with the two associates. I quickly explained what we were up to, noting that she and Viggie would be an important part of our team since they were so close to Ben and were both signatories on his letter.

I reminded her to call me Tuck.

Terry then paused, as if calling up some internal energy. "Oh . . . Tuck, there is something I think you should know. Viggie is my adopted son. It's not really a secret, but Ben and I thought it best not to publicize it. A close friend of Ben's—an Italian who was Ben's European banker—asked him to bring his nephew to America. The child's family had suffered a violent death and the boy had started falling in with a bad lot. Ben couldn't refuse and he brought Viggie here. I had no children so I agreed to take him in. Later I formally adopted him so he could stay in this country. When he was eighteen, he went to work for Ben and has been his bodyguard and driver ever since. They truly love each other."

Her voice trailed off as her eyes got misty.

"Both of us will miss him terribly. We will help you in any way we can."

"I appreciate that, Terry, and I know this has to be very hard on you."

Life for everyone touched by Ben's death was going to be very different and, for some, the future was going to be daunting. Terry was just beginning to process that.

She still spoke of Ben in the present tense.

14

The assistants arrived wearing their traditional associate armor—earnest looks, attentive ears, and proper decorum—which almost covered their understandable sense of unease.

Both would soon be approaching their half-life in the Firm—that point when an associate has enough experience to know whether to move on or stay the course.

The rigors of life as a young lawyer in a Wall Street firm like Winston Barr & Trombley are hard to sustain. Impossible demands are put on young cogs, as they are called by unsympathetic partners who secretly envy their drive, intelligence, and energy.

Advancement within the Firm is like an insidious form of mountain climbing: step-by-step doggedness until you reach the first plateau—partnership—and then without much respite you start up all over again. And those who precede you often plug up the footholds on their way up so the Sherpas won't surpass them. Unfairly, associates are often viewed as overpaid, arrogant, pampered, and cutthroat. That is an outsider's view—probably popularized by Shakespeare.

People tend to hate all lawyers except their own.

My associates were fairly stereotypical. Drew Benson got her undergraduate degree from Barnard College, and her law degree from NYU. Charlotte said she was extremely smart. Her annual reviews, which Charlotte shared with me, noted "relentless drive," "stellar academics," "good instincts," "prioritized," and "New York moxie."

Good traits for this assignment.

An added plus, I noticed immediately, was her embracing empathy. She wasn't a "looker" in the traditional sense; she was a bit too zaftig for that. However, her eyes and her eruptive laughter sealed the deal for me. With her black horn-rimmed glasses and her tousled hair, she seemed intent on cultivating an aura of benign neglect. If she was trying to be retro-chic, it was lost on me.

Frank Dixon was Drew's polar opposite. He was tall, with an athlete's body, and was a double-ivy—Yale undergraduate, Harvard Law. Vigorously metro in his dress and demeanor, he seemed quite self-assured. He was properly reticent and spoke little, deferring to Drew when it came to polite palaver. Eventually he did thaw a bit and told me that his friends call him "Dixie."

Here we were—the five of us, Drew, Dixie, Terry, Viggie, and myself—setting off to solve a potential crime. Throw Nip—our Scooby-Doo—into the mix and the analogy is complete.

After a quick site tour, we settled into the library where I laid out our endeavor. I started by giving them each a folder with the prec letter, Ben's Will, and his prenup.

"The first thing I suggest is that you read the prec letter. Let me try to set this assignment in perspective. Ben wanted to put his life in order. That seems clear from the prec letter.

As I am sure you know, this type of testamentary letter is not that uncommon. The more common ones designate who is to get what bauble. Others are used to clear up some of the ambiguities in relationships and express emotions in ways not appropriate in Wills. This one, however, goes much further. Ben intimates that perhaps someone might try to end his life before he could accomplish some unstated goals. He set forth all this in a letter to his executor—a clever ploy on his part. I suspect he knew that his suspicions would be kept confidential, and that Evan and the Firm would look into these accusations thoroughly and discreetly. A private investigative agency might well have succumbed to the lucre that would flow from leaking details to the press and would be insensitive to the attorney-client relationship issue. So that task has devolved to us. Our client is Ben's estate, as I view it, but we are expected to report to the Firm's Executive Committee.

"A word of caution: What we learn here stays here. This letter and its potential import might involve sex, drugs, infidelity, suicide, corporate intrigue, family struggles, and perhaps even murder, not to mention the impact our findings might have on the distribution of two billion dollars. This I promise you is very heady stuff. Not your standard law firm fare. So as juicy as this may be, do NOT share this with your friends. Zip it up!"

They seemed to get the message.

"The letter that Ben left is full of flourishes that make it difficult to decipher. It is filled with references to the works of three writers of children's classics. The first is Tolkien, who, as you know, wrote *The Hobbit* and *The Lord of the Rings*. Both his stories feature a community of little creatures called hobbits. In both tales, the heroes—Bilbo and Frodo—leave the comforts of home at the request of a wizard to help some elves gain a treasure that is rightfully theirs. That is a gross simplification, but you get the drift."

Both associates nodded, tentatively.

"Two other children's classics are frequently referred to in the letter. One is the *Wizard of Oz* series that L. Frank Baum created. I found out that the author was Ben's ancestor. The other works Ben cites are by Lewis Carroll, in particular his *Alice* books.

"I have copies of the annotated versions of Carroll's, Baum's, and Tolkien's principal works for both of you to take home. It's quite a load. Reading them is your second assignment."

They gave each other quizzical glances.

They were already bonding.

"Let me give you some help with Ben's letter. You will see that he includes a few phrases in Tolkien rune—an alphabet that Tolkien created to use in his stories like a secret code. I have translated them for you with the help of Google. First is the title—'My Legacy.' The second says, 'It is my love for Belladonna that sustains me.' The last rune decodes as, 'My nightshade has saved me more than once.' They baffle me. I've no clue what they refer to, nor do I know the significance of the symbol that appears between them."

My associates were multitasking, writing notes and reading the letter at the same time. To be merciful, I paused for several moments.

"A few other comments. The 'black menace' could refer to Ben's cancer. 'Roäc' is the chief of all ravens and serves as a messenger in *The Hobbit*. Some more. 'Kerberos' is the god Hades's three-headed dog in Greek mythology. It's 'Cerberus' in Latin. *Namárië*, according to Google, is a Tolkien poem written in Quenya, another language that he constructed. Best I can figure out, it means 'fare well.' The rest of the allusions must have some meaning and that's for us to discover.

"Now the cast of human characters: Maude is Ben's first wife. She died many years ago. Tremaine is his current wife. Peter Abelard is her confidant and the executive director of the Baum Foundation. Kati Krkavec was Ben's mistress. She was with him in his suite when he died. Luc is Mr. Grogaman, the recently installed interim CEO of Ozone—Ben's former chief operating officer and the head of ClearAire, Ozone's military contracts division. *Belladonna*, which I suspect is Italian or Latin for 'pretty lady,' may in fact not refer to a person but rather to an herb—*Atropa belladonna*. Hard to tell.

"Well, that's enough for now. I suggest we retire to our desks. I'll check on lunch with Terry and we'll reconvene when it's ready."

Before I did that, though, I went back to the library, closed the door, and spent a few minutes taking stock. I hadn't slept well. Not that I ever did. Worse than usual, though. This matter was daunting. The possibilities kept rattling around in my head like balls in an arcade game.

15

Terry was busy at work in the kitchen. She had just finished watering a massive amaryllis plant that was the kitchen's
centerpiece. She told me it was her favorite flower and that
Ben had given her one thirty years ago. Since then she had
never been without. She had already prepared a feast that
even hobbits, well known for their epicurean conceits, would
have approved of—a large sandwich selection and a medley of
mixed veggies, with sides of homemade potato salad and cole-
slaw. Quintessential comfort foods. She even had root beer
and cream soda.

She had set the table outside in the small yard that separated the main house from the carriage house. That space
had been turned into a country garden, complete with a per-
gola, covered with clinging roses that had long since lost their
blooms. Nonetheless the unusually warm autumn day made
eating outside a special treat.

"Terry, before you serve this feast, I'd like to ask you a few
questions. You know what our assignment is, I assume."

"Mr. Trombley told me that a team of lawyers would be conducting a discreet investigation into Ben's death to confirm that it was accidental or unavoidable."

I suppressed a smile.

Evan was being his controlling self. To the extent that this was a contest, he would want to set the rules, pick the sides, referee the game, and decide the outcome.

Senior partners are like that.

"Well . . . we are approaching this matter with an open mind. The key to our inquiry is the Precatory Letter that you, I assume, typed as well as witnessed. We will be interviewing all those involved, at least to the extent that they are willing to cooperate. You can play an important role in this, as can Viggie. For starters, could you tell me what led up to the letter?"

"Tuck, as I told you this morning, Ben was the most important person in my life and my son's, so you can count on us. As to the letter, Ben had been brooding about matters relating to his business and his personal affairs for some time. They seemed to be more pressing of late. These were in addition to his concerns about his health . . . and his son's health. Before he dictated the letter, he spent a lot of time drafting it. Once it was finished, he burned all of his drafts. To be candid, he seemed to take a lot of pleasure in the process. Ben always loved mysteries, word games, puzzles . . . things like that. Also, he had recently become quite agitated. I overheard several very heated phone conversations over the last several months. He had even taken to closing his study door so I could not make out what was said. That was not like Ben. He was always very open and easygoing . . . until recently."

"Whom were the conversations with?"

"I don't recall them all, but some were with Mrs. Baum, others were with Mr. Grogaman and his assistants, and with Ben's lady friend. Oh . . . and he had several with his daughter's friend, Eloise. Another I remember was with Mr. Abelard. Ben was swearing. That was not like him."

"Did you find his letter unusual?"

"No, not really. Ben loved to write with a flourish. He loved to play with words and he loved riddles. He fancied himself a bit of a philosopher. He felt strongly about life. I think he wanted to create a document that summed up his imagination and his beliefs. You know, deep down, he was a fabulist. He really believed that one could communicate with animals and that spirits are real. He just couldn't quite convince those of us around him to embrace his beliefs . . . at least not completely. I must admit I loved to listen to him when he got going. He had a touch of the preacher in him."

The warmth she had for Ben was palpable.

"Do you think it possible that someone would harm him?" I asked.

"I just don't know. It's the one part of the letter that really bothered me. I tried to ask him about it, but he wouldn't talk about it."

"What about drugs?"

That brought her up abruptly. "Ben never was a drug addict! I can assure you of that! But he was an adventurer—a bit of an aging hippie. I'm sure he experimented with some recreational drugs on occasion."

I sensed that I had gone far enough for today so I eased up.

"Well, I was impressed with your typing of the runes."

"Oh, don't be!" she laughed. "Ben had a typewriter especially altered to put Tolkien's Quenya alphabet where the capital letters normally are. We had fun with that."

"One other thing. What was that symbol all about?"

Terry's head snapped back, almost imperceptibly. "Ah . . . don't really know. Obviously he added that himself afterward. Ben fancied himself the artist."

She then turned back to the food.

I helped her bring lunch out to the serving table and then summoned my lieges. When they arrived the table was set. Viggie had already taken his sandwich and the cannoli that was laid out especially for him and was making his exit, nodding with practiced deference.

Lunch for lawyers is normally done alone at one's desk. The days of martini matinee tastings have passed. Client lunches have long been out of vogue. It was hard for clients to digest food at the rates their lawyers were charging, especially knowing that, in addition, their meal would find its way into their bills as a disbursement.

So lunch outside in a private garden, eating food that was not prepared the night before, and that was served on something other than wax paper, was a special treat. Our break was spent exchanging irrelevancies as a way for us to get more familiar. We adjourned after Terry steadfastly resisted our offers to help clean up.

16

Back in the library, which had quickly become our war room, I began our next debriefing—Ben's Will.

"I have included in your folder a copy of Ben's Will and his Family Trust. The salient bequests are listed there. He leaves his wife whatever amount is provided for in their prenuptial agreement, with a proviso that she vacate the uptown apartment and remove all her possessions from all of his residences within ninety days—a rather harsh provision. Under the terms of the prenup, Tremaine gets a million dollars for every year they were married. Both she and Ben could independently end the union by simply delivering a written notice declaring the marriage over. If that notice was delivered within the first five years of the union, that was all she would get. If it was delivered after five years, she would get a lump sum of $50 million. If Ben died within the first five years without having delivered a notice of marriage termination, she would get $25 million. They would have been married five years this spring. I understand from Terry that Ben had prepared and signed a marital termination letter, but had held off delivering it. If he had done so, she would have received only $4 million—$1 million for each year. But since he did not deliver the notice she gets $25 million. So one could conclude that Tremaine fared well by the timing of Ben's death, although I'm sure she will still feel deprived. Twenty-five million would not keep her in the style she has become accustomed to. And if he had lived just a few more months and not delivered the termination letter, she would have received $50 million.

"Ben then leaves $20 million to Terry and $5 million to Viggie. Additionally, he leaves $10 million to Kati Krkavec, provided she is not pregnant at the time his Will is probated. If she is, then he leaves her nothing, but rather leaves a million in trust for the child, with interest and principal being accumulated and not distributed until the child is thirty years old. He also provides that Kati's child not be considered his issue for purposes of sharing in the Baum Family Trust.

"He then directs that all his real estate be sold, except for the downtown maisonette that we are now in. That he leaves to Terry. The proceeds from the sale of the other real estate plus his securities trading accounts are to then be placed in his Family Trust, which already holds, I believe, about 30 percent of his shares in Ozone. The balance of his personally held Ozone shares was recently gifted to his foundation.

"A few other provisions to note. All of his art, other than anything that Dorothy wants, goes to the foundation. Although he leaves the townhouse to Terry, its contents go to his daughter, Dorothy. Anything she does not want, however, then goes to Terry. His clothes and jewelry go to his son, Leo, except for his Rolex, which he leaves to Viggie. Also he provides that his remains be buried alongside his first wife and his two deceased children, in the family plot, and expresses the wish that Dorothy and Leo make provisions to be buried there as well."

Drew volunteered, "Well, that's not unusual. Parents want their children nearby after they die. My mother wants to be cremated and have her ashes sprinkled around Bloomingdale's. She believes that's the only way to ensure that her daughters will visit her twice a week!"

Even I had to smile.

"By the way," I interjected, "the uptown apartment is an eighteen-room duplex at 740 Park Avenue. It's appraised at about $65 mill. Ben's Meadow Lane, Southampton, compound is worth more than $50 million—it's on the ocean—and his Aspen chalet is worth about $10 million. So they could fetch at least $125 million. When you add this place at $12 million, you get $137 million in real estate, along with the $700 million-plus in his brokerage accounts. They're mostly hedge funds. And about $5 million in personal items—books, cars, and trinkets. Altogether you get a taxable estate of more than $800 million. The feds and the state will take a fair share of the pie, but what's left is a tidy slice. That's not to mention the Baum Family Trust, which has holdings in Ozone worth more than a billion. That's outside the estate. Drew, could you confirm and fine-tune that with Charlotte? Estate tax is not my strong card."

"Sure. Is tomorrow OK? I'll call her tonight when we can talk without interruption."

Drew was on board. I liked her style.

"And Dixie, could you check out what you can on belladonna? And also see if you can figure out that heart symbol in the letter. Enough debriefing for the day. I'm going to make some calls now to Europe before it gets too late. Viggie is waiting outside. I suggest you take your stuff home with you. Enjoy your bedtime reading.

"Oh, one more thing. I've decided to double your salaries for the duration. You will earn them! I'll see you tomorrow."

Ben and Rasputin had obviously obsessed over their Wills. Both included intimations of death at the hands of others. Both were in some sense mystics.

Were they both right?

That answer was our mission.

Complicated stuff.

17

Well, my nose did not grow longer that day.

I did make those calls. Dorothy didn't answer, but I connected with Charlotte. In fact, she was breathless when she picked up.

Seems the despicable Jasper de Vil, Tremaine's belligerent barrister, had just informed her that he had filed a lawsuit in the New York Supreme Court asking, among other things, that Ben's current Will be deemed null and void. His argument was that Ben was unduly influenced by Evan and the Firm, that the removal of Tremaine as executrix and the substitution of Evan was the result of that inappropriate and unprofessional influence. Charlotte surmised that they had somehow gotten wind of the significant changes in Ben's current Will and had concluded that a good offense was their best defense. She promised to fill Drew in with details that night.

Viggie was back, waiting patiently after having dropped off Drew and Dixie. He was more animated than he had been in the morning, although that was not hard. He talked about

Mr. Baum in almost reverential terms, explaining how when he had hit bottom in Brooklyn, Ben had intervened and had given him this job, taught him about life, and made him feel good about himself. He allowed that Ben had sent him to a professional driving school, had gotten him a license to carry a concealed weapon and a membership in a West Side shooting range, as well as a membership in the local gym.

Seems Ben had made him more than just his chauffeur.

When he completed his quick recounting of his life story with Ben, Viggie leaned back and handed me a miniature voice recorder. He proudly identified it as the new SONY UX80, which he boasted held two gigabytes of internal storage. Enough to record thirty-six hours of quality audio. He showed me the pitch control and playback features.

What I did not immediately grasp was that it contained a tape of Drew and Dixie's car ride home.

Viggie found nothing wrong with this, explaining that each night he would give the day's tape to Ben, who would return it after he had listened to it. Viggie would then label his tape and file it at his mother's home.

I tried to keep my dismay and disdain under wraps. This was a rank invasion of privacy. It was not, however, illegal, provided Ben was in the car and part of the conversation.

Corporate executives have been doing it for years. It gets much more dicey when it involves telephones. Both could be criminal offenses and most business titans enjoy their freedom too much to risk it. I'm sure the SEC and the Justice Department would love to get their hands on those. It's the stuff that indictments are made of.

Viggie then leaned back and handed me earphones. My principles dissolved like Alka-Seltzer in water. I rationalized that the Baum matter required the absolute loyalty of those in the group and this isolated invasion was justified to ensure that my team was, in fact, on board. Unfortunately, listening might well have constituted illegal eavesdropping. Nevertheless, I pushed the button. After some initial static, their conversation began to flow:

Viggie, would you please close the divider? Thank you.

Certainly, Miss Benson.

This could really be fun, Drew. A lot better than another Power Authority Refunding Bond! They're so boring, my brain is beginning to fry. This matter is much more interesting. It's like being Sutherland in 24, with double overtime pay!

Dixie, please. It's more like Murder She Wrote. *And I don't think you appreciate the estate complexities. Our heads will be spinning. At least Tucker seems really nice, not like the head of my department. And Tucker's real easy on the eyes—he has a kind of craggy-sexy look and a mischievous smile.*

Not dating now?

I'm dating myself! At least that way I get to pick the restaurant and the movie.

You're right about Tucker, though. I talked with Catherine Rennert. I work with her a lot. She was one of Tucker's contemporaries. You know her, don't you? She said he's one of the good guys. Tucker had a great rep at the Firm—super-smart, hardworking, sense of humor. He was a Golden Goy. And I have to agree, he is fantabuloso, but that outfit he had on was pure Nana Nation. Gave me a bit of the skeeves.

Dixie! If we are going to be in bed together for the next few months—figuratively speaking, that is—you're going to have to talk hetero.

If Big Ben is going to talk to us in Tolkienese, I can sprinkle in a little gayspeak. OK! OK! He's a style-challenged hunk. Is that clear enough for you?

You know about the accident—losing his wife and kids. That had to be really tough. He seems so positive, though.

Drew, that was more than three years ago!

You don't measure that kind of loss in years.

You're right about that. When you have that kind of baggage, you can wear all the polo and rugby shirts you want. And you know, he's old . . . I think he's over forty. According to Catherine, he didn't graduate from college 'til he was twenty-three. Then he spent four years in the marines. Then law school. He made partner in record time—just less than six years. And he's been away from the Firm about three years. So do the math. He's around forty!

You heard what Tucker said about nothing leaving the townhouse.

That was straight out of Michael Clayton. *It was George Clooney's line. You remember, he was the firm's fixer. Maybe this is a Firm conspiracy to paper over a problem. Ozone is, after all, the Firm's biggest client.*

Enough. You've got to admit we have a nice crib to work in.

Yes, but I'm glad we're working out of the table stable. All that tchotchke stuff in the library is a bit creepy. I didn't want to tell Friar Tuck that I had no clue about The Hobbit *or* Alice. *Never read them. I did see the* Oz *movie and I've seen all of the* Lord of the Rings *movies too. Actually I got turned on to the* Rings *books at Yale. The bookstore's best seller my sophomore year was a* Harvard Lampoon *book called* Bored with the Rings. *It was fall-down funny and it got me into Tolkien. I've always wanted to go back and read* The Hobbit, *but there was never enough time. Actually . . . I must confess, when I was young, I was hooked on* Dungeons and Dragons. *I was really into D&D—spells, monsters, gods, weapons. Great for honing skills you need to survive in the law business.*

I thought that was for geeks.

No, to the contrary, no nerds allowed.

Well, I'm kinda in the same boat even though I was a lit major. Of course, I saw the Oz *movies, but not those* Rings flicks—too weird for me. And Alice was my mother's generation. I'm an Agatha Christie addict. When it comes to children's lit, all I remember is Eloise, and the Seuss and Madeline books! And, of course, my favorite book, Charlotte's Web, featured one of my all-time favorite characters, Wilbur. My other favorite was a little doll named Edith. She was in the Lonely Doll series. Lovely Edith with her straight blonde hair and gold hoop earrings. A real shiksa. Finally Mr. Bear and Little Bear came to live with them and when Edith has a tantrum, Poppa Bear puts her across his knee. That's a no-no today so the book was banned. Too bad; it's a great book.

I didn't know you were a spankaholic! Um, what fun!

DIXIE. You are IMPOSSIBLE.

I might be, but let's hope our mission isn't. Tom Cruise would never forgive us. For me, it was The Little Prince. I loved the mystery of it. And the little guy had great duds. It was the only kid-lit that grabbed me. It didn't talk down to you and it wasn't about "good boy meets good girl." It was about things that worried me and it didn't delete the bad stuff of life—like death. Saint X was, as they used to say, one cool dude. What a duo we are, Drew! We're the New Age Bobbsey twins. And we're going to have to be quick studies. You'll have to be my Judy. At least I'll be at home among the fairies.

Seriously, Dixie, do you think this assignment is good or bad for our careers?

It depends a lot on what we unearth, I guess. Anyway, it's only a few months. Our beloved departments—Boring Bonds and Death "R" Us—are not fast tracks to partnership. So it shouldn't matter, I hope.

Do you think we should have gotten some guarantees from the Firm?

Darling! If you want guarantees, buy an alarm clock. Look, we didn't have a choice. Wall Street is just recovering and they're *understandably cost-conscious. The Firm is revisiting this year's bonuses for the worker bees. Partners can't afford to cut back. Word is that the Firm is going to lay off 5 percent of the associates again this year and trim the partner ranks with more early retirements. They're calling it "smart sizing" and "attritionizing." Funny how they always come up with catchy words for crappy deeds. I'm afraid Big Law is going the way of phone booths and fedoras, and on top of that, I heard that a couple of partners, including your boss, got Bernied—Madoff with a sizable chunk of their money. You know what Woolly said: "When the animals are hungry, it is a good time to hibernate!"*

Swell, you're making my day.

. . . Oh, Viggie, thank you. This is my stop. See ya tomorrow, Dixie.

I turned the recorder off, took out the cartridge, and returned the recorder to Viggie.

"Vig, I appreciate your giving me that, but it won't be necessary to record their conversations in the future. They're on our side. I trust them. So let's grant them their privacy."

The truth is, I felt bad listening, almost dirty, like a voyeur outside a bedroom window. Technically, I might have just violated federal and state laws. I would destroy the tape.

No harm, no foul.

Who was I kidding? Some confidences have to stay shuttered—especially between associates and partners. Big Brother has no place in that mix.

I did, however, feel like I had passed their muster—even if Dixie didn't like my cords! And they'd passed muster with me. Quite amusing. Seems associates still live by the rules of Wall Street Woolly. Those cornball word-to-the-wise quips are the oral history of Wall Street associates, handed down to each other and modified to fit the times.

Lady Drew and her Light Knight would serve me well.

18

Dog daze of boredom. That is the major problem for canines and their keepers, since almost all dog sins are caused by it. Slippers get chewed. Rugs get soiled. Papers get shredded.

I was starting to feel guilty about Nip. I sensed that the thrill of being a city girl was wearing off. Eight hours of daytime half-sleep—one eye on Mrs. Grady, the other in repose—were likely to erode her brain.

"Viggie, are you free to work for another hour or so?" I asked as we approached my apartment.

"Sure, Mr. T . . . I don't have no plans."

"Great! Let's pick up my dog and take her to Central Park. We could go to the Seventy-Second Street entrance and walk around the pond. There's always a lot of action there!"

So in less than a half hour, the three of us were paw-loose and fancy free. Well, not quite; Nip had to remain on a leash until nine P.M. Park regulations.

We walked for about twenty minutes, each silent in his or her own thoughts. I could see that Viggie was drawn to

Nip. He was a natural dog whisperer. He knew the moves. He knelt down on one knee and patted Nip's side, making contact at her eye level. Equal to equal; homo to cano—instant rapport.

I believe Nip was actually flirting. She was intent on making another convert.

Viggie nodded to me and smiled when he stood up. There was gratitude in his gesture. It was embracing and made me comfortable with him. In a few moments, his smile vanished and I was looking at a well-worn thirty-eight-year-old, heavy with a history I wondered if he would ever share with me.

As we walked, Nip's attention was drawn to the children. She was ever alert, I suspect, and desperately hoping that JJ and Lilli might bound down the path to embrace her—Lilli leading her brother like Glumdalclitch led Gulliver. My eyes moistened.

"You OK, Mr. T?" Viggie inquired solicitously.

"Oh . . . sorry, Vig, I was just thinking about my family. I do that sometimes."

"Me too," he murmured.

"You had children?"

"No, but I lost my family like you, all at once, and I get real sad when I think about them."

"Would you tell me about it?"

What followed was an unexpected saga.

"I was born in Sicily. My mother's name was Inzerillo. Her *borgata*—family—was at war with the Corleones and their relatives, the Sandinos. My uncle, he killed one of the Sandino sons. He was a real *babbeo*, an idiot. *Capisci?* So the families go to the mattress—war. They killed all my uncles, most of my cousins. Every day a death; every night a funeral. Then one day, they stopped my father's car and they put my father, my mother, and my little brother in front of a wall.

They shot them in the head. Then they hacked off my father's and brother's right hands . . . as a message. 'You pay with your hand for the hand that shot our son.' That's what they painted on the wall. After that, my father's family sent me away to live with my nonno in Pescia, in Tuscany near Collodi. His name was Geppetto Viggiano. He took care of me until I was sent to Mr. Baum. I had to leave or they would have killed me too. The New York Corleone family made a deal with the Italian Corleones that any Inzerillos still alive in Italy could go to New York if they promised never to come back. They called us *gli scappati*—the escapees. *Lo non perdona loro!* Never, never will I forgive them!"

"Viggie, I'm sorry for your troubles. I know a little how you are feeling."

"*Grazie*, Mr. T. I know what happened to your family. Mama Terry, she told me. When they killed my family, I was *pazzo*—nuts—for a long time. Only my nonno, he kept me from doing something real crazy. I learned a lot from him. It was good living with him."

"Tell me what it was like there."

Once Viggie started, there was no stopping him. He gave me a verbal tour of both Sicily and Tuscany. He became particularly animated, almost eloquent, when he talked about the hills, the mountains, and the trees. I let him talk.

As we rounded a path, we came upon the bronze statue of the dog Balto. Viggie came up short.

"This is where Mr. Baum and I came with Argos. It's the *cane coraggioso!* Mr. Ben loved this place. That dog saved many children in the snow."

"Yes, I know the story."

Balto indeed was the canine hero of the twenties, having led a pack of huskies on a three-week trek to deliver antitoxins to some remote ice-bound village to prevent the diphtheria epidemic from claiming more lives.

The feat was considered miraculous. It really wasn't. Unlike humans, sled dogs are virtually fatigue-proof. Their metabolic makeup permits them to run one hundred miles a day and then get up and do it again. Scientists are trying to determine why humans can't do the same.

"*I cani rendono la vita migliore!* . . . *Scusi* . . . Dogs, they make life better, I think."

"So do I, Viggie . . . So do I."

"Mr. T, can we go back around the boat pond to the *fungo gigante* and *grande coniglio*? That was Mr. Ben's favorite place."

That wasn't hard to translate—the de Creeft bronze sculpture of Alice perched on an enormous mushroom talking to the White Rabbit.

Every New Yorker has been there at least once. Every child that visits is drawn into climbing on it. Its gilded patina was proof of that.

I must admit it was a favorite of ours. When we would come with JJ and Lilli, I would have them close their eyes and listen very carefully to hear the tinkle from a cloud of imaginary bats that perpetually hover above. They said they could hear them.

I know I could.

19

The next morning, we had a third in the car. Nip joined the team. Ben's place would suit her well and Viggie would attend to her needs during the day. Terry, already alerted, had snacks, water, and the late Argos's leash in place.

Dixie was there when we arrived. Seems he now preferred to walk. His place was thirty minutes away and he liked the exercise.

"Good morning . . . and THIS, I assume, is the fabulous Miss Nip."

Nip was loving all the attention, but after she engaged in some brief nuzzling with Dixie, I sent her off with Terry. She did not protest. She had already scouted the place and knew where the food was. She would have no problem making the kitchen her home base.

"Drew's going to be late. She's meeting with Charlotte Williams this morning," Dixie announced.

"Let's start anyway. You can fill her in later. What did you find out about belladonna?"

"Well, I checked it out. It's fascinating. The proper name is *Atropa belladonna*, but it is often referred to as 'deadly nightshade.' Both of those terms are in the Tolkienese portion of the prec letter. That has to be more than a coincidence. The herb belladonna has quite a gory history. It's probably what Shakespeare's Juliet ingested. Plutarch reported that it was used to poison Marc Antony's troops during the Parthian Wars. According to one legend, belladonna plants belong to the devil, who is obsessive in caring for them. He takes only one night a year off from tending to their needs. He must be quite anal. I guess that's how he made senior partner in Hades so soon."

He paused, perhaps wishing he could take that flippancy back.

"And there is also a legend that belladonna often takes the form of a beautiful but deadly enchantress. In fact, the famous Roman poisoner, Locusta, killed Claudius by slipping him a mickey of belladonna. She was sentenced to death for that. It's grown primarily in Eastern Europe, particularly Croatia and Serbia. Apparently it is a quick-working poison. After ingesting a lethal dose, a person loses his voice, gets convulsive, and his eyes dilate. You might remember, it was used by Sandra Bullock to knock out Nicole Kidman's bad-news boyfriend in *Practical Magic*, except she overdid it and he died. And in *Perfect Stranger*—a great movie with Halle Berry and Bruce Willis—a character was poisoned by it.

"Now it also has more positive uses. It can be medically beneficial and it's a popular aphrodisiac with certain hippie types. Do you know the British group Queen? Their hit song 'Keep Yourself Alive' boasted that they 'loved a million women in a belladonic haze.'

"It is also said to put more viva in your Viagra. Unfortunately, OD'ing on it can make you hot as Hades, red as a beet, dry as a bone, blind as a bat, mad as a hatter . . . and dead."

I interjected as an aside, "Bilbo Baggins's mother's name is Belladonna Took. I think she is one of the few female characters in all of Tolkien's stories."

Dixie continued, "Oh, and that heart symbol. It's the classic sign for polyamory."

"Polyamory?"

"That's a romantic bond among three people having a loving and intimate relationship, with the consent of everyone involved. The symbol consists of a red heart for love interwoven with a blue infinity sign. It's not to be confused with a ménage à trois or a pajama party and certainly not with consensual group gropes. Those are simply sexercises. Polyamory is considered in some circles as respectable as monogamy, although others view poly couples as ethical sluts.

"In history there are a lot of respectable poly people. Voltaire, Rousseau, Lord Byron, Dumas, Sartre, Dali—not to mention Simone de Beauvoir, Amelia Earhart, Alfred Kinsey, and Warren Buffett."

"You're a veritable Cliffie this morning, Dixie," I quipped, showing my age.

Drew burst into the study and, without any salutations, threw down the files she was cradling, cast off her coat, and breathlessly began.

"I have some late-breaking news! As you know, Tremaine's lawyer filed a lawsuit in the State Supreme Court seeking to invalidate Ben's last Will. His position is that Evan used his influence over Ben to insert himself in place of Mrs. Baum as executor and that Ben's mind and body were not sound enough to make an informed judgment. If he succeeds, he will then make a motion to have Ben's previous Will, which was attached to their moving papers, filed in the Probate

Court. Hard to figure out de Vil's moves. The estate department thinks it's simply to put the issue in the New York Supreme Court. As you two know, that's the lowest court in New York—just a few notches above Traffic Court. The judges there are your least sophisticated but most political judges around. The case was assigned to Judge Babcock. De Vil was a big fund-raiser for her judicial campaign a few years ago. That's the bad news. The good news is it gives us time to complete our investigation as the litigators argue about what is the proper forum. And that will keep the prec letter private at least for a while.

"By the way, the differences in the Wills are dramatic. Under the prior one—the one they proposed should be probated—wifey would get all the real estate outright, except the townhouse. That's probably worth $125 million and would be tax-free to her.

"And that Will also provided for her to get $10 million outright and all Ben's art, except for the art here in the hobbit house—also tax-free. I haven't seen an inventory of that yet.

"Since she would be the executrix, she might be able to control the foundation and influence the vote of the foundation's shares of Ozone. That's a nice percentage of Ozone's outstanding shares.

"And there's more! The real zinger is—hold onto your seats—m'lady is pregnant! And it's a boy, we are advised."

"Wow!" mouthed Dixie.

"Yes, and that could mean another heir. I'm pretty sure that a child conceived prior to death but born after a person dies is deemed his heir for inheritance purposes. Assuming I'm right, the children's share of the Ozone stock in the Family Trust will get divided into thirds—with Dorothy and Leo getting two-thirds and the new baby boy one-third. Lady Tremaine, of course, would be his guardian. She is naming him Bentley

Lyman Baum. Bentley is Tremaine's maiden name—no relation to the car people. Lyman is Ben's first name. When you parse all this out, the merry widow and her little Lord Bentley end up with a lot of shekels, as my dear mother would say. And probably effective control of Ozone, assuming she gets to vote little Bentley's shares in the Trust."

There was a momentary silence until finally I spoke.

"That IS big news. And it makes our job even more difficult.

"Interesting question: Does the Firm have to turn over the Precatory Letter to de Vil? It was not addressed to 'my executor,' but to Evan personally. I'll need help here."

Drew responded with some authority. "I expect so. The Firm will eventually have to turn it over. It was, after all, attached to the Will in which he named Evan executor."

"Potentially, that's a real bummer for the Firm," Dixie volunteered. "If the judge buys de Vil's arguments, the probate work would slide over to de Vil's firm, and even the Ozone work would be up for grabs, unless Mr. Trombley makes some pact with Tremaine or perhaps Luc."

I was thinking along the same lines.

It has always amused me how oddly prioritized lawyers' minds are. My first thoughts were not about the baby, not about the family, but about the Firm's business . . . and I would not even be affected by it. The Firm, however, would be. The loss of the Firm's largest estate as well as its biggest corporate client would alter the Firm's economics dramatically.

Dixie and Drew were animatedly speculating on the effects of all of this, almost oblivious to my presence. Events like this are hot spices in the world of associates.

"Let's get back to work!" I said, cutting off their chatter. "And let's see how this affects our job."

"Well, for one thing, I don't think we'll be able to interview the widow at this point. We might be conflicted, even though technically Dixie and I are on leave from the Firm for three months."

I agreed and added, "One way to look at our task is that we are not practicing law, but rather doing investigative fact gathering. It may be at some point advantageous to view it as that. In any case, that doesn't preclude us from interviewing the others. Evan told me that Dorothy, Luc, Leo, Abelard, Eloise, and Kati met with Ben in his suite the day he died. I'm afraid that we are going to have to ratchet up. I suggest that both of you leave immediately for London. I'll have Terry make reservations for you. We'll see if she can get the same suite that Ben used, if that's all right with you two."

No objection was forthcoming, but I did notice a sudden pallor appear on Drew's face.

"Drew, I think you should contact the investigators who were retained by the Firm's London office and see if they have had any success in finding Kati.

"Dixie, you should work with Patricia Stewart. She's in charge of the London office. See if she can get you into the coroner's office. Her brother's a constable in London. See how we go about getting the medical reports and what it would take to do an autopsy quickly. Also, talk to the doctor who attended to Ben in the hotel. Hopefully, you can get all this done in a week.

"Take an evening flight. You're both young and we can't afford to lose a day. In fact, would leaving tonight work for you? Viggie will take you to the airport. Meanwhile I'll work the stateside witnesses as best I can."

I took their lack of protest as acquiescence.

20

I had forgotten how imposing the Addison Racquet Club was.

Its massive granite edifice, unchanged for a century, straddled almost a whole city block. It was a Florentine palace staring down with evident disdain at the hectic hubbub of city life.

When I called Evan, he suggested we meet "off campus"—meaning outside the Firm—for, as he put it, "delicacy reasons," and suggested the "Club," which he felt needed no further identification. It's a stodgy, fraternal—read men only—club, located on Fifth Avenue.

It was there that Evan felt most at home. If he had any social failings, one could ascribe them to time warp. He seemed stuck in the eighties, the time when Madonna first hit the charts and Ronald Reagan was president. That was when Evan became a senior partner and a member of the Executive Committee.

The only change in those thirty years at the Addison was the flowers.

Evan was waiting on the second floor, indifferently leafing through the *Wall Street Journal*. He rose and greeted me with his signature firm-gripped handshake, left hand massaging my shoulder.

The "old boy" salutation and salute. No bear hugs here.

The club's main reception hall was pure *Masterpiece Theater*— twin functioning fireplaces, paneled walls boasting foxhunting scenes in ornate frames, and antique tables showcasing well-polished trophies that testified to long-forgotten athletic prowess.

The room's ceiling was supported by twenty-foot Tuscan columns, painted mottled black with gilded details and illuminated by four great coach lamps.

Warm brown leather chairs and sofas populated the dark interior of the great room where Evan was holding court. Fortunately the arched ceiling-high windows ushered in enough sunlight to ensure that the mildew of the past was kept at bay, at least until the seasons changed and the walk-in fireplaces could do that job.

Evan offered me tea from a nearby sterling silver urn. Muffins and jam could accompany it. I demurred.

"It's quiet and uneventful here . . . not like the Firm," he volunteered, with a self-satisfied grin. "Everything here is based on tradition: Monday night, bridge; Wednesday, billiards; and Saturday, a classic movie in the study. And the menu never changes. Cream of chicken on toast is my favorite. It's like an oasis—no iPhones, iPads, iPods. And the members are . . . ," he paused, searching for the most politic words, ". . . so much like me. They leave their attitudes and agendas at the door."

Peering over his glasses, which had settled at the base of his very patrician nose, he allowed, "You would love it here!"

"I'm sure I would."

We both knew I was lying.

He was clearly in no hurry to discuss my concerns for he launched into a reverie about the Club, his sanctuary he confessed, from the demands of Big Law—the twenty-first-century term for white shoe Wall Street large-firm practice. That was a more appropriate handle.

Large law firms were no longer on Wall Street, having moved uptown, and they no longer exclusively employed those white-shoed ivy school boys who honed their writing skills editing their prep schools' literary journals, the ones that J. D. Salinger so cunningly maligned.

No firm today could compete—or even survive—if it were populated predominantly by WASP male ivy-educated effetes.

Today's big firms are, in fact, exceedingly efficient legal factories that employ—or more aptly consume—the most accomplished and the most eager associates they can find, regardless of family, school ties, gender, or ethnicity. These beaver kits are promised professionalism at the pinnacle and, to seal the deal, they receive annual salaries and bonuses that range from an entry-level law school graduate at $180,000 to more than $300,000 for a senior associate.

So as not to make them feel too guilty for this largesse, ample pro bono and indigent legal-aid assignments are always available for them in their spare time.

Of course, there is no such time, unless they can learn not to sleep during the week.

No matter how mercenary these institutions have become, they are still able to ingest the best and the brightest, the silver-spooners and the overachievers, and turn them into pantry maids and foot soldiers, spitting out 90 percent of them within ten years—older and more weary than their biological ages.

Law firms were spoiled by the baby boomers, who had an inexhaustible appetite for hard work. The millennials and the

whatevers, albeit just as hungry, seem to want to pursue their
personal passions at the same time they work. And today's
associates want to be included. Many of the older partners
resent that. Doesn't augur well for billable statistics and
subservience.

"You know the history of the club, don't you, Jonathan?"

"No, sir."

I knew that was the response and excuse he needed.

"Well, let me share it with you," he began, as he poured
himself another cup of Earl Grey, savoring its orange fragrance.

"It's a rather regal monument to the art and pleasure
of racquet sports. Tennis is truly the game of nobles. Those
tennis terms, you know, all find their origin in the royal
courts of Europe. In fact, the word 'tennis' derives from the
French word *'tenez.'* Roughly translated, it means 'May I have
your attention?' You used to call that out before serving to
put your opponent on alert."

He droned on, much more donnish than I remembered
him.

"Here at the club they play tennis the old way. We call it
'court tennis.' Unfortunately my playing days are over—too
many herniated disks."

That, I knew, was a nose-extending canard.

Evan has never been a competitive athlete. I suspect he
found losing unacceptable and didn't like to sweat.

"I've always recommended that young lawyers take up the
sport. It requires not only a practiced skill, but also guile, a
considered strategy, and the strong will to win. All the quali-
ties one needs to survive at the Firm."

He looked up to see if I was still enraptured.

In fact, I had tuned out on his soliloquy awhile back.

I found it more amusing to observe the depleted gene
pool of Binkys, Dickies, Barclays, and Alistairs scurrying off

for a shower or a massage. I suspect they were still wearing their prep school ties.

No dress-down here.

"If you'd like, I'd be delighted to sponsor you for membership," he offered disingenuously, privately praying for my demur, which I quickly gave to him. I saw no need to make him uneasy.

Enough, he's had his moment. Now for mine.

"Evan, I wanted to discuss my engagement and get your take on the latest bump-up—Tremaine's pregnancy. And, also, de Vil's lawsuit." It took him a few seconds to process my request.

"Oh . . . well, I don't take de Vil's suit seriously. They have no grounds to claim undue influence. Ben was his own man. He was in fact very lucid until the end. Anyone involved will testify to that. I have been the executor for the last twenty years, with the exception of two of the last three. That was Tremaine's doing. She had a fit when he told her about my position. She gave him no peace until he named her. Once the honeymoon was over, Ben insisted we revert to his original preference. You can confirm that with Charlotte. When Charlotte told de Vil, just before the funeral, that I was the executor, they shouldn't have been surprised. This is just legal posturing. Again that old expression applies. The best offense is a good defense."

"Something like that," I responded, mercifully not correcting him. He had reversed the famous Von Clausewitz line.

"They're just, I suspect, trolling for a generous enhancement over what Tremaine got under Ben's last Will, hoping that we pay up to avoid a sordid public media event. The rags would relish that. Look at what happened with Astor."

"Particularly, I would think, when they see the Precatory Letter."

Evan stiffened.

"Why on earth would we give them that? It's addressed to me personally, and if I'm not to be the executor it would not be relevant. Additionally, it should be considered a privileged letter between a client and his attorney and out of their reach."

"I understand, but arguably the letter goes to Ben's state of mind, so the litigators and the Trusts and Estates folks might feel differently."

"That's absurd! They can all go fuck themselves!" Evan countered, with a turn of phrase I'd never heard him utter before. Obviously this matter had settled in his stomach like a prickly pear.

"That seems like something Charlotte would dream up. As for the child, I'm happy for Tremaine. It'll give her something to remind her of Ben, other than her inheritance."

"Don't you find it odd that they would have been intimate at the same time he was essentially writing her out of his Will, terminating their marriage, and carrying on with Kati?"

"Jonathan, I don't speculate on a client's libido. You know as well as I do that Ben was always in high fervor. Sex may be the poor man's polo, but it was the only sport Ben cared passionately about. And Tremaine, after all, was his wife."

"Well, do you know if he was seeing any other women besides Tremaine and Kati?"

"Jonathan, you should know—better than most—that Ben and I were professional friends, not social friends."

I believed Evan. Thinking about it, I cannot remember his ever referring to a single non-client-related person. I'm not sure he had personal friends. He was a true legal monk. The Firm was his ministry, this club his chapel. He needed no more.

I sensed this line of inquiry was over as far as he was concerned.

"Evan, the principal purpose of meeting with you today is to debrief you about the events that took place the day Ben died and get your input on them. You're the only impartial person who was there." I thought the last phrase might lubricate his response.

"Well, what would you like to know?" he asked. With Evan, a little sucking up goes a long way.

"Let's start with the purpose of the trip to London."

"Ben, Luc, and I were meeting with Darren Russett's people about the possible sale of ClearAire. You know, Ozone's private security and military assistance division—Luc's baby. You haven't been around in the last few years to witness its extraordinary growth. ClearAire benefited dramatically from wars and global unrest. It's now surpassing the entertainment division in profitability. Ben wanted to sell. He feared that in time Washington would significantly reduce its dependence on hired guns. Deep down I think Ben found it dirty business. Luc was adamantly opposed. I tried to be a matchmaker, even suggesting at one point that Luc consider leading a buyout of the division. Luc rejected that. He felt the business needed to remain part of Ozone to succeed. Ben remained unpersuaded, but agreed to think further on it. Anyway, Russett's offer was well below what Ben would accept. They're hard bargainers, but I'm sure they'll be back with more. Their courtship is just beginning."

"Did you in fact meet with the Russett group?" I asked.

"Yes, in the morning, just after Dorothy left. As I recall, the meeting lasted about two hours, and after that Luc, Ben, and I huddled on the subject. Luc and Ben went at each other for about an hour. Darren and Ben go back a long way. They became very good friends—primarily through their common charities—UNICEF and the Boy Scouts. Ben idolized him. You do know that Russett is now the richest man in the world—next to Gates. Ben was very upset by Luc's conduct at the meeting, even though Darren wasn't there. He feared that Luc's abrasive attitude would get back to Russett."

"After that meeting, what came next?"

"Luc left, and Ben spent some time with Leo alone. Then he and I had lunch with Peter Abelard, the executive director of the Baum Foundation. He happened to be in London on foundation business and asked to have lunch. Ben fired Peter during dessert."

"Why?"

"Ben wanted to change the foundation's mission purpose from promoting the arts and amassing a collection back to its original mission purpose—fostering a better understanding of autism and enhancing children's welfare and the appreciation of literature, particularly the study of how children's books speak to adults. Subjects, I suspect, Peter had no expertise or interest in. And Ben wanted to make them not just guidelines but binding on the trustees."

"Was that a reaction to the flap over Leona Helmsley's millions to her dog?" I asked. "Remember that case? The trustees essentially ignored her direction and went their own way. That reminds me! I should put provisions in my Will relating to my dog and ensure that my executors don't ignore my wishes!"

Evan seemed disdainfully nonplussed. So I proceeded with my inquiries.

"How did Mr. Abelard handle his termination?"

"I must say, Peter was quite the gentleman about it. I sensed he had been forewarned.

"After that, let's see . . . " Evan paused.

"Oh, I left to go make some stateside calls while Ben and Peter finished up. Then Ben met with his daughter's friend, Dr. Thompson. She's Leo's psychiatrist—or psychologist of sorts. I was not needed for that."

"Did you overhear what that was about?"

"Not really. My room had a door to the hall and a door into the living room of Ben's suite. That one was a double so you could hear only loud sounds."

"Did you hear anything loud during the meeting with Dr. Thompson?"

"Now that you ask, yes. Seemed like the two of them were having a blistering exchange. I could not make out what it was about. I presumed it had to do with Leo, but I am not sure. It was quite heated.

"I then left for a few hours. Went to Nutter's on Savile Row to pick out some new shirts. They're still the best. Later I returned to the hotel suite to report stateside on some corporate developments. When I got back, Kati had already arrived. I joined them for a quick drink and then went back to my room to freshen up. I was going to Harry's Bar for cocktails with Sonia Shüller. She's a new partner in the London office and later I had planned to have dinner with Jocelyne Masters. She is the widow of the former head of that office. She's a lovely woman. Do you remember her?"

"No, not really."

"Well, just as I was about to leave, Ben came out and asked if we would fetch the house doctor. He said he was not feeling well. We called the doctor, who came immediately. He and Ben retired to the bedroom. After a few minutes, the doctor came out and told us Ben had died."

"Must have been very traumatic."

"Yes, we were close, as you know . . . I suspect the day was too much for him. His ticker just gave up."

There was something hollow, detached, and matter-of-fact in Evan's description of Ben's last moments. I would have expected a little more angst, even from Evan.

"It's unfortunate that his death occurred, but it was going to happen sooner or later anyway. You know, of course, about his condition. Perhaps it was a godsend—may have saved him a lot of pain."

"On that subject, his cancer, who knew about that?"

"It was a tight circle—Dorothy and, of course, myself. I expect that Dorothy told Dr. Thompson—Eloise—and perhaps there might have been a few others, but I don't think Luc or Kati or even Tremaine knew anything about it. Oh, and I expect his secretary did too."

"One last question, Evan. What's your take on Ben's letter to you?"

"It was typical Ben. You know . . . as hard-nosed and serious as he was in business, he was quite quirky in his personal views and hobbies. He didn't discuss them much with me. He really was into that fantasy literature. Can't say that I am. I suppose it was his way to let off steam and have fun. I don't make anything of the letter. As far as his demise, I certainly don't think foul play was involved. For god's sake, he had a heart attack."

He paused, realizing that his annoyance was getting the better of him.

"The letter—just the jokester in him creating a little havoc. I'm sorry that Charlotte didn't simply file it away. Then we wouldn't be involved in this nonsense and wouldn't have had to impose on you."

He leaned toward me, his eyes staring straight into mine.

"Jonathan, you're like a son to me, always have been. This inquisition that the Firm roped you into is pure partner posturing. The sooner you conclude this matter, the better for all concerned. Wrap it up quickly. We're only doing this to placate the pantywaists at the Firm. We really owe it to the shareholders of Ozone to get back to business and to Ben's heirs to let them get on with their lives."

That was his summation and the signal that we were done.

21

"Yes, we're on the road again. This time to Washington. *Like a band of gypsies, on the road again!*"

Nip didn't respond, but Viggie did. *"I zingari? Non capisco!* They live like wolves in the woods," Viggie murmured.

Italians are not very hospitable to Romas.

"It's a song," I lamely tried to explain. Willie Nelson wasn't in his vocabulary so I changed the subject. It was too early in our relationship to work on tolerance issues.

I had decided to have Viggie drive us down. It would give us a little break from Ben's place and give Terry some time off to sort out Ben's files without constant interruptions. Nip loved the car. And the Willard Hotel was very dog-friendly.

"Vig, I'm surprised you've never been to Washington. It's America's Rome. Quite beautiful." And it was. Some view it as the first tangible manifestation of the City Beautiful Movement in America. That movement's proponents believed in the power of fountains, statues, and tree-lined boulevards as an antidote for moral decay and social disorder. Not that it

worked all that well in that last regard, but it's still a stun-
ningly beautiful city.

I was off to debrief Luc and garner some documents at
Ozone's Washington operation. Its elaborate offices are housed
in the Evening Star Building on Pennsylvania Avenue, just an
hour away from ClearAire's principal training facility, which is
located on 2,000 acres in rural Virginia. These two locations
were Luc Grogaman's fiefdom.

Luc had responded with undisguised disdain when he
agreed to meet. He was a legend at Ozone. A former Navy
SEAL who, after a short stint in the service, earned his MBA
in record time. He then joined Ozone and rose quickly within
the ranks. Grogaman was not one of my favorites. He seemed
infected by a malevolence that I could not comprehend. Perhaps something had happened during his service days. I found
him the opposite of Ben. Perhaps opposites do attract. And, I
have to admit, they made an effective team.

We had a long ride ahead of us. Nip was no diversion.
She had fallen sound asleep as soon as we cleared the Holland
Tunnel.

So I engaged Viggie in more stories about Italy. He seemed
to brighten up when he talked about his youth—other than
his immediate family.

"Vig, what was living with your nonno like?" He looked
at me curiously, but after a moment, took the bait.

"My nonno, he was a *gradevole persona* . . . a good man,
a happy man. He had no one to live with so he liked to take
me in. He would tell me stories, especially about *la tratta delle
marionette*, Pinocchio. You heard the story, no?"

"Yes, it was one of my favorites."

"But it's not like the movie. That's for *bambini*. The real
story is about a boy who does bad things. He acted like a
sciocco—an idiot. But he always comes back to his father,

who—you know—had the same name as my nonno. Maybe that's why he liked the story so much. Pinocchio, he had many adventures. You want me to tell you about them?"

"Sure . . . beats talk radio."

"C'era una volta un pezzo di legno," he said with a broad smile. "Once upon a time there was this piece of wood."

Then we tramped through the somewhat sordid stories of a rebellious child who hated school, rejected authority, refused to learn, and took pleasure in laziness, a child who was occasionally cruel and dishonest, with barely a trace of integrity. He, of course, falls in with the wrong crowd.

The way Viggie told the story, the little wooden orphan was indeed very selfish and ungrateful, his "father" understandably hot-tempered, and the Blue Fairy quite hard-hearted.

Viggie told me, through these escapades, the story of his life—his pain, his outrage, his search for family. It would seem that the wood from which Pinocchio was carved was really humanity itself.

The only real difference between Viggie and the puppet was that Pinocchio was looking for his family tree and Viggie was running away from his.

"Do you know, Mr. T, that Mr. Baum gave money for a statue in the Pinocchio Park that was built on the river Pescia, right near my nonno's house? It is beautiful, but not as big as the park in New York."

"Yes, Terry told me a little about it."

Viggie was a good talker as well as a good—and fast—driver. He could do both at the same time and without taking his hands off the wheel, a virtuoso performance for an Italian.

"How did you get to be such a good driver?"

Viggie beamed as he told me the story of his adolescence.

"You know, when I was young, before my family was killed, I was what they called *un cattivo ragazzo,* a bad boy. All

I wanted to do was drive faster, shoot better, and run faster than anyone else. I thought that would keep me alive . . . and maybe if I was with my family that day they too would be alive. My hero was Mario Andretti. You know him? He was the greatest race car driver ever and, like me, he came to America when he was young. I only knew America from the movies—lots of fast cars and everyone had a gun. My nonno said no guns and no driving, but he let me go running. I ran many kilometers every day. And when my uncle told me I could come to New York, I was very happy. Mr. Ben, he was a lot like my nonno. He was hard on me but good. He said he would pay for me to go to school for race car drivers for three months. It was my dream and now I go there every year for two weeks to practice.

"He also helped me get a gun license and put me in a shooting club in Chelsea—not far from where we work. And he also got me into a gym. He was a good—a great—man. I loved him . . . and I loved his dog, Argos. Now they are both gone. I only cried three times in my whole life and these were two of them. Now I only have Mama Terry. And you and Dixie—er, Mr. Dixon. You know, he and I go to the gym together and for long runs on weekends. Sometimes in the big park where we went to with your dog and sometimes we go to Roosevelt Island and run along the water. Dixie is strong like me. He makes me work hard. I like that . . . I like him."

That was news. Dixie had never mentioned it. I smiled. These were not my children. Each was his own person. They didn't need my permission.

Just as he finished, we entered the Fort McHenry Tunnel in Baltimore.

We would soon be in the capital.

I scrolled down my e-mails, past the spam that had slipped by my filter, until I got to Drew's missive.

She reported success with locating Kati. She would meet with her the day after next. She advised that Dixie had interviewed the hotel doctor and had an audience with a deputy coroner the next morning. She indicated that she had other interesting info, not appropriate for e-mail.

We came into Washington and proceeded down Pennsylvania Avenue. The National Gallery was to our left with its subtle yet imposing modern wing. It had been Alice's favorite museum.

Moments later, we pulled in front of the Willard, one of Washington's most prestigious hotels. The "residence of presidents" is its tagline. It is fair for it to be boastful. The Willard has hosted every American president as a guest since our twelfth, Zachary Taylor. Lincoln stayed there with his family for the ten days leading up to his inauguration. The bill, including meals, totaled $773.75.

Only the prices and the plumbing have changed since then.

It's a national treasure, full of history. The public rooms befit a place for the powerful and privileged. The grand foyer shows off its mirrored panels, marble columns, period chandeliers, and intricate marble mosaics, while a harpist serenades.

The private rooms are as one would expect—heavy curtains, high four-poster beds, mirrors, and TVs discreetly but strategically placed. The management had a sterling silver water bowl awaiting Nip, with a bottle of beef-flavored water.

Nice touch.

Nip surveyed the bed's height. It was a giant leap for dogkind, but she was game. And after one aborted assault, she made it. She sensed that Washington was a place where it was best to be on top.

I sent Nip out with Viggie for a walk, around Constitution Avenue, of course, routing him past the Ellipse and the White House while I hurried to the National Gallery before it closed. I thought a little aesthetic nourishment was in order. It would fortify me for what I expected would be an unpleasant breakfast with Luc tomorrow.

The walk was not only invigorating but enlightening. Gone in large part were the government geeks and policy wonks that I remembered populating a stodgy city. Rather there seemed to be a younger, more vibrant crowd milling about. You have to, of course, discount the steady stream of weary tourists, loaded down with souvenirs and looking for more.

Maybe it has to do with that young couple from Chicago that moved in a few years ago.

Before I knew it, I was there, at the entrance of the National Gallery. Calder, Moore, Noguchi, Serra, and LeWitt stood witness to the visitors as they entered. I was drawn to the Edward Hoppers. For me they showcase how the bittersweetness of being alone can be assuaged by embracing familiar surroundings. I had experienced that biting isolation and the depth of that feeling in the preceding three years.

Looking at the Hoppers, I sensed that they were telling me it was time to move on.

22

I'm an early bird and apparently so are the pigeons of Washington.

Nip and I crossed the hotel's lobby just as the sun had broken through the cloud cover. I found a bench in Pershing Square. A passel of pigeons was already there—the only other occupants. A few scattered when we approached but most held their ground. After all, we were just visitors. And they had seen millions of us pass by.

Washington's rock pigeons are different from those of Paris and New York. Their gray bodies and dark blue necks are set off by their snow-white rumps. With wings that boast two black epaulets, they have an almost military look.

Across the street, a congress of crows sat on the phone lines taking all this in. I smiled when I thought that among them might be Roäc—the crow Ben had referred to in his letter—watching over us, about to give me some sign.

If he did, I missed it.

Nevertheless this was a good time and a good place to gather my thoughts about my breakfast with Luc Groga-man. There were subjects that I could not broach with him professionally—Ben's testamentary dispositions and his Preca-tory Letter. Both fell within the attorney-client privilege so I had to have a cover for the conversation.

Suicide? I could query him about that. It could invali-date Ben's insurance policy, presuming it was a new policy. That, though, seemed far-fetched. Suicide by heart attack just doesn't seem plausible.

I needed another subject that would engage him. The potential sale of Ozone's military assistance subsidiary, Clear-Aire. I was sure that would get his attention.

We met as agreed at the Café du Parc, the Willard's power breakfast haunt. I scheduled it early enough for us to find a quiet corner. Surprisingly, he was on time. For some clients, tardiness was a marker of importance—too many more impor-tant things to do than worry about annoying your attorney. The truth is we are hardly ever annoyed. We charge by the hour and the meter turns on when scheduled. Dusting our heels doesn't diminish our fees. In this case, I wasn't charging by the hour—and he wasn't late. He arrived with a lieutenant, whom he curtly introduced as Alessandro Sandino.

Sandino was short and stocky. His frame seemed steel-cut. His hair, latte brown with blond streaks, was already reced-ing. His nose had a slight tilt, probably from a break long ago. A stubborn chin and protuberant eyes rounded out an unwelcoming demeanor. His visage reinforced his prizefight-er's body—bull neck, barrel chest, and knock-kneed shanks.

I had not seen Luc for more than three years other than fleetingly at Ben's funeral. Up close, he was still tight and mus-cular. His salt-and-pepper hair was trimmed military short; his pallor was grayer than I remembered. It was his eyes, however, that defined him. They were as I remembered them—colorless and remorseless. I sensed in them a volatility that could turn malevolent given the right impetus. It may sound a bit melodramatic, but he heralded a dark destiny.

"I just read about your Patriot Award from the National Rifle Association. Impressive! I was unaware of your interest in the plight of the eagle."

I always Google a person I'm meeting beforehand. You never know what you'll find. The National Rifle Association is essentially a lobbyist for the gun industry and I would expect that ClearAire is a very good industry customer. And, I surmise, to dress up this organization's agenda, they give awards for activities that nonmembers might find appealing. For an assortment of reasons, bald eagles were threatened with extinction and in 1967 Congress declared them endangered. In 2007, they were taken off that list, but they are still protected.

"Ha! You're well informed, Tucker. We have adopted the bex eagle—what most call the bald eagle—as ClearAire's logo and mascot. They are fierce fighters. A good visual reference for what we do. The eagle has his talons around the globe just like ClearAire has its operations all over the world. We have given a sizable sum to organizations promoting the protection of eagles.

"I'm a big game hunter myself. It's my only hobby. Nevertheless, I have never killed an endangered species . . . well, hardly ever," he added, smiling at Sandino who shot him back a knowing grin.

"I've got a place near Benin City. Nigeria is a great place for big game hunters. And ClearAire is very active there. So I get special access. But enough of this shit. What are you here for?"

He made it apparent there would be no more small talk so I launched into my inquiry.

"I've been engaged by the Firm to help facilitate the administration of Ben's estate and as you might expect, federal and state taxes play an important role. Since Ben left a considerable amount of his worth to his children, the estate taxes will require the estate to liquidate considerable amounts of his assets. One alternative we are exploring is to recommend that Ozone spin off its military operations and pay the net proceeds out to shareholders as a cash dividend. That would provide the liquidity necessary for the taxes. We would, of course, need the board's approval to effectuate such a plan."

My pronouncement about the potential sale of ClearAire produced an immediate and expected rejoinder.

I quite enjoyed his unease.

"Listen, Tucker, I don't have the bandwidth to deal with your Firm's crap right now. I'm wall-to-wall since Baum died. I have made some great strides in calming the shareholders' shitfits that followed his death. I have no intention of circling back to satisfy your partners' prurient curiosity."

He then glanced down not particularly furtively at his array of mobile devices—multiple gadgets simultaneously active were the new symbols of power.

Any good lawyer understands body language. It's part of the skill set that separates one from the pack. I always watch the eyes. His weren't bulging anymore. He had checked his anger.

"That makes no sense. The idea of selling ClearAire is idiocy. You may have heard that Ben was toying with the idea of selling off the division, but he was not serious. I like to think he was more titillated by the fact that the Russett group was interested than anything else. Our government contracts group is on the cusp of real growth. There is no reason to sell it now—or ever. Our public shareholders aren't clamoring for liquidity; we haven't yet reached our potential. And our biggest competitor, Blackwater, is on the run. They recently agreed to pay the government forty-two mill for fuckups in Afghanistan and Sudan. Five of their execs have been indicted on weapons and obstruction charges, and two of their guards are up on federal murder charges. Their CEO has exiled himself to Abu Dhabi. Congress is constantly holding hearings on their offshore activities. Do you see what an opening this is for us? Of course Russett is interested. This is big."

"Perhaps Ben was concerned with the prospect of the government shutting down the wars," I volunteered.

"Look, it's a win-win for us. There will always be wars somewhere and, if America is involved, the Democrats will want to outsource as much as possible. That's what we do. If the hawks ever have their way, we have a hundred-year annuity. ClearAire may be the only option."

He paused for a caffeine hit, then continued.

"You know, Tucker, these are delicate times. The board is skittish. I need to keep them placated. They were all very close to Ben. I don't want Ben's death to spook them and your poking around won't help."

He was right to worry. Ben owned the Ozone board like every successful CEO does. They were handpicked people of impeccable pedigree whose loyalty was prized more than their insights. Without Ben, they were leaderless. He'd kept the board in a tight corral.

"I assure you we will be discreet," I said. Then I abruptly changed the subject, hoping to catch him off-guard. "It must have been hard for you being there when Ben died," I said.

He quickly, and I sensed quite defensively, countered.

"Look, I had left the hotel long before he died. In fact, I was at the airport when Trombley called me. I left shortly thereafter on business. There was nothing I could do. Why do you ask?"

Malignity was evident on his face. His countenance became Putinesque. He was like that—one moment seemingly exuberant, almost sympathetic, the next openly menacing.

"We're just trying to rule out foul play and suicide. Either could possibly affect the disposition of his wealth. You were with him for what we understand was much of the day, so I'd like your insight about the people he came in contact with that day."

"Look, Tucker, I don't know what you're really after, but you can tell those fucking partners of yours they're on a short leash. I will not allow this company to be brought down by its lawyers' ghoulish curiosity. Ben is dead. He was an old man. These things happen. I saw nothing out of the ordinary that day. But the company goes on and as of now that responsibility is mine. I intend to meet that challenge. And I better not find any of your time on our bill. We have enough problems with the SEC and Justice right now, especially the fucking SEC. It's like mud wrestling a pig. After a while, you realize that the freakin' pig is really enjoying it. We don't need you and your goddamned associates diverting our attention. Understood?"

There was that implacability showing through those piercing stone-gray eyes. I couldn't shake the feeling that something was rotten in the State of Ozone.

And Luc knew it.

He stood up archly, signaled his capo, and turned to me.

"Copies of the documents you requested have been assembled at ClearAire. We'd rather you and your people didn't spend time there. Do you have a driver?"

I nodded affirmatively.

"Well then, I suggest your driver go pick them up. And if you don't mind, could he take us with him? Our car broke down this morning and it will take too long to get a car service this time of day. We have pressing business out there and it would save time."

"Yes, of course, my car's out front."

With firm shakes and almost imperceptible clicks of their heels, we were off.

Nip was waiting with Viggie in tow. I introduced Viggie to his unexpected passengers and immediately sensed that something serious had agitated him.

23

Something was amiss. The breakfast conversation and Luc's attitude just didn't calibrate. Beneath it all, he was cold, distant, and unreadable.

Nip willingly came to my side. I sensed she wanted no part of Luc and his goon. We set off for a long walk, hoping to clear my mind. It would be a good hour and a half before Viggie returned.

"Let's first go see this bex eagle, Nip. It's across the park."

Eagles are not my favorite fowl. They're big, with a wingspan of over six feet. I'll give them that, but they are carnivores. They eat fish, ducks, turtles, and even their own. And they feast on carrion willingly. Not like my feathered friends at Twenty Acres. They're almost all vegetarians, although they're known to eat roadkill and leftovers when the opportunity presents itself. I think on the whole, though, compared to eagles, the denizens of Twenty Acres are much less aggressive.

I like it that way. Nevertheless, the bex eagle became our national emblem, winning over the objection of Ben Franklin, who had thrown in his vote for the wild turkey.

Washington was graced that day with perfect weather—no clouds, no humidity and a breeze that was embracing. I thought it an ideal day for a walk in the verdant open space that makes the capital so inviting—the Ellipse, Washington's monument, and the National Mall.

But before we did, we traversed the park to see the sculpture of the bex eagle, ClearAire's mascot and symbol. A voracious carnivore for a company of mercenaries. It lived up to its reputation. Wings and claws extended, intent on the kill, it was truly menacing. Nip ignored it; inanimate objects were of little interest unless they smelled.

I had almost forgotten how beneficial these walks could be—therapeutic, if not aerobic. Nip was more into information retrieval than exercise, yet any invitation to roam was met with excessive enthusiasm, manifested by a little dance-like ritual. She then settled into her sniff-and-anoint routine. Somewhat petulantly, I slid back into my happy Hamlet mode and contemplated death—a subject I had become conversant with.

One thing seemed sure. Magic can't bring people back, not even in the wizarding world. Life seems unfair. The words of Tolkien keep bouncing about in my head. "Many who live deserve death. Many that die deserve life." Alice and the kids deserved much more than they got.

Enough, I told myself. I'd been wallowing in this for three years and counting. I really didn't want to make my life an ode to my paradise lost. So what had I done? I'd immersed myself in another death. Seemed an odd way to stop thinking about the subject, but it was too late to change flight patterns.

To make matters worse, my gut was rumbling and it wasn't from the food at breakfast. It was the company. Luc did that to me. He treated me with neither seriousness nor respect. I never minded being challenged by a client—you expect that. But I was sensitive—perhaps overly—to slights, real or imagined. Yet in a perverse way, that failing served me well. It was a great stimulus to keeping my guard up and any objectivity intact.

Luc seemed more than uncomfortable this morning. He was aggressively abrasive. He was dismissive of my inquiry and particularly annoyed at our document request. I had explained in my request letter that we had only nine months to file the estate's federal tax return. We needed to gather all of Ben's assets and income streams and we had to get it right. An estate of this size would automatically be audited. That is why we asked for documents relating to all payments to or from Chimera, Cerberus, and Hydra. These foreign companies appeared to receive recurring consulting fees from ClearAire or partners related to it and we needed to know if Ben had any direct or indirect interest in or relationship with them. I had noted references to them in the files that Terry had shown me so I added them into the document request. I had remembered these companies from the SEC inquiry I was working on for Ozone just before Alice's accident. ClearAire's unresponsiveness back then was the catalyst for my abrupt departure from Disney and return to the Firm.

I always suspected those entities might be conduits for facilitation fees or recipients of kickback payments. I got a bit of perverse pleasure in adding them to the list, even though they probably had no relevance to our task. Perhaps it was just a case of curiosity interruptus.

Client hostility was nothing new for lawyers. I had experienced Luc's dark moods before. Many clients—normally those who operate just below the boss—have animosity toward their lawyers. All lawyers do is slow their progress, place hurdles in their paths. CEOs tend to be more appreciative. They know the buck stops with them. Chief operating officers have shorter horizons, more tactical goals.

They prefer to muscle lawyers rather than massage them.

Luc had become interim CEO, but he was still the bully. He hadn't mellowed since I'd left the Firm. But was he so venal and ambitious that he would kill his mentor? Of all those who were possible suspects, Luc might be the only one who meets the traditional tests for the culprit—motive, opportunity, and temperament. He has a kingdom to gain, he was alone with Ben the day he died, and he had killed before. I had heard him boast of his lethal exploits during his days as a Navy SEAL, and his only known hobby was big-game hunting. Those experiences may not have made him a murderer, but they did make him a killer.

Perhaps I'm not being objective. Other than the letter, we had no evidence that suggested murder. Was my disdain for Luc coloring my objectivity? There are a lot of vice presidents who are a heartbeat away from the throne who do not hold a pillow over their boss's face.

If Ben was really intent on selling ClearAire, Luc might well have panicked. It's not the kind of operation that shows well in sunlight. Additionally, acquirers like Russett have histories of replacing top management in their acquisitions. Russett in particular believed in putting his homegrown lieutenants in charge; he trusted only his own thanes.

That would not be a surprise to Luc. He was the same that way. Everyone at ClearAire swore loyalty to him.

He was a man with an excess of talent and an absence of conscience. And I suspect at times Ben was glad to have him.

On our walk to my car Luc had reiterated that our inquiry was unnecessarily intrusive and that he would make his displeasure known to Evan. "Tucker, this is bullshit and you know it. You had better watch yourself," he mouthed close-up, intentionally encroaching on my private space. Those words resonated in my mind. He had served notice that he was my personal monster. I feared that our success might well be measured by how we handled him. It was not going to be easy.

My life had changed dramatically. A whole raft of new friends and old enemies were populating my days. Nip and I had lived for three years as a party of two. To better insulate myself from the silent chill that permeated me, I clung to her.

Nip and I have become a unit that no one has coined a collective noun for. Dixie came the closest—borrowing the words of Forrest Gump—"You two go together like peas and carrots."

24

As we returned to the hotel, I saw Ben's car approaching fast. It lurched to a stop a few feet away. Viggie bolted toward me. A freeze-frame of anger was etched on his face.

"*Stugot! Bastardo!*"

"Viggie, calm down!" I implored, putting a hand out to brace him. He was hyperventilating.

Nip sensed that something was very wrong. She quickly moved behind me again. Her instincts signaled retreat; her tail was wagging but her eyes were bulging. They never left Viggie.

"That shithead Sandino! His uncle killed *mia famiglia*. I told you about the man who killed my family—Greco Sandino. The Sandinos did Corleone's killings, you remember. That bastard must be one of the Sandino sons. Now he's capo to that man Grogaman.

"I listened to them. I know you said I shouldn't, but this time it was about family. Mine . . . and yours. I turned on the recorder. They gave me no attention . . . I didn't matter to them."

He started shaking again.

"Vig, keep calm. Remember you're my capo now and I need you. You're no good to me like this."

His head snapped back perceptibly as he exhaled. I thought I saw momentarily a flush on his face. I think he understood, perhaps for the first time, that he was valued for more than his driving skills and storytelling.

"I'll be OK, Mr. T, but it was—how do you say—a shot to me."

"I'm sure it was, but how do you know he was part of that family?"

"Oh, you can tell. The hair! Blond men in my country they come from the North. That is where the Sandinos live. He has their hair. He carries their hate in his heart. Some things you just know."

Again rage began to spread across his face like the onset of hives.

"Did they ask you for your name?"

"No, I wasn't important enough. Now you can hear and you will understand." He handed me the recorder; I handed him Nip's leash. She wasn't so sure, but she gamely sidled up to him.

"Meet me here in forty minutes, you could stand a little fresh air."

As they walked away, I called Dixie, advising him of my early return and asking him to meet me at Ben's place. I then packed, paid our bill and had the concierge put my stuff in Viggie's room. I waited for them at the steps of the park. This time Viggie arrived noticeably calmer. I knew Nip would calm him down. I then told him to drive back to New York, with a stern admonition to take care—no speeding—and to drop off the Ozone papers at Dixie's apartment.

"Nip may get antsy when she realizes that I'm not going. Have her sit in the front and just tell her more stories about Tuscany. She won't understand, but she'll listen."

I then cabbed it to the shuttle.

As the plane leveled off at cruising altitude, I reached for the recorder. Fortunately it was a clear day as I headed to New York—no turbulence. I had about forty minutes to listen to the tape.

I was crossing the line again. Each time it put me closer to where I did not want to be. Yet, again, with only the slightest pause, I hooked in the earpiece and turned on the recorder.

. . . what a freakin' asshole idea, selling ClearAire. Russett would love to take the cream from Ozone and leave us with the dregs. He knows what he's doing. Goddamn! This is all Ben's doing—the old fart! It wouldn't surprise me if he probably put that in his Will. It doesn't matter. I can stop this at the board if nothing new erupts. Baum was the only person pushing for the sale. I don't like Tucker nosing around. He's been trouble before. I really thought with Baum out of the way, we could rest easy with the Madeira operation. No one's inquired about them for years. Now Tucker's guy is asking for those files. This could be trouble.

This, on top of the government sniffing around. The SEC doesn't really worry me, though. They're so full of shit, they couldn't smell a rose if you shoved it up their nose. What does bother me is Russett. The brokers say that he is continuing to buy Ozone stock and lots of the hedge guys are following him.

Maybe they figure he'll do a back-end run—go for the whole pie. If he can't get ClearAire alone, he'll take Ozone and sell off the other pieces! His stock holdings are getting close to 5 percent. Smells like he's lining up for some friendly fire. I will not give this up. Not now. Not ever!

Russett will play hardball like he always does, but he's picked the wrong dog to fight with. Trombley played it right in London— he came up with the idea to let me buy ClearAire. He knew that Baum would resist that. Now, with Baum gone, I suspect that control of his shares will shift to Trombley since he's the executor. He'll want to keep things the way they are.

So, Boss, what do you want me to do?

With Tucker and the SEC fishing around, and the Swiss gnomes going soft on secrecy, it is a good time to close down Barcelona. Where's Trig? We might need him.

Boss, I guess you didn't hear. He took it in Fallujah last night, got in a street fight with three locals but a fourth guy popped him from a window.

No! Too bad! But you know he was a bit over the top even for us. Well, what about you, Sandy? You up to that kind of task?

You can count on me, Boss.

Damn it to hell. Never expected Tucker back. Didn't like him before, don't like him now. Too bad he didn't go down with the missus . . .

Now I was the one hyperventilating. The woman next to me edged closer to the window. I was afraid she was going to reach for the attendant button.

I forced myself to appear calm, but my mind was in overdrive. My animosity toward Luc was metastasizing into hatred. What did I expect from him? He liked to kill. Some humans—too many—do. Whether it's an animal like Snowdrop or a human they decree to be the enemy, they get a rush when their prey is in the scope of their rifle.

Some people are just that way. It kind of explains why we are the only species that kills its own on a regular basis. Perhaps Luc and his ilk are the denizens of the dark side that Ben was alluding to in his prec letter . . . "too despicable to speak of."

This matter had just gotten very personal. Somehow, I had to get a collar on my emotions. Either that or resign this job.

A bumpy landing mercifully distracted me and I quickly exited to the relief of my seatmate. This tape I was not burning—or returning.

This one was mine.

25

The fleet of curbside taxis was endless so the wait was short. The ride back was your standard New York experience—a crabby cabbie, pushing maniacally through city traffic, spouting cynicisms all the way in a dialect I couldn't understand.

Luc's comments hung around in the back of my mind like a harbor bell in the fog, making idle thought impossible.

I didn't handle our meeting well. I must admit he'd made a good brief for ClearAire, proclaiming that his division was now the largest private military support company in the world, with 20,000 advisers in training at all times. "Balance and Support in the Battle for Security" was its slogan. He boasted that they had more than 18,000 operatives—each commanding an annual fee of $400,000, and double that amount for sensitive duty.

In the past, I had tried to suck up to Luc, to no avail. His personal defense shield was impenetrable; there were no fissures. He wouldn't submit to flattery; he wasn't looking for an alliance. He never, at least in my presence, mentioned anything personal.

He remained as I remembered him—drum-tight, fit, and always on the offensive.

The Marine Corps had almost done the same to me. Military demeanor is all about physical prowess and respect for authority—programmed perfection, tight lips, and creaseless comportment. That was why I didn't reenlist. Four years was more than enough.

I found the law firm the polar opposite. The muscle mass was above the collar; fealty was only conditional. Professional standards had to govern your actions. The means had to be as justified as the end.

Being more Thomistic than Sophistic, I really thought I had found my place.

Unfortunately you quickly learned that compromise was constant; rationalizations and exhaustion often overrode caution. Sometimes your standards got as wrinkled as your suits. Those were some of the reasons that kept me from rejoining the Firm.

My vibrating thigh-mate beckoned, breaking my torment. I smiled ruefully. Nip wasn't around to give me that look. She was unnecessarily jealous of the iPhone. "Nip!" I laughed silently. "Don't be jealous. You're not losing your place. Remember, I never turn you off."

The message that popped up was from Dixie, advising that he was on his way to the townhouse and would await my arrival. We lurched to a slow crawl as we passed the site of the world's fair. The slower we went, the louder my hackie's rant.

Both were rankling me so I hit "D" on my speed dial and closed the partition. Dixie's effervescence and benign irreverence made him easy to like, and his quiet savvy was earning my respect. He immediately launched into his report on his visit to the coroner's office.

"Lucky you had the foresight to get the letter from Evan . . . er, Mr. Trombley. Normally they won't speak to anyone but the next of kin. The London office also helped in getting me quick access. Seems the coroner's staff wanted no more to do with the Baum matter—but more on that later. Normally in London corpse removal is handled by funeral homes or crematoriums, under the direction of the deceased's doctor or the hospital administrator. The coroner's office gets involved only if there is something fishy—or, as in this case, if the decedent is a foreigner.

"The officer assigned to this case, Dr. Blakely, was friendly but not very forthcoming. He said that his office received a call from the hotel's physician asking them to process the body. Shortly after the body was released to the funeral home, he received a visit from Mr. Abelard, armed with a letter from the widow authorizing him to make arrangements for Ben . . . excuse me, Mr. Baum's burial."

I smiled. For associates, working out the protocol for addressing clients and partners is an important part of their maturation. Deference must be rendered to both but the salutation is not to be excessive or fawning. And partners are rarely helpful. They seem to relish an associate's unease. The first week every partner is referred to as "sir," until you begin to blanch at your own obsequiousness. Out of earshot, partners are simply referred to by either their last names or their first—the former to register distance or disdain, the latter to suggest an enviable intimacy.

"Dixie—let's set some ground rules. The three of us are going to be up close and personal for the next few weeks. You can call me Tuck, Jonathan, or Mr. Tucker—just never Tucker.

I prefer Tuck; my friends use that. And as for the Wiz, let's just call him Ben. Nicknames seem best for the living."

"Thanks, that makes it easy . . . and I'll advise Drew."

Dixie quickly resumed. "Next I visited with the hotel doctor—Dr. Cornelius. He asked if I was aware of Mister—Ben's—medical history, and when I responded 'his cancer,' he relaxed and opened up. Seems he arrived in response to Ms. Krkavec's call. He examined Ben in his bedroom, confirming that he was dead. He volunteered that there were no signs of contusions or injury and, in the absence of any other indicator, he concluded the cause was a coronary event. He then called the coroner's office, following the protocol for deaths of foreigners. He indicated that Mr. Trombley and Ms. Krkavec were present when he arrived, but that she left shortly after he confirmed Ben's passing.

"He told me that the widow's assistant, named Abelard, had later advised him that the widow wanted the body buried at sea. When told that was illegal, she opted for cremation and directed that the ashes be immediately scattered at sea without any ceremony.

"The hotel doc. He is a bit of a character. He is small and very officious. He told me that although he was Austrian by birth, his father was English and that he has worked in London in his present position for eight years. He reminded me of the Munchkin coroner in the *Oz* movie. I almost expected him to proclaim that Ben was 'really most sincerely dead!' But it didn't take him long to loosen up. He considered himself Ben's London doctor and friend. He often provided Ben and his son with prescriptions for an assortment of pills, including Mr. Blues. Not sure that Pfizer would welcome that endorsement. He also advised that this was his last week at work and that he was moving to Africa to work with the poor.

"A few other points. The good doctor confided that the body was exceedingly moist with sweat when he arrived. Then following hotel protocol, he stayed with the body until the ambulance arrived and he then accompanied the body to the morgue. He seemed very genuine. I think he really cared about Ben. He said he didn't spend any time with Evan. He noted that just before the body was removed, Mr. Abelard arrived, apparently dispatched by the widow. He insisted on staying in the living room until the body was gone. According to Evan, Abelard then went into the bedroom and removed all of Baum's clothing, jewelry, papers, and personal items and he remained until the maids came and repaired the room.

"Dr. Cornelius told me that he has had more than thirty guest fatalities, every one of them due to heart issues. He explained there was a hotel protocol for making the process as discreet as possible. They had to respect the living. I assume he meant the other paying guests.

"So those are the highlights. I'll write up my notes tonight in memo form. One last thing that might be of interest. I asked the doctor for his personal feeling on the event and his response was pretty fascinating. I had used my pocket recorder to help me when I wrote my report and I copied his last comments verbatim. I then destroyed the tapes. I had not gotten his permission. I'll read it to you."

. . . so sad. He was having a harvest of trouble. To me, though, he was, as my grandmother used to say, mein gute alter Freund. He had been slipping a bit lately, and his memory was failing him. I wonder if he might even have had early dementia.

Did you order an autopsy?

Oh, heavens no! Unless there was physical evidence of trauma or a wound, our protocol is to release the body to the next of kin. That was Mrs. Baum, and if she wanted an autopsy, she could have requested the coroner's office to conduct one. He was a good

*person, a generous person. I'll miss him. He still had a lot of life
left in him. He should not have let all of this happen.*

"He wouldn't elaborate. I felt he wished he could have
taken that last comment back."

"Dixie, thanks, but I have to get off. I'm pulling into my
apartment and I'm off to see Charlotte for an update. It's too
late to meet with you now. Oh, before I forget, would you
check with Terry to see if she has any executive travel records
relating to any trips to Florida in the last four years and also
to Spain—Barcelona in particular. Also can you find out if
there is much office buzz about Russett's interest in Ozone?
And finally, call a Mr. Sandino, in Grogaman's office, and find
out when we can get the complete file on those Madeira companies. It wasn't included—notwithstanding our request—in
the files given to Viggie when he went out to ClearAire."

I thumbed my phone off. It was becoming apparent that
Dixie was a good and patient listener. He makes people feel
he is giving them his full attention. That's a seductive trait
lost on many young lawyers. And his humility, candor, and
humor are disarming. They cause people to take him into
their confidence.

He was, as we say, a keeper.

26

I have a set formula for selecting my attire. Shirt from the top of the pile, shorts with the most elastic, trousers with remnants of a crease, shoes with a semblance of polish. Then I top that off with the sweater with the least lint balls and the jacket with the fewest dog hairs. Finally, double-checking that the socks are a close match, I am ready to roll.

Style tips from the fashion-challenged.

That evening, though, I was obsessing over my sweater, which for me was abnormal. Nip found my fussing quizzical and fixated on my ritual, her head tilted to the side in puzzlement.

"Don't give me that look! I am not going on a date. This is business . . . and no, you're not coming. Why don't you just butt out!"

The fact was that I was looking forward to dinner. Charlotte was one of the few links to my past. Other than Nip, she was the only one who knew my family. When I lost Alice and the kids, we became good friends.

Nip just doesn't like it when I leave. She really never got used to being alone. When I wasn't there, she always had Alice and the kids and she still misses them. I tried to visualize Alice's reaction to all of this. I could no longer quite see her with the clarity of three years ago.

It is upsetting when memories fade.

I looked at my watch. "Nip," I said in my best White Rabbit voice, "I'm late, I'm late, for a very important date. No time to say hello, good-bye. I'm late, I'm late, I'm late."

And, in fact, I was.

I had made the reservation for six thirty at the East Side Social. The restaurant was not too far a walk for me, but too short to cab it. So I had to hustle. It was a good place for us to meet. The food was excellent, the decor nonoffensive, and the tables sufficiently spread apart that we could talk in other than whispers and code. Dark wood, dark tables, no tablecloths—except in the booths. The most distinctive wall art was the neon exit sign. I picked that time to meet—much too early for the latte-lite crowd and little chance of meeting any Firm personnel. Its rigorous ordinariness made it comfortable for me.

To my dismay, Charlotte was already there. She was wearing loose black slacks and an oversized gray cashmere turtleneck that cradled her cascading black hair. Her hands were almost white, unblemished by sun or age. She didn't walk in the woods, I surmised. Her long fingers held no jewelry. I liked that. I'd always found her great-looking, but on this particular evening a tenseness diminished her beauty. After a brief exchange of mea culpas and absolutions, we ordered. Pork, lamb, strip, and rib eye were the menu's mainstays, garnished with an assortment of mushrooms, marsala, and parmesan. I, as always, ordered the Sunday Spaghetti—Grandma's Special Recipe, which when decoded meant meatballs and spiked with an abundance of garlic, chili, and a touch of cream. Charlotte demurred and settled on mixed baby lettuce with lemon and olive oil—a feast for a size three.

"So, whassup?" I uttered.

"Tuck, I don't know where to start." There was stress in her voice.

I smiled lamely, then launched into another White Rabbit routine. "Begin at the beginning and go on 'til you come to the end: then stop!"

That elicited a wan smile.

"OK, I should start with the Will contest. As you know, Tremaine has filed a broadside complaint in Supreme Court, alleging that the most recent Will Ben executed was invalid for a number of reasons and that the earlier Will naming her as executrix should be probated. Additionally—and this is new—she wants to be appointed Leo's personal care guardian as well as his property guardian and she wants her yet-to-be-born child recognized under the Will and the Trust as a full heir.

"Tuck, this really could be serious trouble. If Tremaine can successfully argue that Ben did not have requisite capacity to execute his most recent Will, or that Evan and I inappropriately induced him to change his previous Will so that Evan replaced her as executrix, then Tremaine would take Evan's place under the old Will and in all likelihood gain control of Ozone. It could break just right for her. The board of Ben's foundation consisted of Ben, Dorothy, Evan, Tremaine, and Abelard. With Ben gone, and if Evan is knocked out for conflict reasons, then it's just the wife, the daughter, and the executive director—and my strong guess is that Tremaine has Abelard in her pocket . . . and other places too. So she would control the vote of the foundation's 800,000 Ozone shares."

"What are the chances that she'll succeed?"

"On the law and the facts, she shouldn't. I know of no medical evidence that would corroborate her claim that Ben lacked capacity. Ben may have been fox crazy, but he still had his marbles. As to undue influence, that is laughable. Ben came to me. I didn't reach out to him. And luckily, I had two associates present when we conducted the Will planning sessions who will testify to that effect if necessary. To create a binding and valid Will, all you need to know is the nature and consequences of a Will, the general nature and extent of your property, and who you want to leave it to. Clearly Ben passed those tests. And his prec letter in many ways further validates that . . . and that was quite recent."

"So you've decided to produce the letter?"

"Tuck, we just don't have any choice, no matter what Evan says, especially in this court. I'm sure the judge will side with de Vil. They go way back.

"As to the other issues Tremaine raised, it is not that clear-cut. Ben was appointed Leo's guardian when he turned twenty-one and there was no successor appointed at that time. I had asked Ben to put his wishes in the Will, but he told me he was taking care of it. He brooked no conversation on the subject. He didn't like to acknowledge Leo's condition. I felt it was part of a lifelong denial. Tremaine's position is that as Ben's wife she has been involved in the selection of doctors and caregivers for Leo. In fact, she did introduce his doctor, Eloise Thompson, to Ben. She is going to argue—I understand from conversations with de Vil's office—that they consider Dorothy's lifestyle and relationship with Eloise to be disqualifying. They are also seeking a court directive ordering Eloise to have Leo brought back to New York. He's presently in Paris with Dorothy. Even if Tremaine wins on that motion, I doubt seriously if a French court would act quickly on this. And they're also suggesting that Dorothy may be conflicted because of her position at Ozone. They will argue that she might not be objective when it comes to voting Leo's shares.

"Concerning the child Tremaine is carrying, the inheritance rights are complicated. New York law has an odd provision on children born after their father's death. They have a right to an inheritance only if the deceased father had no children, which is not the case here. If he had children and provided for them in his Will, then any after-born child would be entitled to only what was left to the father's other children. In Ben's case, his children were previously and amply provided for in the Family Trust, but all Dorothy and Leo get under the Will are a few of his personal possessions.

"Another factor is that there doesn't seem to be any evidence—or even allegation—that Ben knew Tremaine was pregnant. If he did, I'm sure he would have made provisions for the child. The issue could also be complicated by the provision in the current Will that leaves money to Kati's child, if there is one at the time of probate, but specifically precludes that child from being included in the Family Trust. If the current Will is rejected, it will be a windfall for Tremaine."

"Any other news I should know about?"

"Plenty, Tuck. It just keeps coming. This could not have come at a worse time. If Tremaine wins on all counts, control of Ozone could go over to her. Think about that. She would control Leo's shares, the foundation's shares, and the shares, if any, that would be allocated to baby Bentley. The math is compelling. She would then be able to vote all those shares except Dorothy's. She would be the new Ben!

"In that scenario, Evan is toast. He loses the estate business and the foundation business and even Ozone itself as a client. And he will, as you know better than anyone else, be looking for a scapegoat. He has already complained that I should have had Ben provide for Leo's custody and that I should have read the prec letter the day Ben gave it to me, notwithstanding the direction to the contrary on the envelope, and then destroyed it, or at least given it to him. He had one of his hissy fits and it was really painful for me, considering he was very involved with Ben's Will prep. You should have heard him."

I could empathize.

Old WASPs sting hard, especially their own.

Even though he was good to me in many ways, Evan was quick to lash out if things did not go well. I have felt his sting several times. The most abusive was when I took off for Disney.

Charlotte's eyes went moist.

Reflexively I reached over and took her arm, rubbing it the way I did with Alice when she was upset. It seemed the natural thing to do. She closed her eyes for a long moment and then rebounded.

"Sorry, I didn't mean to get weepy, but they're heaping a lot of bad stuff on my plate. And there is really no one else I can talk to. Forgive me?"

"No problem. Now how 'bout another glass of that pinot. It's pretty good, don't you think?"

She nodded, her lips reluctantly parting to form a weak and sad smile. Drawing a long breath, she pushed on.

"It's just not fair. I've played by their rules. You know the deal for women partners here. Loose suits, flats only, no open toes, no burgundy nails, no name brands, no pink. Only jewelry from grandma—dainty not dangly. If you assert yourself you are a feminazi. If you let your intelligence be too obvious, you're a cliffichick. The men's idea of dress-down is to shed their coat and tie. That doesn't work for us. Our only option is to lose the pearls. My mother always said that beating boys will not make you happy or married."

Unfortunately she was right. As embracing as Big Law presents itself as being today, in reality it still remains mad-men-centric.

Most women are relegated to servicing the clients of rainmakers. They get the work but not the rewards.

Men get the plums; women get the pits.

More than 50 percent of the lawyers in the Firm are female. Five percent make partner. And none are on the Executive Committee. Some argue it's a gender thing—familiarity is tantamount to flirtation; flirtation invites harassment; harassment ends your chances of moving up the ladder. Most male partners are leery of championing a woman too vigorously—afraid of rumors, and fearful that the demands of motherhood will pull them away just when you need them. And adding to that was Charlotte's innate paranoia. She once confided in me that she had changed her last name from Cavatica to Williams. Felt her family name was too ethnic and would diminish her partnership chances.

It's nice not being part of that bull dung anymore.

"The word is that Russett is preparing some kind of takeover of Ozone. I'm not privy to what's going on. I can hardly get a word in edgewise with Evan. He's always huddling with the corporate guys."

I understood her frustration. "Big Law babes"—women partners in large firms—remain a step behind and below. Virtually all of the Firm's corporate clients have male CEOs, like Ben. They all want their primary lawyer to be their confidant, collaborator, confessor, and if you're not lucky, coconspirator. The partner who brings in the business ends up being part-time buddy, part-time shrink, and full-time quarterback. When it comes to personal matters, he's a lot like your favorite bartender. CEOs want to talk about their personal life as well as their business life to someone who doesn't remind them of their wife.

Charlotte lowered her voice. I suspected she had realized it was too shrill.

"Tuck, you didn't hear this from me, OK? Our gray-haired leader Wiggie has announced he is retiring at the end of the year. And he has not anointed his successor as chair of the Executive Committee. So the battle is on to replace him. The partners are all a bit edgy, praying to land on the right side of his successor."

I was all ears. This was high drama. Regime changes rarely occur voluntarily, and when they do, succession is usually pre-ordained.

"Trombley has put himself forward as you might suspect. His claim is seniority and billings. Hard to argue with either. He will be the last remaining partner named on the masthead who is still practicing. And Ozone and the estate contest will assure his position as top biller again this year. Gordon Brady is his main competitor and is lobbying to be cochair with Dan Finn. They are both very popular. They are waging a whispering campaign against Trombley, suggesting he's going to get dirt on himself as the Baum case progresses. You know he doesn't really have many friends in the Firm."

She wasn't calling him Evan anymore.

"Unfortunately for me, it's all about the Will contest. Tremaine's guns are blazing. She's even claiming Ben had lost it, mentally and physically, which are distinctly different allegations from 'lack of capacity.' They are alleging that he recently became unbalanced. They're even trying the spittle and piddle offense."

"The what?"

"That he was incapable of controlling his bodily fluids—involuntary dribbling and incontinence—signs of advancing Alzheimer's. They allege that his secretary was his de facto caregiver. You can see that all this circles back to me and the Will."

"Charlotte, you're being . . ."—I almost said hysterical—"too hard on yourself. Those charges are utterly groundless."

"I know, but hindsight doesn't help. Ben had been so ada-mant about his decision to get rid of Tremaine that I assumed the letter of marriage termination was prepared and on its way out, which is what he told me. And, you should know, Trombley wants your investigation closed down immediately. He's playing hardball. If I have to, I just might go to the Bar Association and the DA with this. Ethics trumps con-fidentiality here. Of course, my career at the Firm—or any firm—would then be over. I'm horribly depressed over all this. If people keep putting you down, you start believing they're right."

"Whoa! Despondency, depression, and despair . . . these are not in the lexicon of future senior partners. You know that. The appearance of confidence and calm in the face of this is even more important than competence. Don't let Evan up the emotional ante. He is a master at using guilt as a weapon. You'll survive this, I promise. And don't make Evan your mortal enemy. Remember—a fight to the end rarely has a winner. I'll protect you from Evan . . . somehow. Now, let me ask you a few questions, OK?"

She quickly agreed.

"Do you remember the provision in Ben's Will about being buried with his original wife and his two boys?"

"Of course I do, Tuck. Ben felt very strongly about it. I remember him specifically mentioning it at both Will sign-ings. Tremaine was present for the signing of the previous one. Why do you ask?"

"He was cremated in London and his ashes were spread at sea."

"You must be kidding! What a vindictive bitch!"

"Enough about her."

A change of subject was needed.

"All this talk of Wills woke me up to the fact that my Will is obviously outdated. Would you have someone call me and I'll go over it. Need to make provisions for my dog, Nip. I'll have to think about what I'll do with my estate now."

"Sure, I'll have Mimi—you know her, she's one of my favorite associates—call you next week. You don't want to die intestate. All your money will go to Albany. Lord knows, though, they need it."

"Oh, while you're at it, could you have her send me a copy of Alice's accident report?"

"Of course, but why bring that up now?"

"I don't have a reason. I've never seen it."

Truth is that I'm still in denial. It's not like Alice to be involved in an accident. She prided herself on her prowess on the road. Maybe the report will shed some light.

In what seemed like a few minutes, three hours had passed. Our dinner was over. I had long surpassed my self-imposed two-drink limit and I sensed it was time to go.

"Thanks, Tuck. This was good for me. I'm sorry I had to share this with you. I don't know why you put up with me."

"You've always been a friend, Charlotte. That in itself is a tremendous thing."

"You're right about that. You know who your friends really are when you have trouble. And you have always been there for me."

She stood and leaned over toward me. She had a natural odor of allure, a scent I had almost forgotten. Our eyes fixed and she kissed me, letting her lips linger a few seconds longer than appropriate as her body pressed into mine.

I did not recoil.

27

All were in attendance in Ben's study—now dubbed the Hobbit Hole. Dixie was his cheerful self, sporting a black blazer with sleeves ending well above his wrist and trousers that never met his ankles. A bit too Pee-wee for me. Drew was her usual economy-size bundle of energy. I wouldn't hazard a detailed description of her attire. She had quickly moved away from Big Law regulation dress to another look. Bohemian-hip, urban-workable were the best I could come up with. And to finish off our team, Nip was there. She had taken to joining us, settling on the Oriental in the middle of the room. It gave her the best vantage point. For what, I am not sure, since she dozed off within minutes.

"Perhaps I should fill you two in on last night's dinner with Charlotte first. Things are getting testy in the court proceeding."

I then summed up de Vil's legal assault as best I could, leaving out any reference to the partners' power-play machinations.

"A few questions about the Will issues. Drew, what was your reaction to the burial at sea?"

Drew responded. "Well, really not too much other than it was totally contrary to Ben's stated wishes. Perhaps Tremaine was not aware of that provision, or more likely, she found it repugnant and just opted to ignore it."

"You're probably right on your surmise. And Drew, could you get up to speed on the right of inheritance for children born after the testator's death? According to Charlotte, the issue is not all that clear."

"Will do," she said. "There's been a lot of press about that over the last several years. Heath Ledger's Will was executed before his child was born. Same with Anna Nicole Smith's daughter. This stuff isn't all that novel. For the rich and famous, Will contests are as much a part of their lifestyle as champagne and caviar."

"OK, Drew, now for your report."

"First off, London was awesome. A lot to report. I don't know who to start with. Best to do it chronologically, I think. So that means the maid. You were right, Tuck, to have us stay in the Baum suite—the ick factor notwithstanding. The staff appears indentured to specific rooms. The hotel has quite a helping of wonderful maids. I met Pervy the first morning. She is a joy. No problem prying info out of her. I straightened up the room before she came in. Didn't want her to think I was a slob. Her full name is Fleur Pervesie, but she prefers Pervy. We became rather well acquainted during my stay and I found her observations amusing and sometimes quite insightful."

Out of the largest pocketbook I had ever seen, with enough belts and buckles to restrain a gladiator, Drew extracted three dictation pads, selecting the one that had a large "P" sketched on the cover.

"Excuse me while I get out my pads since I take almost everything down in shorthand. It makes life easier. You know, it's a lost art today; no one gives or takes dictation anymore. We all prefer to peck at our desktop. My mother made me take steno in high school, just in case things did not work out. Not exactly a confidence builder. Still find it very useful when I can't record interviews. I like to be precise on a client's or witness's comments.

"Seems Pervy is a bit of an institution at the hotel. She's been there for sixteen years! Her husband is housebound with a disability and takes care of their little 'ankle-biters'—children."

"He can't be that disabled if he's still a breeder," Dixie observed.

Drew continued, dismissing Dixie's flippancy.

"We would have a cup of 'rosie'—tea—each day when she came to turn the bed down and she would regale me with stories about the Baum suite guests.

"She absolutely adored Mr. . . . Ben. Seems he left her a 'ton'—that's a one-hundred-pound note—every day he was there, and at the end of his stay she would always find a box of sweets with her name on it. I think she had a crush on him. Doesn't seem she liked any of the other suite regulars—except Ben's son, Leo. She particularly disliked Peter Abelard. Apparently he was all over the place the day Ben died. First he had a meeting with Ben, then she saw him standing in front of the door 'Tom peeking,' and later in the room when she cleaned it after Ben's death. In the case of a guest's demise, house rules require a full cleaning as soon as possible. Claims Abelard stayed with her and another maid while they did their work, hovering over them like a vulture waiting to pounce and peppering them with questions—all the time collecting Ben's personal items, including clothes, jewelry, books, magazines, toiletries, medicines, and what she described as 'playthings.'

Sexual aids, I suspect. He even looked under and behind the bed. She thinks he was looking for something important and even pressed her on whether she had removed any items—an inquiry she considered tantamount to an accusation of theft. As for Tremaine, Pervy had an equally low opinion—'a sad arse excuse for a wife. Always left her scanties about. Nothing but a shagbag in fancy clothes—all fur and no knickers!'

"Pervy had been in and out of the suite three times the day Ben died—cleaning up after breakfast, lunch, and late afternoon drinks. And she overheard several 'argy-bargies'— arguments. One with Mr. Grogaman and another with Dr. Thompson. She couldn't really recount what they were about, but said both had big rows with Ben. Wasn't fond of either. Nor was she particularly fond of Kati, whom she less than kindly called Ben's 'pikey jam tart.' She volunteered that Kati was Ben's source for 'kisses and hugs,' which I later found out meant drugs.

"One thing seems clear. Pervy's not a suspect. She had access but clearly not motive. I suspect Ben's largesse was a nice supplement to her earnings. Enough on Pervy."

Pulling out the next pad, which had KK on the cover, Drew allowed that she was able to find Kati Krkavec by simply calling a number that Terry gave her. It was Kati's cell phone. Although apprehensive at first, she agreed to meet Drew at a coffee shop, after Drew explained that she was working on Mr. Baum's estate and that Kati was included. When she arrived at her appointment, Kati's brother was with her.

"Kati is a serious person. I'd guess she's in her late thirties. Her English is excellent. Can't say the same for her brother, who looked like every Soviet gangster you've seen in the flicks—three days' growth, about the same length as the hair on his head, black jeans, cheap leather jacket, ugly macho knockoff shades.

"Kati—unlike her brother—was quite stylishly dressed, although perhaps a little on the flashy side. She was very respectful and open. She listened to my questions and answered them, always glancing at her brother for validation. I expressed my condolences on Ben's passing. Told her we understood that he was very close to her and admired her very much. She thanked me and confessed she was very much in love with Ben. She said that she was still in shock from his death. I asked her to tell me what happened that day as well as she could. Hesitating for a moment, she said she had a drink with Mr. Baum and his lawyer—I assume she meant Mr. Trombley—and then she and Ben retired to his room, where they rested and talked. Ben was very agitated and she wanted to relax him, but he persisted in talking about Mr. Grogaman. At that point, Ben asked her to ring up the house doctor. She did and Ben spoke to him and asked that he examine him. On his arrival, she returned to the suite's living room and waited with Evan. After about twenty minutes, the doctor stepped out and announced that Ben had passed away and that he would attend to the body.

"I then asked Kati if we could speak alone for a few minutes. After a heated conversation with her brother in what I presume was Montenegrin, perhaps Albanian, he went about thirty feet away and lit a cigarette, never taking his eyes off her. He just stood there sulking and smoking.

"I told Kati that I understood her pain, that I was with my father when he died—the first time I had seen a dead body of someone I loved. Sadly she told me it was not her first and went on to share with me her extraordinary story.

"She came from Peroce, a little village she described as down from the mountains in Montenegro, and was traveling to Granica in Kosovo. She was on the road with her husband and their four-month-old child when some Serbian militiamen accosted them. They gang-raped her in the snow on the side of the road, forcing her husband to hold their baby and watch, promising her that they would be spared if she didn't resist and enjoyed it. I'll read her exact words. 'You can't imagine it. After they were done with me, my husband's pockets were emptied. He was spat on. I watched their spit run down his face. Then the captain shot him and my little boy with his pistol as the others laughed. The bastards! They didn't keep their devil's bargain.'

"She was only seventeen! They eventually dumped her at the Albanian border. There she was forced into prostitution and eventually consigned to an Italian pimp. She finally convinced an English john to help her flee to London, where she was able to locate her brother.

"She's quite a survivor. You wouldn't guess she'd had such a life by looking at her. She's truly beautiful. Great eyes—the Bette Davis kind. Her hair is raven black without even a trace of curls. That's the one thing I really envy about her.

"It was her eyes that were her giveaway. They are deep black. You had the sense that she was watching you, her brother, and every stranger, all at the same time. She was always on guard.

"We engaged in some small talk and after a while I felt she was starting to relax so I asked whether they were romantically engaged at the time Ben died. Without any hesitation—or any embarrassment—she said no. She had wanted to, but Ben was too agitated.

"Here is how she put it," Drew continued, flipping over her pad: "'He talked about his enemies, not really to me but more to himself. I think he meant Mr. Luc and his friends. He also said that the "twit"—that was what he called Mr. Abelard—was a "pussy," not much of a man. And he laughed, adding that his son's doctor was too much of a man.' She then said when the hotel doctor stepped out of the bedroom she knew right then—another man she loved had died and again she could do nothing. It was, she said, her *sudbina*. That means destiny," Drew added. "I looked it up.

"Now the important part—for us. She finally asked me whether Mr. Baum had left her money. She told me that Ben had given her the name and number of his banker, Andreas Amaroso, should she ever need help. Apparently she has been unable to reach him. I then told her about the bequest of ten million dollars in trust for her with income paid annually, contingent on her not being pregnant when the Will was probated. If she were, the amount in the Trust would be reduced to one million, with the income on that accumulated and paid out to her child at the age of thirty. She was stunned and asked what probate meant and when it was done. I explained and told her it could happen in about six weeks. She erupted. These are her words. '*Kopile Ubijin*' or something like that. I'm not sure what that means, but it sounded profoundly nasty. 'The fucking bastard lied. Damn him. Damn him to HELL. They are all evil! Men—they make the rules; they change the rules. That lying son of a bitch. He will burn and rot in hell. He promised . . . he promised . . . no man will ever kill my child again!'

"She pushed over her coffee, stood up stroking her stomach, and walked away.

"And for the record, I agreed with her."

28

Sensing that the three of us could use a break, I called a time-out. Clearly Drew could use a breather. She was obviously stressed by her session with Kati. The ploy proved effective. We all gathered back at the Hobbit Hole, like a clout of cats, eager to hear about Drew's encounter with the curious Mr. Abelard.

"Sit back. The story of Peter Abelard will take some time in the telling but it's worth it," Drew promised.

Sensing she had grabbed our attention, she began.

"I had some luck locating Abelard. I had noticed in the coroner's report that he listed Brown's Hotel as his London residence. So I simply rang them up and asked for him. Maybe I caught him off guard . . . whatever. But he was quite friendly and, to my surprise, asked me to join him at the hotel for tea. I took him up on his invite. I had assumed that he wouldn't talk to us—considering the Tremaine litigation— but he seemed genuine in welcoming me.

"I knew of Brown's. I think it's the oldest hotel in the city—all Chippendale and chintz. You have to love it," Drew exclaimed. "And it's in the heart of Mayfair, right near the Bond Street and Regent shops and the theaters and Hyde Park. I'll stay there next time for sure . . . if I can. It was started by Lord Byron's valet with money from his wife, Lady Byron's personal maid."

"That must have been a cozy kitchen. I guess there's hope for Pervy after all," Dixie noted.

"You two should know," Drew paused. "I'm an Agatha-holic. My favorite Christie mystery is *At Bertram's Hotel*. She modeled her fictional hotel on Brown's.

"Anyway, when I arrived at the hotel, the concierge directed me straight into the tea room. It was, as you might expect, wood paneled, with working fireplace, Jacobean plastered ceiling, and a baby grand in the corner. The maitre d' led me to what he called the Abelard table.

"Peter wasn't quite what I expected. He is good-looking in a goyish way. He had anchorman hair. And his tan was chemically enhanced to set off his butter face, blue eyes, and caramel hair. He seemed very fit and had a little barbed-wire tattoo on his left wrist. He was manicured to perfection. Throughout the meal he maintained a charming nonchalance. Yet under all this I sensed an ulcerative colitis was lurking. You see it all the time in New York—part flirt, part con, out on the town feeling good about their hair. He is—to use one of Lewis Carroll's favorite words—slithy, kind of slimy yet soft.

"At this point, I think it's best to listen to the tape. When I arrived at the table I asked if he minded. He didn't."

She then pulled out her recorder and turned it on.

I appreciate your seeing me on such short notice. I know well the indelicacy of calling on you at this time. You must believe we would not intrude upon your and Mrs. Baum's grief if it were not a matter of such importance. We are questioning those close to Mr. Baum to help establish the cause of death, or at least rule out certain causes, for insurance purposes, as well as to marshal information on Mr. Baum's assets for the estate probate.

I understand.

Can you tell me about the day Mr. Baum died from your vantage point?

Well . . . sure. Our office—that's to say the Baum Foundation and my art advisory business, which is unrelated to the foundation's work—are located only a few blocks from the hotel where Ben died. That's why he and Tremaine used that particular hotel. Ben and I usually met there when he was in town. On the day he died, I met with him there and he advised me that he was changing the foundation's mission purpose in a direction that I wouldn't be appropriate for. He wanted to concentrate on medical research and helping children. That would not be for me.

Pausing her recorder, Drew summarized Abelard's recitation of his résumé—from art lover, to gallery owner, to foundation professional.

"He loved his job as executive director of the Baum Foundation and explained that its mission purpose is to support art institutions rather than artists individually. He adored London for its art scene, particularly Frieze, which he described as London's hippest art event: 'Art Mardi Gras for the Rich and Randy.' According to him, it's become one of the most important contemporary art fairs in the world. Hedge fund managers, magnates like Ben, pop stars, sheiks and shiksas, babushka babes and their 'oiligarch' billionaires, old, new, and stolen money—his words—all stampede there.

"Again according to him, Fischl, Struth, and Sherman remain the hotties. As crazy as it sounds, he assured me that this is how the market works. Love it or loathe it, doesn't really matter. How soon and for how much can you flip the art? That is the question—according to him!

"When I asked what happened the day Ben died, he responded in a very open manner, telling me more details about his firing, rather matter-of-factly. He made two other visits to the hotel that day—one at about four. He was passing by and thought he'd try to get Ben to revisit his decision to alter the foundation's mission purpose and lobby that at least a portion of the foundation's activities remain art-directed. When he got to Ben's door, he overheard a violent argument raging between Ben and, as he described her, 'his gypsy whore.' Feeling nothing positive could come of interrupting it, he left, only to be directed back sometime later by Tremaine when she received news of Ben's death. She wanted none of Ben's belongings to fall into the hands of Kati or the hotel staff, particularly the room maid, whom she could not abide, allowing that she was a disrespectful cockney know-it-all gossip. He said that Kati—whom this time he described simply as 'the escort'—had just left. When I asked why there was no autopsy, he bristled, rather visibly, stating that there was no need, that death in the sack with one's mistress is in the tradition of Nelson Rockefeller and was commonplace, especially considering Ben's condition. He refused to elaborate."

"Excuse me, Drew," I interrupted. "Abelard's and Kati's stories don't quite jibe. Remind me to talk to Ben's New York doctor. We should get a better read on his health than one can get from a hotel physician."

"Will do and you're right. Kati claims that she and Ben did not engage in sex that day. So, back to Abelard. When I asked him about the funeral arrangements, he said he was simply following the widow's wishes. Claims cremation and burial at sea were a tradition in her family. She remembered that it brought closure when her father, a naval officer, had died. He then volunteered that the last year hasn't been easy for Tremaine. Ben's actions were becoming increasingly bizarre and his indiscretions much more public. She had been trying to maintain the appearance of marital normalcy for the sake of Ben's reputation and his son's stability. With evident pride, he called her a brave woman.

"I then asked him for a list of all of Ben's art, allowing that it probably would take him some time. Told him we would need cost and current value appraisals for the estate tax returns. He then dropped a not-so-little grenade. He said that would be easy since the only things in Ben's name were the three paintings in his New York office and the 'crap in his townhouse.' All the other art was gifted by him to Tremaine when acquired, noting that his advisory firm had handled the purchases for Tremaine and billed Ben directly. According to Abelard, Ben didn't buy significant art until he married Tremaine. That information changes the estate dynamics rather big-time! Tremaine already has a lot more than we'd speculated. Abelard refused to guess at the value. We hadn't factored that in since Ben's Will indicated that all art that Dorothy did not want was to go to the foundation. I'm surprised that Abelard was so forthcoming—again with the litigation pending. That may not have been too wise. He didn't have to provide that info."

Dixie chipped in. "He seems a bit like the Donkey—had the right to remain silent but, I suspect listening to you, not the ability."

"Shrek," smiled Drew. "You may be right. He's not too smart, but I kind of like that in a man."

"Time out, kids! My mind is spinning."

Even Nip was getting anxious. She does that when she thinks people are arguing. She can't distinguish anger from good-natured banter. One of her few failings.

Drew fussed with her hair for a moment, and returned to her debriefing.

"Peter went on to talk about Tremaine in terms normally reserved for candidates for sainthood—her class, patience, spirit, fidelity, and long-suffering. And he outlined her widowhood plans. Apparently with the exception of the new apartment she bought in New York, she plans to sell everything and settle in Antigua. He informed me that she was there now scouting out places and arranging for her residency."

"Clever lady!" I added. "If my memory of international tax law is still correct, a British citizen who does not spend more than six months in England and is also an Antiguan resident is not subject to any tax—in England, the United States, or Antigua. Nice deal for our Lady Tremaine."

"She'll set herself up with barrels of money from the sale of the art goodies—ALL without a farthing for taxes. I suspect she may have been planning this for some time. You need time to have your lawyers and accountants vet a plan like that," Dixie added.

"Sorry, Drew, didn't mean to interrupt your report," I said.

"No, that's OK. In fact, I'm fascinated. Maybe there is more to the merry widow than I thought. Anyway, where was I? . . . Oh, my conversation with Peter was terminated by the arrival of two of his buds.

"He introduced his guests—Jeremy Lerot and Patrice Lapin. They're partners in an art gallery and appear to be Peter's good friends. With their arrival, the tea party could begin and the waiter appeared as if on cue with flutes of pink champagne. Lerot oddly complained before even sitting, 'No room, no room!' In fact there was plenty of room for all of us.

"I must take a moment to describe what the three were wearing. Peter had a pink-collared shirt with white cuffs, a green plaid Edwardian vest, a tweed smoking jacket, and dark purple slacks. I noticed when he crossed his legs that his socks were not matching—one orange, one bright purple. That can't be a mistake. He had tan suede wingtips and a really hip hat. It looked like a Langston Panama, with black suede trim and a super stingy brim that he wore throughout our meeting. Really cool. You're going to see a lot of them in New York next spring, I'm sure."

"God help us. The chapeauistas will be thrilled," Dixie muttered. "More Kiddie Lids! Are we all supposed to look like Kid Rock?"

"I think fedoras are sexy. They're so old Hollywood—Indiana Jones, Clark Gable, Humphrey Bogart—and I sensed that dressing up was a tradition at these afternoon teas.

"Lapin was the more serious one. He launched into a 'state of the art market' soliloquy. Here's how he put it: 'Art is a true commodity now. The number of global millionaires has increased by 200 percent. Investing in art is the most attractive place to park cash. It's the new gold. It's tangible and cash-convertible. If you buy the best, it almost always works.'

"There's apparently been a mass migration of heavy money—Chinese, Russian, Arab, Indian—into the art market. The way Lapin put it was the world is 'reshuffling the goodies.'

"During most of this discussion, Lerot seemed distracted, glancing at the window ledge where two very large black birds were preening themselves."

I interrupted, in part to give her a break. "They were probably ravens or large crows. The venery term, by the way, for a group of them is 'an inconvenience' or 'a murder.' Never liked either phrase myself. They are quite common in London. Charles II once sought to exterminate them. They reminded him of his wife Anne, who, as we all know, failed to give him a male heir. His extermination efforts were almost successful when a royal astronomer warned that if all the ravens were killed, his kingdom would fall. So he decreed that six ravens would be spared and kept in the Tower of London. Not wishing to tempt fate, English rulers have always made sure that there are a goodly number of crows in the tower."

Drew continued. "Well, the boys weren't paying these ravens any respect. Lerot took his spoon and chased them away, tapping on the window. That led Lapin to start up a riddle game. The question was 'Why is Peter like an elephant?' The two of them fired out answers. Because his skin is thick! Because he has a long memory! Because his nose is long and brown! I must say, Peter took it well.

"It then turned nasty. Peter posed a riddle. 'Why is a raven like a gypsy?' He was slyly but obviously referring to Kati. The answers again came out rapidly. Because their hair is black and shiny! Because they both can cast an evil eye! Because both steal shiny things!

"By this point I had had enough. 'Gentlemen,' I said, 'let me solve your riddle for I have to leave. Crows and gypsies are alike because both are shrouded in mystery, both are exceptionally wise and beautiful, and both are often misunderstood and unnecessarily reviled. Thank you very much for tea. I'm late for a very important date.'

"I then left. It was all uncommon nonsense. I can only suffer fools for so long . . . and Agatha was starting at eight!"

29

"Oh, uh . . . hi, Tuck," Terry said awkwardly as I entered the kitchen, still struggling to address me in a familiar way. She has always been unfailingly deferential and especially formal to Ben's lawyers.

Old habits are hard to break, especially when they are tied to old memories.

"What can I get you?" she asked, fidgeting with the wire bowl of cherries she had placed next to her prized amaryllis.

"Would you like some? Ben had twenty a day when they were in season. Had a touch of the gout and was told they would ward off another attack."

"Did they?" I asked.

"Seemed to for him . . . he loved them anyway."

"Terry, I would like to talk to you confidentially. A number of things that are coming up in this investigation seem a bit odd. Drew and Dixie have left for the day so I thought if you have time we could just talk."

As I settled into the chair opposite her desk, I could feel a welcoming warmth emanating from her. She was what one called 'a good person'—always affable, never seemingly on edge, and obsessively orderly. The table testified to that. Papers stacked neatly in piles, an appointment calendar prominently displayed, and a small picture of her and Ben, off to the side in an ornate antique frame. The pens were all the same, upright in perfect harmony in a wicker holder next to her ever-present plant.

"Is everything OK, Tuck?"

"Yes, we're making some inroads, but so many puzzles remain. It's almost as if Ben purposely set them out to test us," I lamented.

"Maybe, just maybe, he did."

"Ben keeps bringing us back to his favorite books. Do you know what attracted him to them?"

An even deeper breath prepared her as she launched into her story.

"It was in 1967. Ben and I were literature buffs in high school. We would go out to the hills and read for hours. We didn't talk much at first. We would just hide from the world up there, often reading late into the night. Now, you understand, late then was usually nine o'clock!

"Ben used some of the inheritance from his parents to buy a red Ford Cortina. Gas was around thirty cents a gallon. We considered that appalling. I chipped in for the gas. It was the least I could do. It got us to the woods.

"There was one night that I remember most distinctly—it was in the summer. Ben had somehow managed to buy a copy of a new book called *The Road Goes Ever On*. It was a book of Tolkien's English and Elvish poems set to music. I remember asking him why he was so interested in Tolkien. He said he had read *The Hobbit* over and over and over again and also *The Lord of the Rings*. He couldn't explain why. He just said he found magic in them. They made him feel like a different person. I'm a little at a loss to explain. We were used to doing lots of heavy reading—Ayn Rand, Kerouac, not to mention Harper Lee, and even some light reading, Sendak and Seuss. Most of our gang weren't into that kind of stuff. They were more into being hip and fashionable—miniskirts and hot pants. I wasn't the Twiggy type. I was more a granny dress girl. Both Ben and I loved bell bottoms, even if we could not quite get ourselves to adorn them with love beads. Ben was kind of straight. Some of our less kind classmates called him a nerd because he would often wear a short-sleeved white shirt and tie to school. But that was just so he could go directly to work without changing his clothes. I thought it was unfair. He was anything but, though I have to admit Ben's idea of being hip was a turtleneck. I guess in some ways we were both on the square side," she confessed with a smile.

"Still, Ben was in his heart and soul a rebel. He found an ally in Tolkien. Maybe that explains it. I remember him saying that the stories were bigger than the books, that they were about things that mattered. Tolkien spoke to young people in the sixties. He painted a picture of peace and natural beauty and its desecration at the hands of evil, and he did it in a way that felt real. No one had ever read anything like it. Ben would read passages to me for hours. I really believe it was meant to be read out loud. Its cadence and tone can only be really appreciated by hearing it, the same as with Dickens and Woolf. I suspect it is difficult for people today to understand that impact. Tolkien claimed us as no other writer had done before . . . or since. When Ben would read to me, that was magic. He was hooked on Tolkien and I was hooked on him.

"The truth was I was madly in love with him and it never faded."

She paused, enjoying a private reverie.

I didn't blink—a well-developed nonreaction, heeding one of Woolly's most helpful words of advice: "Leave your galoshes and your emotions at the door." Surprise, disappointment, and anger are best submerged when dealing with clients, partners, or witnesses.

But I must confess, their relationship was a bit of a stopper. And I was disappointed that I had not suspected it from the start. Prom Queen, trophy wife, voluptuous vixen. Terry was missing from my chauvinist picture.

"Well, as for the other writers. You know Oz is—was—in his blood. He once told me that it was the first word he ever spoke. For Ben and me there was never a time before Oz. I still have his battered copy. It's like my first Teddy. When I leaf through it now, it's like a yellow-brick roadmap back to our youth.

"As for Lewis Carroll, he read the *Alice* books as a child and he reread them to every one of his children many times. He thought they would give Dorothy a role model in Alice. And he found in the nonsense parts a way to connect with Leo when he was young.

"But really, it was Tolkien's books he was most drawn to. He took them as his own. He also felt they liberated him a bit from his family's obsession with Oz. Ben was not a religious person but he was spiritual. He felt the *Book of Common Prayer* got it wrong. He wanted a Lord that was not jealous and who would not visit the sins of the father on the children. For Ben, his ancestor preached vitality and happiness and Tolkien taught perseverance and humility. And he loved elves, their traditions and their fondness for nature, and he reveled in the idea of elfish reincarnation. He was fascinated with what he called 'dark evil.' He always felt that one was not born evil; rather, it was an acquired vice. Many years later, he told me that those books continued to fascinate and influence him, that they helped him find strength amid the storms that he encountered and that they kept alive the inner child in him. I remember another thing he said before he left for London: 'I will not go gentle into that good night. I will not stop for death.' He thought it was Tolkien but I thought it was Dylan Thomas. Both our memories are developing black holes. It happens. He said he had a mission to right some wrongs and ensure his legacy. He wouldn't elaborate but allowed that if he let shame come to him, it could spread to his family and even to his revered great-great-uncle. Am I getting too maudlin?"

Without waiting for a response she continued.

"That summer night Ben and I stole away to read the new book of Tolkien's poems. Ben had just bought a portable machine that let us play the music that was written to accompany the poems. It was like Gregorian chant. Just wonderful. That night we shared some mary janes—that's what we called pot—and stayed 'til sunrise. It was a very special night. At the end we had finished off a bottle of very bad champagne and toasted JRR. That was Ben's nickname for Tolkien. I remember his toast: 'We will always walk together in Frodo's footsteps.'"

Her voice and visage strengthened as she leaned forward.

"Tuck, for you to really understand Ben, I'm going to have to be very frank with you. I have in fact been trying to gather up the courage to do so. And this is as good a time as any," she announced, wiping her hands on her apron, which she then promptly removed.

"The things you will have to know are very delicate and very personal. I never imagined myself having this conversation, but I feel it may be essential. So I'm just going to let it all hang out."

She talked more slowly as she began a tale that grew in the telling.

They met in high school, drawn together as she had said by their common love of literature. But it was not until the long night she and Ben celebrated Tolkien's book of poems that they became intimate. After graduation Ben went to work full-time at the local electronics store, his mother and father having died in his teens. As an only child, Ben inherited a decent-sized estate, which was administered by the town's only lawyer. The store owner, having no children, "took a shine" to Ben. When he died later that year, Ben bought out his widow. He and Terry worked together. He was the brains; she was the organizational brawn—so to speak. Quickly they made the business quite profitable. Ben was in fact a wizard when it came to marketing electronics. Terry got pregnant, but before they could get married, she lost the child. She found out then that she could never have children.

"Both Ben and I were heartbroken," she said. "Even though he was very supportive, I knew he was more than devastated. He absolutely revered his great-great-uncle and was hell-bent on perpetuating the Baum line. He was obsessed with having a male heir. I didn't quite understand it, but he was everything to me."

They were clearly more than just lovers. They had developed a true partnership, turning one store into a chain of stores. They were busy and quite happy, but Ben's overarching drive to have a male heir drew him to Maude. She was a classmate of theirs—likable but boring. Maude came from what was called "good stock." She had six brothers and five sisters, from which Ben divined that she was very fertile and he was right. In short order after Maude and Ben were married, they had Dorothy, Leo, and the twins. Terry wasn't happy but was not about to leave Ben over it.

At this point, she added, "Tuck, the story gets even more delicate. I'd like a glass of sherry to help me get it out. Would you join me?"

A bottle materialized and she served us both generous portions.

I learned that Maude had grown progressively more introverted over time and detached from Ben's life. She was very proper but pedestrian. As soon as she got pregnant, she insisted that all intimacies cease. It was during what Ben called the "dry periods" that Terry and Ben reconnected physically. She acknowledged that most people would find that unhealthy, but she and Ben did not. After Maude gave birth, they would cease their intimacies until the next dry period. They worked out what some would consider a Faustian pact.

Then a tragedy occurred.

As Terry put it, "Those wonderful twin boys somehow got themselves caught in the current of the river that ran near the house and drowned. Earlier that day, Maude, who was again pregnant, had come upon us at the wrong time. She was understandably quite upset. I was devastated. I always thought she might have suspected, but now she was sure."

The boys dying caused Maude to miscarry, losing the baby. It was a boy. Three days later she killed herself.

At one point in her grief, Maude lambasted her daughter, Dorothy, blaming her for the drowning—for not being there with her brothers to protect them. Ben did nothing to counter that. He was fearful that Maude would blurt out something about his infidelity and Dorothy would never forgive him. Terry said it was one of the few times she didn't respect him. She allowed that there would be others.

With the air of relief that confession can bring, she stared at me, and with the small hint of a wry smile said, "I assume by now you have figured out that I am Belladonna."

30

I hadn't. I don't know how I missed it. The amaryllis, the polyamory sign, and the Tolkien rune: *It is my love for belladonna that sustains me.* It now seems so obvious.

She beamed, somewhat sheepishly, adding, "I've always had Ben's back and I still do."

I was nonplussed that I'd been oblivious to their relationship. I am aware that corporate executives and their private secretaries have very special bonds. Their fealty almost always is to their boss, not the company. It is often a love affair, emotionally and sometimes physically. But here, perhaps because of age and Ben's notorious philandering, it had escaped me.

In a law firm, it is different—more like brothers and sisters. Associates often have affairs with other associates, but rarely with the secretarial staff. Fraternization with a secretary is taboo—a career killer for the associate. Less fatal for partners; sufficient billings will grant them indulgences.

"Perhaps I'm not up to this task," I proffered.

She countered with conviction. "Yes, you are. Ben never made it easy. He had become very leery of those around him.

I'm sure he would have wanted you to look into this. He was very fond of you and so am I. So let's get to the bottom of this if we can."

She'd just put herself on the team.

Seems we could use the help.

"OK," I said. "Here's our approach. Ben's death most likely occurred from a coronary event—at least that's what his personal doctor, the hotel doctor, and the coroner's office surmise. I suppose the issue is whether that event was facilitated by nature, by Ben himself, or by someone else. If it's a third party, then in all likelihood it would be one of the people who spent time with him that day—Abelard, Eloise, Kati, or Luc. The only other ones were Dorothy, Leo, Evan, the Russett people, and the maid. They don't seem germane.

"So I would like to learn as much as we can about each of them and the issues, if any, they had with Ben at the time of his death. Let's start with Luc. He is not a favorite of mine."

"Nor mine—or Ben's either," Terry added. "Their relationship had become strained. The company has three revenue streams—electronics, its original core business and Ben's baby, followed by Luc's division, and the entertainment division, which Dorothy now runs. To Ben's annoyance, Luc's ClearAire was quickly becoming the most profitable and fastest growing, with electronics suffering from the competition. Dorothy's division was doing well but the global economy wasn't helping that business. Luc was getting pushy. He wanted total control over his division and Ben just didn't trust him."

"Do you think Ben was prepared to sell ClearAire to the Russett group?"

"Eventually," Terry replied. "But he felt it was complicated and had to be sorted out. I always thought Ben was a bit afraid of Luc. Did you know we have a little surveillance group that works in the carriage house beyond the kitchen? One of its favorite targets is Luc."

"I knew you had some staff there, but wasn't sure what their jobs were. What do they do?" I asked, trying to temper my titillation.

"Well, it's not part of the company. Ben installed it years ago and personally paid for all of it, expenses as well as salaries. There are three wonderful people who work there. I'm very concerned for them. I told them that they can stay on for the next six months. I'll cover all those expenses personally."

"Can you put Dixie in touch with them? He's our tech mouse and could certainly make use of their data."

"Sure. I can set that up."

"Would you elaborate on what the surveillance team does?"

"Generally they try to spot any unusual activity at the company. They monitor all travel, disbursements, and communications, including company e-mails and telephone calls, to see if any patterns create concern. For example, they monitor communication frequency and timing to unearth possible breaches of the company's policies or insider stock trading. They're particularly watchful for any excessive communications with investment bankers or brokers who did not represent Ozone. Ben believed that where there's smoke, there's fire. Now you have to understand they do *not* eavesdrop on actual conversations, they only analyze objective data. Ben wanted to stay within the law."

"How was Ben handling these issues in the last few months?"

"Ben was a moral—and, as I said, a spiritual—man, even though he did not believe in a wrathful god. His beliefs were more basic. Good acts trump good intentions. There is no devil but the one that lurks within us. He would quote things like that all the time. And he believed in simple things. He said he didn't want to inhabit a universe of ambiguity. That was where he felt Luc resides.

"Don't get me wrong. Ben was no saint. He had become moody. He recently said that no man is rich enough to buy back the sins of the past and he was feeling the impotence of his wealth."

I felt she was falling back into a personal reverie so I changed the subject. "Let's talk about some of the others. What can you tell me about Abelard?"

"I have no use for him!" she snapped. "I suspect he's become Tremaine's lover. Ben stopped all intimacy with her months ago. I found him a twit. No more than an errand boy. He came here a few days after the funeral, demanding all of Ben's personal items other than those specified in the Will to go to others—items like his clothes, even his combs and toothbrushes. He and Tremaine treated Viggie and me as domestic help and I had no standing to complain. Fortunately I had time to gather up those items that were important to me in the days after Ben's death. Tremaine, of course, did not invite us to the funeral."

"What was your relationship with Tremaine?"

"I didn't have one. As I said, to her I was simply the help. She did not engage me. She even had her own secretary."

"Did you speak to her when she called?"

"She rarely called of late. For Ben the marriage was over. He had come to believe that she was infertile. He didn't marry her for her companionship. She was into all the things that money could buy . . . and none of them interested Ben.

"To be candid, I resented her. She was not like Maude. I understood that and I made accommodations. I thought his quest for a male heir was over. After Maude died, I had a full life with Ben. I became 'Aunt Em' to Dorothy and Leo. I raised both of them as if they were my own. And then after

Dorothy left, we adopted Viggie. My maternal desires were fulfilled. And Ben and I remained very close in every way.

"I'm sure Tremaine was very annoyed when she found out how much Ben left me. She has no clue as to our relationship. I despise that woman. Hated her from the beginning. I warned Ben, but he was on his male heir hunt again. Didn't work this time either."

"Well, I'm not sure if you know, but Tremaine's pregnant. Claims, of course, it's Ben's and it is a boy."

There was a deadening silence while she processed this news.

"I can assure you her child is *not* Ben's! He had long ago given up on her. That's why he took up with Kati. Ben was spending lots of time in Europe of late and Kati was a better diversion than Lady Tremaine ever was. In fact, Ben had me prepare the formal letter terminating their marriage. He was to sign it on his return from London.

"As I said, I had a full life with the only man I ever loved. And I'm not the first woman to share her lover's affections with others. I wasn't happy about it, but in life and in love, you have to make compromises. We remained partners in every sense of the word, including intimacy.

"This is an awkward subject. I know young people view older people as asexual but that is just not the case. If anything, Ben and I grew even more intimate as we matured. It wasn't routine; it wasn't obligatory; it wasn't daily. But it was always wonderful. The big difference was our reticence to talk about it. We zealously guarded our privacy.

"You know, Tuck, Laurence Olivier said that inside, we're all seventeen, with rosy red lips. Ben and I never obsessed about aging. Our sex was not about passion or drama. It was about mutual pleasure. And we didn't need any medical assistance. That was not the case for Ben with others."

I sensed that I needed to change the subject. She had made her point. Her brief was compelling, but she was now gilding the lily.

"Terry . . . a delicate question. Could Ben have accidentally or intentionally killed himself?"

An emphatic *no* was her response. "Ben's cancer wasn't going away, but his death wasn't imminent. He was a realist. He had to plan and the fear of its interrupting his mission was like a stone in his gut. He felt he would have to rush and was only worried that he would lose his stamina. He was more driven than ever. He was not forthcoming as to what his concerns were, but I could sense they involved Luc, Leo, and Dorothy. As to its being an accidental overdose of something, Ben was too much in control to abuse himself beyond his limits."

"What about Kati?" I asked.

"I really don't know much about her. Ben rarely talked about her. As close as we are—were—there was a place in his soul that I never gained access to. I accepted that."

"And Eloise Thompson?"

"Again, I was never really involved with her. You know she was introduced to Ben by Tremaine. After Maude died, as I said, I became—by default—mother to Leo and Dorothy. Leo was always a problem. He was diagnosed as autistic. He had anger and attention problems. Yet he had many moments when he was just wonderful. Those moments became fewer and fewer and his moods got darker and darker. He got hooked on the occult—Merlin was his fixation, almost to the point of obsession. You've never seen his room upstairs, have you? Perhaps it's time for a break and then we can reconvene up there. It's best you see it. It will make it easier to understand."

"Fine. I've got some calls to make. Say fifteen minutes?"

31

I was beginning to question who Ben really was. My picture of him might have been just that—a picture. Clearly he wasn't the totemic presence I came to admire. Perhaps he was the ultimate flimflam man—a huckster hiding behind a curtain of power. Maybe he was the wizard his great-great-uncle had envisioned.

Terry poked her head in, interrupting my musing.

"Ready to go upstairs? Best we take the stairs. The elevator struggles with two adults. It was meant only for Argos and Leo."

"I'm ready. I never miss an opportunity to take the stairs. It's the only exercise I get these days. But before we go, I'd like to cover a few more matters."

"Sure," she said as she sat down next to me.

"How is your relationship with Dorothy now?"

"Well . . ." she paused, seemingly organizing her response.

"We were very close while she lived here. I always treated her as an 'adult,' even in her teens. When she went off to boarding school, she became distant. I suspected it was a coming-of-age thing. Later, when her sexuality evolved, I think she found our closeness awkward. But don't misunderstand. She has always remained cordial, solicitous, and loving. She was the only one who called to console me when Ben died. I always felt she knew more about Ben and me than she let on. I am very fond of her. And I admire what she has done with her career . . . and her 'coming out.' Ben, of course, did *not*. He was very upset at first. It further deprived him of that elusive heir. Another instance when I wasn't proud of him."

"And did you have anything to do with the Precatory Letter?"

"As I told you before, I typed it. Ben must have added the love symbol later. The Elvish script I typed in and the letterhead we borrowed from a Tolkien drawing. We had fun doing it. Ben wasn't morose about it. If anything, he enjoyed it. One thing though—he refused to explain it. At least now you know who Belladonna is. That's actually a nickname that Ben pinned on me early on. Bilbo Baggins's mother's name was Belladonna Took. She is the only woman of strength in all of Tolkien's books."

"What do you make of the letter?" I asked.

"To me, it's kind of a word game, confessional, manifesto and wish list . . . all in one."

"There was an odd reference to the Dark Lady. Do you think that was referring to Kati?"

"No, no," she smiled. "That has something to do with a basilica on top of a mountain, near Barcelona. I think it's also a spiritual community. The Dark Lady is some kind of saint. Not sure, though. Ben was more into that kind of thing than I was. He was drawn to mysticism and religions. Ben would go to Barcelona—stopping over on his way to somewhere else. I think ClearAire may have some operation there. He visited a Father Jeronimo. He's a priest at the monastery. In fact, he had a stopover there on his way to London this last trip."

That was news!

Again trying to keep my curiosity in check, I asked her matter-of-factly to forward me his itinerary for that part of the trip . . . and also Luc's. I remember his telling me he was on his way to Barcelona when he learned of Ben's passing.

"No problem, that is all at our fingertips in the carriage house," she proudly proclaimed. "I'll e-mail it to you."

"What about the last few paragraphs of his Precatory Letter that are directed at Dorothy?"

"Can't help you much there. Other than the obvious. I think it might be a message to Dorothy. They had—since her teens, maybe earlier—a secret language between them: coded words, obscure references. It was their private place and no one else could go there. The diaries were where he put most of that. I'm transcribing the last two weeks of them for Dorothy, along with the Precatory Letter. Do you think it's OK to send her that? I suppose I should ask Mr. Trombley."

"I'll do that for you. And I'll also check with Dorothy. I'm not sure Evan ever sent the Precatory Letter to anyone outside the firm. As you know, it does contain language that could be read to suggest that someone might do Ben harm. That, in large part, is what generated this assignment."

"I know . . . and it bothers me. Ben prided himself on being slow to anger, but I sensed from the tone of his letter that he was very agitated. I'm not sure if it was his displeasure with Luc or Abelard or perhaps Tremaine."

"Oh, two other matters on my list. Do you know anything about any European bank accounts?"

"Not really. Ben had a European banker, Andreas Amaroso. He is a good friend. He's Italian but he lives in Zurich. Andreas was the one who asked us to take his nephew Viggie.

I have never actually met him, although we have talked many times on the phone. I think that there were accounts for Dorothy and Leo in Zurich."

"Could you give me his contact info? Dorothy mentioned him to me. I'd like to reach him."

With a flick of her iPhone, she announced "Done" as she hit SEND.

"OK, enough of me doing Perry Mason. Time to climb the stairs."

I followed her. It wasn't that easy. She had no problem, but I was panting. I really had to get back in shape. I missed those long walks with Nip. Unfortunately the city is not conducive to trekking. Too much sidewalk traffic. Perhaps late-night jaunts would work.

Finally we entered a labyrinth of nooks and cupolas that constituted the attic. It is best described as Merlin's college dorm—a place of myth and magic. The decorations consisted of gryphon posters and an assortment of what I was told were "sacred Stonehenge bluestones," all obtained, according to Terry, from eBay. The tables were strewn with vials and cans with homemade labels as well as grinding bowls, pumice jars, and incense burners. On long shelves above the desk there were ornamental daggers, wands, and what appeared to be a chalice, as well as several bells. An old leather binder held what Terry described as Leo's *Book of Shadows*—a diary of handwritten invocations, spells, chants, and remedies. A large round wooden disk with five-pointed stars enclosed in a circle dominated the walls.

Seems that Leo was homeschooled. Essentially his education came from Ben and Terry's readings of children's classics.

"He got hooked on Merlin when we read the Arthur legends. Of course Ben generously embellished the stories more to his liking. Merlin became Leo's Gandalf. When we read

Connecticut Yankee to him, we edited out the references to Merlin because Twain had made him a villain.

"For Leo, Merlin was his personal wizard. Someone his father couldn't preempt or quote. Leo wanted to be a magician who could heal the sick and infirm. He saw Argos suffering the ravages of old age. He had seen his mother die and now he sensed his father was ill. He was not retarded; he was very perceptive. Surprisingly so. He was able to buy whatever he needed through his eBay account. So he accumulated all sorts of potions, elixirs, and herbs that he blended to cure the afflicted, particularly wounded birds.

"Tuck, I love Leo, but as he got older, he became more and more morose and too difficult for me to control. On Dr. Thompson's advice—you know she became Leo's doctor—he moved to Europe to live with Dorothy and her. You see, well . . . we had another tragedy.

"You never met Argos, did you? She was Ben's other love. And mine too. We had her for sixteen years. I'm convinced she was put on earth to adore the two of us. You know what Labs are like. She was so much like Nip. In her last years, her hips began to give out. That's why we installed that little elevator. When Ben wasn't here, she would follow Leo and me around. And when Leo would go to his room, she would often lie at the bottom of the stairs and whine. The elevator solved that. She would stay the night with Leo, even sleeping on his mattress. They became inseparable.

"Oddly, I was more worried about Argos's health than I was about Ben's. I just loved her so much. She was utterly sinless. I kind of agree with Kundera—one of my favorite writers—that perfect love can exist only in the love a person has for his pet. I never forgot how he put it: 'Mankind's true moral test . . . consists of its attitude towards those who are at its mercy: animals.' I think Ben, Leo, and I passed that test.

Argos's death was one of the most unbearable things that we have suffered."

Dabbing her eyes with the side of her hand, she gained her composure and continued.

"Did you know that autistics and animals think in pictures rather than words? You could feel the bond between Leo and Argos, especially since Ben was away so much. He became so desperate to help her when she became ill that he conjured up some potion. He found it in his sorcery book. It consisted of oils from Stonehenge, schnapps, vodka, lots of chocolate brandy, and cocoa beans. We later learned that Argos died of theobromine—chocolate poisoning. Her lips turned blue, she had a seizure and died. By the time Viggie got to her, it was too late. We never told Ben how it happened. It would have broken his heart if he knew that Leo had killed his Argos."

32

I arrived early for my meeting with Eloise Thompson. She had insisted that we meet at the Plaza Hotel's Palm Court. I didn't demur. In fact, I was intrigued. The Plaza is one of New York's signature landmarks. Its ownership has always titillated me. For more than one hundred years, it was at the epicenter of Gotham society, sitting regally at Fifth Avenue and Central Park South. The Vanderbilts were its first guests and it quickly became the hotel of choice for the well-heeled. Conrad Hilton bought it for $4 million in 1943; Trump later bought it for $400 million. He sold it for $325 million when Ivana left him. The buyer later sold it for double that to an Israeli-Saudi combine, which in turn sold control to a fabulously wealthy Indian.

My reverie was interrupted.

"Hello. You must be Mr. Tucker. I've heard so much about you from Dorothy. I welcomed your call and dreaded it all at the same time."

"Thank you, Dr. Thompson, for seeing me on such short notice, and you can call me Tuck."

"All right. Settled. You don't have to call me Doctor and I won't call you Friar."

The verbal jousting loosened up the atmosphere.

Eloise Thompson was not what I had expected. Tall, thin, with short blonde hair that seemed to haphazardly frame her face. Black horn-rimmed glasses drew your attention to her prominent and welcoming eyes. She was smartly dressed— a white tailored shirt set off her black pantsuit, and black pumps completed her highly stylized androgynous look.

Without any prompting, she entertained me with the life saga of her only aunt, Kay Thompson—"Kitty" to her close friends. Seems she was a modern-day Alice on steroids. Aunt Kitty, I learned, was Judy Garland's mentor and best friend. And yes, her aunt was the same Kay Thompson whose enduring fame came from her *Eloise* children's books, which, the good doctor volunteered, were inspired by the antics of her aunt's goddaughter, Liza Minnelli. Her aunt had passed away a little more than ten years before, and like her, Dr. Thompson had made the Plaza her not-so-humble abode—and office—in New York.

That was how I met Eloise at the Plaza.

"Before we start, let me state that I'm hopelessly conflicted. I'm Dorothy's partner and soon-to-be spouse, I'm Leo's doctor, and I was Ben's adviser and Tremaine's friend—and that's just for starters."

"As I explained yesterday, I would like to debrief you about the events leading up to Ben's death," I began, hoping not to sound too formal.

"I'm looking forward to this opportunity. I have a lot to say. I realize—mostly from talking to Dorothy—this is a serious investigation and there are real concerns as to how her father actually died. I'm right in the middle of this. So let me start with my story."

I let her keep rolling. Never shut off a witness. Every litigator will tell you that. More information flows from unprompted narrative than probing interrogatories.

"This was my home—before Dot. Have you seen it since the restoration?"

I gestured a negative.

"I get to go to all of the charity events here—a sort of family perk. The hotel management has a long memory. It was here that I met Tremaine. We struck up a friendship. We had a lot in common in those days—Chanel for dresses, Gucci for leather, Manolo for pumps—and it was here she announced she was seriously dating the famous Ben Baum of Ozone Industries. After they married, she introduced me. We hit it off and he engaged me to work with Leo. You see, my specialty is counseling children and adults with autism. Through that engagement, I met Dorothy and the rest is history—in the making.

"So much for the background. Now for more meaty matters.

"Let me share with you my thoughts about Ben, Leo, and Dorothy, from a psychiatrist's point of view. I will have to reveal things told to me in confidence, as well as my observations based on hours of therapy. I've discussed this at length with Dorothy and she has given me her consent to be open with you on her behalf as well as Leo's. Nevertheless, I'm walking through a minefield of conflicts here. Don't know if I should get a lawyer or a shrink," she mused.

"I've often asked myself the same question."

The repartee again seemed to put her at ease and she launched into what would turn out to be a fascinating profile of Ben Baum's family.

To gain a modicum of privacy, we moved from the Palm Court into the main reception room, overlooking Bergdorf's. The court was never empty and the tables were too tight.

Heads would be leaning to hear this tale. The reception room was perpetually Christmas. The high-back chairs were decorative, if not comfortable. She preempted a part of the southeast corner. The large room was in constant motion with guests and sightseers. Lots of little Eloises posing on the stairwell for their adoring mothers, a blush of boys not far behind.

"I suppose we should start with Leo. Technically he is my only patient in the Baum family. He is what we call a mid-spectrum autistic. He has difficulty forming friendships. He's often nonverbal and oversensitive to stimuli. He has limited interests. He loves a consistent routine, gets upset at change. As you may have learned, he is hyperfocused on medieval sorcery, for which he has savant skills. At his core, he is a true prince of a person. Several years ago, we all mutually decided it was best to bring him to Paris. You know about the Argos problem?"

"I only know what Terry told me."

"Well, perhaps I should add to that. Leo has a very big heart. His three big loves were Ben, Dorothy, and Argos—and in all fairness, Terry too. She did her best with him. After he accidentally poisoned the dog, Dorothy and I convinced Ben it was time for Leo to leave New York. We never mentioned the poison. But it was clear to us that Leo could not be left alone.

"He is now bigger and stronger and at times becomes violent. With Ben gone so often and Dorothy almost always in Paris, Terry wasn't up to the task any longer. She had a full plate as Ben's personal assistant. So Dorothy's place in Paris seemed best—at least for the time being. She has room, two male assistants, and me. Ben begrudgingly agreed, with the proviso that we bring Leo over to stay with him whenever he visited London or Paris. It seemed a fair compromise.

"Leo has had a difficult life. His mother's and brothers' deaths alone were quite traumatic. Being homeschooled and

without contemporary friends, all his formative life references
were based on children's literature. So he evolved into a kind
of Harry Potter, going through the wardrobe, down a brick
road, without any idea where it might lead. And his father,
for all of Ben's doting, was often more harmful than helpful. Candidly, Ben proved wanting as a parent—for both his
children—due in my opinion to his overarching obsession
concerning a male heir. He lost three boys with his first wife,
and Tremaine has been unable to conceive, leaving only Leo
surviving. The same Leo that Ben found so 'defective' that he
had him neutered!"

She caught my lower jaw dropping.

"I gather you didn't know that. He allowed Leo to be cir-
cumcised when he was a teen, but added a vasectomy to the
procedure without informing him. He feared that any child of
Leo's might also be challenged and not fit to be groomed as a
proper Baum successor. You can't make this stuff up!"

"Let me interject, if I may," I said. I sensed that this was
going to be a long session.

"Do you think Leo is capable of killing his father?"

That brought her up short.

"Well, that's a difficult and highly speculative question."

After she unclenched her jaw, clearly annoyed at the
interruption, she continued. "Leo is an intensely caring and
loving person. He worships his father. I do not believe he
would be any more inclined to hurt or kill his father than
would a normal, loving son. In fact, the instances of autistic
patricide are the same as nonautistic patricide, although some
argue it's less detectable. But the Argos incident was a wake-
up call. And now he is being medicated to take the edge off
his anxiety."

"I understand that Leo and his father had an argument in
London?"

That brought her up short again.

"Well, Ben and I argued too, but that doesn't make me a suspect, does it?"

Maybe I was pressing too hard.

"Of course not! I'm sorry if that sounded adversarial. It wasn't intended to be."

I wasn't sure that satisfied her.

"Leo was chafing at his 'house arrest' both in New York and in Paris and he was lobbying for more freedom. He wanted to go out on 'dates,' but his father would not hear of it. Leo was blooming sexually. Helping to navigate love for a person on the spectrum was alien to Ben. I think he was afraid the vasectomy might have worn off. Even though he knew the chances were exceedingly slim, Ben's fear of an unplanned heir from an unknown mother and Leo haunted him.

"Unfortunately my assessment of Ben, from a psychological standpoint, is also dark. In my opinion, Ben suffered from Narcissistic Personality Disorder. His relentless need for adoration from all those around him was evident. The real clue was his excessive self-absorption. Ben was admittedly intriguing, charming, and even charismatic. Yet he insisted that all roads lead back to him.

"Dorothy felt the constant need for his validation. Yet Ben's approval of her accomplishments was rarely given. Surprisingly the literary Dorothy's journey through Oz is an apt metaphor. She believed the Wizard was the only person who could help her find her way home, but when she sized up the man behind the curtain, she realized she would have to get there on her own. And that's what is happening here. Dorothy finally came to see her father as the imperfect mortal that he was—a visionary business genius, a self-made man of letters, and, in no small part, a humbug. Remorse and guilt had no meaning to him. They were feelings, emotions—not ideas. Ben put a blindfold over his feelings.

"Here I am on the most sensitive ground because of Dorothy's and my personal involvement. Dorothy had witnessed the essential 'primal scene' when she secretly observed her father and Terry having sex. However, she eventually came to understand that she had to come to terms with her own sexuality.

"And yet she has never quite satiated her 'father hunger.' There was a lot of King Lear in Ben's life. To a large degree, he abandoned Dorothy for his business while at the same time demanding of her excessive flattery and testaments of love. The more he tried to control her, the more she rebuffed him. Yet he was the only light in her heaven. Yes, she adored him. It is a classic Cordelia complex.

"Don't misunderstand. Dorothy is not just another dysfunctional. To the contrary, she is highly functional. Witness her success in a man's world. She has quickly and efficiently quieted the doubters. She proved that she is much more than the boss's daughter. It took Dorothy a long time—peering through the looking glass of life, so to speak—to realize that there was no Oz. There was no Wonderland. She is just now coming to terms with the child she was and the woman she has become. She has finally stopped looking for herself in those books. She now realizes that she can in fact take over the empire, not as regent to Ben's grandson but rather as Ozone's Queen Victoria."

"That's quite a story. The family dynamics are complicated."

Lame, but it was the best I could come up with.

She paused and leaned forward and smiled. "And they are going to get more complicated. Dorothy and I have decided to have a child. We are convinced that for her to come full circle as a person, she has to stop being the perpetual child and become a mother. That is the best way to close the book on the past.

"The plan is for me to carry the child. Dorothy felt a familial obligation to tell Ben. To our amazement, he was elated and supportive—particularly after I signed a tight prenup.

"Then to our utter surprise, he volunteered to be the sperm donor. His genes, my gender, a successor to Dorothy finally assured. Once we got over the 'ick' factor, we agreed. The prospect of happy endings carried the day. Ben rushed off and made deposits in a New York sperm bank. He was anxious to do it before he started chemo, which he knew was inevitable, although not immediate.

"The day he died, Dorothy and I went to see him at his hotel to complete the formalities. Leo was with us. Ben had by then consumed more than his fill of his favorite 'Hemingway highballs.' It was late in the afternoon. He was agitated at something and was awaiting the arrival of his banker friend. He announced that there was one detail he hoped Dorothy and I understood. His participation was conditioned on our agreement to abort if the child was female. Obviously for us that was unacceptable and just plain evil. Typical Ben, especially when he's tipsy."

She paused.

"That's what the fights were about. First with Dorothy and me, then with Leo, who had pieced together what was happening. His father wanted to make another boy! One that wasn't broken. He lost it. 'You want to get rid of me and make a better son!' Luckily, Emir, one of our house assistants, had come with us. It took both of us to subdue poor Leo.

"And yes, on that day, there were at least three people who wanted to kill Ben Baum."

33

"We've got a lot to talk about!" I alerted Dixie and Drew as they made their way to the round table. Actually it was a rectangle, but Ben's antique desk now served as our conference table. Dixie and Drew were having a hard time balancing their iPads, iPods, MacBooks, and notepads while sitting in Victorian high-back chairs.

"And we do too," Drew responded with a tinge of the dramatic in her voice.

I went first and gained their attention quite quickly. Terry's love story, Leo's sad saga, and Eloise's revelations were even more riveting in the retelling. Glancing at each of them, I could see that they were enthralled. This was, in associate parlance, "good stuff."

"The plot just got a lot thicker, eh?"

"And we have a few more facts that will make the poutine thicker yet," Dixie added, matching my Canadian slang.

"My turn," said Drew. "I just received some info from the police officer I spoke with in London—the one the London office put me in touch with. Seems he's dug a little deeper.

Kati's brother is apparently even more sinister than he appears. He heads a gang of Eastern European thugs. They are loosely aligned with the Mafia Shqiptare—not sure how to pronounce it. They have taken over the sex trade in Soho. Their trademark skills are blackmail and murder—particularly assassinations and usually by poison. It's the preferred method for settling disputes, I'm told. They are the killers of choice for Russian oiligarchs. Also, seems Kati has been hauled in for questioning several times on suspicion of blackmailing johns. They have not been able to make a case yet. Her alleged targets aren't talkative, much less cooperative.

"And," Drew continued, "I've done some snooping on Jeremy Lerot and Patrice Lapin, Abelard's tea party guests. I have a friend who works at the Tate Museum in London. My friend checked them out with a number of big-time dealers. Seems the boys are not held in high esteem. Some questions have surfaced about their integrity. He won't elaborate, but did suggest we stay clear of them. So I decided to do diligence on the prices of some of the art acquired by Tremaine and also by the foundation. I don't remember Peter's mentioning the foundation's being a buyer of art. I got the invoices from Terry and checked Artnet. That's a website that gives you access to auction results. The prices for the art Ben bought for Tremaine are more or less in line, but not the foundation's purchases. The ones I could get comparables on were over on the buy-side by 60 percent! More than half of the art that the foundation bought was owned, at least according to the invoices, by the boys—Lerot and Lapin. Nice work if you can get it. Then, just for the fun of it, I searched some social image sites looking for them."

She pulled out a dozen image printouts for us to view. They were all couple pics—Abelard and Patrice, Jeremy and Abelard, and several of the boys together.

"I presume that each took turns with the camera. The most interesting was one of Jeremy and Abelard arm-in-arm beaming a thumbs-up sign in front of a building in the Caribbean with a discreet but readable sign—*Royale Development Banque*. The metadata file on that photo embeds info on the images you take with a digital camera. It gives you a lot of stuff about any photo you take. For me, all I wanted was the date and the place. It confirmed that the image was taken on Saint Kitts a MONTH after Ben's office overpaid for the art Abelard bought for the foundation."

"Interesting," I said. "OK, Dixie, your turn."

"Well, my story doesn't have the salsa that Drew's does. I've been working with Frank Mack, the head of Terry's geek gang in the back carriage house. They're quite a crew. I'm pushing them beyond their comfort zone. And they are cool with that and so is Terry. They've been able to trace some deposits that relate to the companies that Luc's goons are stonewalling me on. Cerberus and two others that they noticed had identical activity—Chimera and Hydra. I've become intrigued by them. They're all references to Greek or Roman mythology. Cerberus, as you know, is a three-headed hound and referenced in the prec letter, spelled with a "k." Chimera is a fire-breathing creature and Hydra is a water beast with many heads. Happy little family of monsters.

"They are three foreign corporations whose ownership is unknown, but they appear to have all received funds wired from various ClearAire clients, service providers, and unknown third parties. So far our info shows that they all in turn wire-transferred these funds to unknown banks. What caught Frank's attention was that at a point about a year ago the transfer amounts for each account were about the same. Those companies are all incorporated and registered in Madeira. Then Frank hit a dead end. So far there is no way for us to further access those accounts. Seems that the transfers of funds out of each of those corporations can be effectuated only in person by the holder of its bearer shares, and we have no idea who that is. There is another name that appears from time to time in e-mail chatter—'Typhon.' In mythology, he is the Father of all Monsters. We suspect that entity or person is somehow connected."

"Help me—I'm lost," begged Drew. "Madeira? I thought that was a cheap Portuguese wine."

"It is, but I'm talking about the country, which is south-west of Lisbon, near Morocco. Its capital is Funchal, and it's an autonomous region of Portugal. It has very advantageous tax benefits—minimal annual taxes, under 2 percent, and minimal accounting formalities. A perfect tax evasion environment. Each of the companies is incorporated by a single shareholder, which in this case was a Spanish sole proprietorship with a local law firm listed as its address and agent. There is no requirement that the beneficial owner be disclosed in its filings. So far, it's a dead end as to who owns these companies or who has the bearer shares."

"How does all this relate to us?" I asked.

"Well, not sure it does, but it's an unexplained anomaly. It seems that the wire transfer deposits—as well as we can trace them—emanate from either ClearAire itself or clients or subcontractors of ClearAire. And it's too coincidental that these three entities each get virtually the same monies and that they are all named after mythological gods. And I suspect Typhon is the godfather of them all—sort of. What all this is about, we just don't know, but it doesn't pass the smell test. As you've said yourself, Tuck, coincidences don't happen twice. Here it happened three times."

"OK, Dixie, I agree. Stay on that and see where it leads."

Drew's head was spinning and mine was too. I ran my hand through my hair trying to dislodge whatever was colonizing in my brain and suggested that we take a break and regroup in fifteen minutes. We would need clear heads to survey where we were.

34

"Now is not a bad time to assess where we are. We have pulled back the curtain on those closest to Ben and we have found things a bit darker than we started with. Natural causes, accidental, self-inflicted, or foul play—all are still on the table. We should not count on being lucky and we've got to guard against overanalysis. Incongruities are part of everyone's life, including Ben's, so don't obsess about them. And remember, we are not district attorneys; we are not judges. We're more like a grand jury. All we need to determine is whether there is sufficient cause to suspect foul play. Then it's the Executive Committee's job to decide what to do.

"Looking at things objectively, we have no forensic evidence as to what caused Ben's death. No autopsy. The doctors at the hotel and at the coroner's office both fobbed it off as a coronary event. Perhaps more a guess than an opinion, although that would seem logical. His New York doctor is more skeptical. Ben had no history of heart issues, and other than his recently discovered cancer, which admittedly was potentially serious, he had few health problems.

"And suicide, at least to me, doesn't seem probable. The Precatory Letter, at best, mildly suggests it as a wistful option, but a man who was about to finally get the perfect male heir—mothered by an intelligent, highly educated descendant of a well-regarded author of kid-lit classics, married to his daughter, and who by written agreement, I am told, ceded sole custody and control over any children to Dorothy—doesn't seem a suicide candidate."

"Perhaps that's not as pat as you think," Drew said. "I'm not so sure. All this talk about heir creation could be academic. Is it all right for me to talk to Charlotte? I'd like to see Eloise's agreement and check the law as to whether that child—or children—would have any rights to the estate or the Trust at all, and, if so, whether a parent could bargain it away."

"I'm not sure Charlotte or Evan even know about this proposed agreement," I allowed. "The agreement was done by another law firm. You could check with Terry to see if Ben had a copy and any correspondence from that firm and I will check with Eloise. She would certainly have one."

"While I've got the floor, I want to make one thing clear," Drew announced. "I am changing my opinion about the deceased. It's appearing more and more that he was a plaster-cast hero . . . and a self-absorbed humbug, and I'm not buying the splendor of polyamory if all you get is an occasional call to service and a potted plant."

"You do have a point," Dixie added. "It does seem Ben was very conflicted. He had to know that death was coming, but probably believed that an exception would be made in his case. That's a Saroyan line."

"Well, I'm not buying the possibility of suicide, period," Drew countered.

"Don't be so dismissive, Drew," Dixie said. "Ben was on the verge of possibly losing control of his company and maybe his legacy. He was smart enough to know that artificial insemination of an over-thirty-five-year-old with the sperm of a sixty-plus-year-old was at best a long shot—so to speak. And being somewhat estranged from his daughter, having cancer, and losing his beloved dog had to have taken their toll."

I then added, in a whisper, "When you lose all those you love, suicide is much more viable than you might think."

"In all due deference, Ben was no Jonathan Tucker," Dixie said, looking down.

Trying not to sound awkward, I said, "Let's get back to our analysis. Let's list the possible candidates other than Ben. That universe would have to include Luc, Kati, Abelard, and even Leo. Eloise and Tremaine have to be included, but they seem like longer shots.

"So starting with my favorite, Luc Grogaman. He's a professional soldier, and killing is an accepted consequence of that trade. Ben's death was Luc's gain. He ended up in charge of the whole show and now controls his own destiny. To the extent there is any serious illegal dirt at ClearAire, which I think there may well be, he could now keep it buried or clean it up. And he was present in London that day. I would not rule him out."

"I'd put Abelard on the list," Dixie volunteered. "He was there several times. And he lost the best job he will ever have and, if Drew is correct about his buds, it may have been much more lucrative than we thought. My only reservation is that he does not seem too smart and I'm not sure he has the *cojones* to kill. Yet if greed is the biggest tool in his box, then he just might have sucked up enough courage to do it. I'll cede the floor to Drew on Kati. Another one of my favorites."

Drew snapped to attention.

"My approach to this is simple. 'What would Agatha think?' These events actually fit her classic motif—a suspicious death with multiple suspects who have secrets that eventually get discovered. In this case, we are not going to gather them in a room and announce the guilty one. If Ben's death is foul play, it was most likely murder by poison, and if so it was most likely added to Ben's food or perhaps put in his Bloody Marys. Agatha believed that poison was the easiest way, especially when others were present. According to her, no one notices the person waiting on you."

I rejoined the conversation. "It may not have been over money. Financial gain is not the only reason people kill. In fact, it is not the principal reason. From what I've read, revenge is.

"If we follow the motive trail, Luc and Abelard might have acted in fear of jeopardy. Abelard clearly was out of a job, and his personal transactions might not stand the light of day. And the same may be said about Luc. Leo or Kati could have done it in anger or for revenge. Ben was jettisoning Leo and making a more perfect son. Kati must have known that Ben did not want her to have his child. Neither could change Ben's mind. Eloise and Dorothy don't seem to have any motive. There are plenty of sperm donors around. And Tremaine? Well, assuming Abelard was her accomplice, I'm not sure what she gained. Why make herself perpetually beholden to Peter? She would have wanted Ben to live at least a bit longer so the full amount of the prenup kicked in."

"There is another possibility," Drew added. "Leo could have been trying to save—not kill—his father. He might have concocted another Merlin cure, hoping to make his father better."

"Good point," Dixie allowed.

I nodded concurrence and added, "I think we need to do a little more legwork. Drew, could you call Pervy and find out if she recalls who visited Ben the day before he died? It dawned on me the other night that he did not just arrive in London the day he died. I expect he arrived midmorning of the day before. Might prove helpful to know who he met with that day, if anyone. I'll check with Terry and you check with Pervy. Probe her a bit more. Now that time has passed and there were, hopefully, no adverse consequences for her, she just might be even more forthcoming.

"Also check with Kati. What I haven't mentioned is that Eloise and Dorothy are really incensed about Ben's infanticide provision as it relates to Kati. Dorothy is going to ask Evan if there could be a way to make Kati's choice less draconian. She's willing to waive some of her share of the estate to accommodate that. She's even willing to personally gift her the difference if she elects not to abort. She may have reached out to Kati already. So without promising anything, you can fairly give her a little hope."

"If it's not too late," Drew murmured. "Her genes weren't good enough for Ben. I hope it won't offend you, but he really was a creepster—a serial aborter, a chronic Romeo sniffing up every woman he met, a terrible father, and a scuzzball with an outsized ego. I'm not sure he could handle rejection. Perhaps when he couldn't select the gender of his daughter's child, he finally offed himself."

"I fear we're circling the drain. Drew, talk to Abelard again. See what his temperature is now. I once read that murder—if that's what we have here—turns a bright light on and a lot of people are forced to walk out of the shadows. What they do after a murder is often more telling than their conduct before it.

"I think we all have to be careful not to be proprietary about our personal theories. That can frustrate the process. For now, keep your mind open and just gather info. Dixie, pursue the Madeira companies. You may well be onto something, but it may have nothing to do with Ben's death. We'll see.

"OK, back to the trenches. I have to see Evan early tonight for cocktails at his apartment—a command performance. I've never been there before; don't know anyone who has. And Dixie, can you come by my place about nine thirty tonight? I want to hear more about ClearAire. I should be home by then. Ask the doorman if I'm in. I may be out with Nip. He'll know. We're now doing our constitutional down to the UN every night. Join us."

35

Four-fifty Park was not imposing from the street—it was not even on Park Avenue. Close enough, however, to use that address. But as the doorman personally delivers you to your host's floor and the elevator opens directly to his apartment, you quickly sense that this is a place for quiet money.

Evan greeted me with his signature handshake and embrace, careful not to draw me close enough to penetrate the boundaries around his personal space.

"So good of you to come. There is much for us to talk about and I thought it best done away from the commotion at the Firm. It's unrelenting these days, but I'm sure you realize that. It's been a trying few weeks, to say the least."

In the gray early evening light, the color was wrung from his eyes and he looked older than I remembered. Big Law can do that. His silver hair, not quite as thick as I remembered, hung unkempt around his ears; his incessant attempts to slick it back were to no avail.

"You look tired, Evan."

"C'est la guerre!"

That was a sure sign of fatigue. When he got tired or stressed, his pigeon French would come out. I often thought it was an annoying affectation that he used to gain time and gather his thoughts.

He was certainly in his element. The apartment was undeniably old-school charming. He introduced me to his furniture—two Louis XV high backs, an extravagant Bella Italianate sofa set, a nineteenth-century museum-quality grandfather clock that, he proudly pointed out, was made of marquetry wood. He allowed that these all came from his recently departed spinster aunt—his last living relative. He then led me to his trophies—as he called them—an Antoine-Louis Barye sculpture, a Maurice-Quentin de La Tour, a small Henry Moore, paintings by Tiepolo, Picasso, Degas, and Dubuffet. Again all the largesse of his beloved auntie.

Seems his genes swam in a different pool than mine.

I was sure this was not a social visit and as if he could read my mind, he announced, "Jonathan, things are getting out of hand. *Quel dommage,*" he sighed, with a gleam of worry in his eyes. A closer observation confirmed my first impression. He had aged overnight. He was a husk of the handsome man he once was. A trace of sag in his bottom lids and cheekbones revealed his anxiety. His narrow smile hadn't altered, but it seemed a tad meaner.

"Well, let's get on with it. We have a lot to cover. You know Russett has been amassing shares in what the Street is convinced is a takeover bid. And the Street has been following suit. The brokers are buying any shares they can get. He would never have done that if Ben were alive. The board is already gearing up. Ozone's super voting B class shares lost their weighted value with Ben's passing. The shares owned by Ben's Trust and the foundation now return to parity with all the other shares from a voting standpoint. And even though they remain a potent voting bloc, we may find them neutralized.

"Tremaine's attack dog, de Vil, is challenging my position as executor and trustee, and even as a director of the foundation. He wants the old Will probated, putting Tremaine in as executor and, in the interim, a court-appointed crony made temporary executor. You know that person would likely abstain from voting in this case. In the foundation, we could have a stalemate even if I'm not removed—Dorothy and me against Tremaine and Abelard. Peter was never properly terminated. His contract required formal written notice, so he remains as executive director and trustee, again deadlocking the board.

"The Street thinks Ozone's parts are worth more than the whole. If Russett wins, he might just keep ClearAire sans Luc and sell off the electronics, which is not a growth industry now, as well as Dorothy's division, which is going great and would bring a healthy price. Just those two divisions generate a billion in earnings before interest and taxes, and the market, even on a multiple of only ten, would value it at over several billion. Russett would get to keep ClearAire for nothing. I'm afraid Ozone's in play. The daily volume has almost doubled. The stock is up 18 percent since Ben's death.

"Add to that board unease. It's more than just post-Madoff nerves. The SEC is all over Luc's operation. Some members of the board want us to appoint a special counsel and Justice is nosing around. Luc is understandably worried."

Evan continued, "It's not that we are without defenses. We can seek a white knight if we have to. We already staggered our board seats and issued some poison-put bonds that require buy-backs at three times the purchase price. At worst, we have only made Ozone more expensive and at best bought time to find alternatives."

He droned on about bear hugs, poison pills, sandbags, shark repellent, and sleeping beauty—Wall Street jargon for these battles.

"And as if that's not enough, I have the succession issue at the Firm. Wiggie's departing at the end of the year and the young turks are mounting campaigns to block my ascendancy under the banner of partnership democracy. In our business, as you well know, it's billings that matter and I'm making the most rain right now. I'm the only masthead partner left. And I've offered to serve only one term. I'll retire in three years and settle in Zurich. Love that city—it's clean, food's great, the old city's charming, and people are proper and polite. I like that. These upstarts can wait. Not to worry though, we've faced worse—you and I," he whispered as he placed his hand over mine.

He usually avoided physical contact. I always viewed it as an egalitarian conceit.

Maybe I was being too harsh. I was once his fair-haired boy. He was my Firm rabbi. I owed him. I was ambitious and street-smart. He called it "moxie."

He poured another sherry for himself and offered me one. I demurred as he began to muse about the "old days."

"You know, Jonathan, when I started, senior partners could recall the time when their predecessors refused to have phones in their offices, when appointments were still made by letter, and their first year's income was $2,500. Everyone was a gentleman. Mutual respect was a given. I know this might sound a tad biased but there were no micks or hebes in the Firm. People didn't act pushy or crazy. They were patiently waiting for their turn in the spotlight. People didn't poke their *nez* where it didn't belong!"

As hard as it was, I held my tongue. Evan could get like that when he was under pressure. White shoe law firms when he was young were exclusive—read restrictive—clubs. White male Ivy Leaguers from well-heeled, socially connected families were the only ones admitted. It was not until clients began to demand prowess instead of pedigree that they opened up to the rest of us.

"Evan, I need to ask you a few questions before we continue. I suspect you have a long agenda, so if I could interject." He bristled at my rudeness, but acquiesced. "When did you, Luc, and Ben arrive in London?"

"I'm pretty sure it was the day before Ben died. I came in a day early. I believe Ben stopped in Barcelona and arrived later in the afternoon. Not sure when Luc got there. He stays at the Hamilton House. Can't stand the place personally. It's really not five stars anymore—filled with Africans and Arabs.

"Ben called a meeting with Luc and me that afternoon. After that I left and didn't return until rather late that night.

"Jonathan, is this visit about your investigation? You know my position. Ben was under great stress. Kati wanted a commitment, I gather, Tremaine wanted the ranch, and Luc wanted the company. Not to mention his daughter's lifestyle, his son's challenges, and his own health concerns. I was there. He died of a heart attack. This so-called investigation you've been roped into is purely political. Billings breed bitterness. Don't make yourself part of it.

"That is really what I needed to talk to you about. The Ozone board has set a special meeting for a week from now. It's going to be a full-day session and, to keep the press away, it's being held upstate at the convention center in New Paltz. You know where that is, don't you? Everyone is staying at the Mohonk Mountain House. So since more than half of the partners will be up there to consult with the Ozone board and its committees, the Executive Committee decided to hold its meeting there too.

"We want you to give us a final report on your findings.
We've decided that dragging your investigation out any longer
will make it too much of a distraction. Luc is relentless in his
harping about it, especially after today's tawdry incident."

"What incident?" I inquired, with an edge to my voice.

"Well, your associate, Dixon, apparently assaulted one of
Luc's key assistants, Mr. Sandino."

"I . . . uh . . . do not believe Dixie would do that."

"It wasn't fatal. I'm sure it has been exaggerated. Anyway,
I've handled it. So just wrap up your project and prepare your
report. And by the way, Sandino's just been appointed the
interim head of ClearAire now that Luc is the interim CEO
of Ozone.

"So now that you've gotten your walking papers, so to
speak, I have a proposition for you. I would like to invite
you back to the Firm as a senior partner. That would include
membership on the Executive Committee. Your comp will
be pegged at senior status, so if business holds up you'll be
making upward of three million plus next year.

"All of this investigation business should never have happened. Jonathan, it's time for you to rejoin our world. You
have so much to offer and to gain. And it's more than that.
I know how you like challenges. Well, that's what is facing
firms like ours.

"And you won't have to worry about Luc and his ilk. In
deepest confidence, I'm brokering a deal to get Russett to give
me a price to buy ClearAire and then we'll give Luc an opportunity to match that number on terms he won't refuse. Luc
will have his baby and Dorothy will then take over the reins
at Ozone and you will work directly with her. Solves everyone's problems except Russett's, but he'll get over it."

36

A lot to digest.

Evan at his puppeteer's best, pulling all the strings. I needed some air. Luckily the night air was refreshing—temperate and windless. It had rained earlier and the sky was vivid as it often is after a rain. Only an occasional cloud and a moon sliver blemished its perfection. A perfect night, yet Nip was anxious. She sensed that all was not right with me.

She was right.

I was roiling with anger. Evan's offer was tantamount to a bribe. I felt this had less to do with Luc and Russett than with Evan. He was orchestrating his final moment in the sun and wanted me to be his concertmaster. I couldn't even consider his offer until I finished our assignment.

Pure conflict. He knows better.

Dixie was on his way. He had e-mailed me and called, but I had turned off my phone in deference to Evan, knowing his aversion to them, and forgot to turn it back on. I could see that Dixie was agitated as he half-ran down First Avenue. Nip and I had already arrived at the UN. I let Dixie catch his breath.

"I heard about Sandino. So what's the story?" I asked, trying not to show my concern.

"What exactly did you hear?"

"Just that you 'assaulted' a client," I replied.

"Well, in a manner of speaking that's true."

"Was he looking?" I asked.

"Kind of," Dixie admitted.

"Oh, well, you know Woolly's last words of advice— 'Never hit a client—if he's looking.'"

He answered with a wry smile, "I'm not perfect."

"So what happened?"

"I was trying to get information on the three companies we spoke of in the carriage house. We call them the three Furies—Frank Mack's term.

"I was pushing for payment invoices and wire instructions for those three companies and after being stonewalled for three hours, I was told they all involved 'diplomatic security contracts' so that I needed approval from a senior Clear-Aire officer to override 'the need to know' ban. I asked for Sandino—he's the only one I knew by name. He came and took me into a conference room, where without much provocation, he pressed me against the wall and grabbed me between my legs. He wanted to make a point, I guess. Tuck, no one does that without permission so I kneed him hard. When I left the room he was still wincing on the floor. I'm surprised he had any balls left to tell anyone what happened."

"Good God! Are you sure you're OK?"

"I'm fine. I can take care of myself. I expect I'll have to leave the team. I understand."

"No! You are definitely not leaving. You're family. We need you. It's all moot now anyway. The Firm is pulling the plug on us next week. We all have to appear upstate and present our findings—as inconclusive as they are. So this is almost the end of the last quarter and we need a good tight end to catch a Hail Mary, if we are going to succeed."

"Well, I was the best tight end Yale's ever had—and I'm talking football."

"Dixie, I don't really know anything about you. Let's forget about Ozone and the Firm for a while. Stop hyperventilating. Relax and tell me about yourself."

Before he could begin, a hover of great horned owls started hooting. It was mating season and they were, if anything, persistent. The UN park provides the owls with both privacy at night and ample leftovers from lunch. They were in high fever, making themselves heard. Oddly this seemed to settle Dixie, if not Nip.

"OK, you asked, so here's my story," he said with a certain resignation.

"I was raised on the Florida side of the Gulf of Mexico, in a small town near the Alabama border. It was, as they like to say, as far south as you can go without getting your boots wet. Not sure if it was heaven or hell, but it was what I called home. The only viable business in my hometown was metal recycling. So we affectionately called it 'Junkville.' It was populated by 'good old boys' whose only interests were ball, booze, and bigotry—and broads if you had any time left. All the woes of the world, they were sure, were brought on by 'fag politicians.' My buddies were all coked-up cowboys sporting guns and spouting alibis. I spent most of my time listening to Jimmy Buffett. He was my bard; his words were my bible. Like him, I had a 'schoolboy's heart, stout legs and nomad feet.' I knew that to survive, succeed, and maybe escape, I had to do ball—football. It was the only thing respected down there. I was tall enough, quick enough, and scared enough to make all-state tight end and runner-up High School All-American East. Good enough to get a scholarship to Yale. That was my one big chance. It was time to leave—too many people were curious as to who was climbing under my mosquito net.

"All went well at college. I was one of the top receivers in the East in my junior year. I was on my way to the pros. Then boom—my knee blew out. ACL. My dream was dashed so I sidled over to the law school for no good reason. And I was surprisingly happy there. I loved the competition. And it didn't hurt as much as football. I wanted to be successful even though my father said it would ruin my life. He was wrong. I'm always looking for challenges. That makes me happy. It's what I want—at least every now and then.

"I'm happy right now doing what we're doing. When it's over, I suspect I'll move on. Even if the Firm would have me back, which I seriously doubt, I'm stifled there. It's not like football. There the quarterback, tight end, and tackle are all pulling together. In the Firm, you're on your own. You have no teammates. You work ten hours a day for seven, eight years and hope somehow you make partner. I was starting to miss the banana wind in my hair, excitement in my life. This assignment woke me up to what the practice can be like."

Dixie was real. I liked that. If JJ had lived, I would have wanted him to be like Dixie. Stanching my emotions, I glanced away. That's when I saw it coming—a small black motorcycle approaching fast. Odd at this time of night, I thought. Then it happened. The driver raised a bar and swung it at me. Nip went wide-eyed, snarled, and lunged. I heard the crack as it landed on her head. She fell to the ground without a sound.

Ugly, awful silence followed. I reached down. There was no life in her eyes—those same eyes I depended on to see what I wanted to see, what I hoped to see, and what I didn't see when I looked into my own.

Once again life as I knew it would never be the same.

37

"You're going to be fine, Tuck. You passed out when Nip went down. She's going to be fine too. Vet says she has no permanent damage. X-rays and an MRI confirmed that. Apparently dogs have surprisingly strong heads and quick reflexes—so the blow probably was just glancing, even though she passed out too. At worst she had a concussion. When she regained consciousness, she was wobbly and disoriented so I left her at the animal hospital overnight. Viggie picked her up this morning and she was resting back at the Hole with Terry and Drew doting on her. Drew told me she's loving the attention.

"And as to what happened? Well, the guy on the cycle pulled out a billy stick and my guess is that he was aiming at Nip, not you. I heard him shout, 'Careful or you're next.' He was gone before I could get to him. Police arrived within minutes. They brought you here—NYU Medical. I cabbed Nip to the animal hospital up on Sixtieth Street. And then got hold of Drew. She stayed with you until early this morning. You were sedated with some strong stuff. Drew went back to the Hole when I got here this morning. Viggie's been busy shuttling us all around. Also Terry got some security guys they use to keep eyes open around the house. Probably overkill, but she doesn't want to take any chances."

"I've got to go," I said. I tried to get up, but Dixie restrained me.

"Whoa, Kemosabe. You have to be checked out first. The nurse said it should take about an hour. So just relax. If you're feeling OK, I could give you an update on our favorite friends at ClearAire. I've spent some time getting info on them. The company came into its own when Blackwater, now known as Xe Services, ran amok. If you remember, the feds indicted its former president and four other senior officers on weapons violations and making false statements to federal officials. This unleashed a barrage of bad press for Xe and its founder, Erik Prince, who, like Luc, is a former Navy SEAL. When a series of 'extrajudicial' killings was laid at Blackwater's feet, particularly the killings of five Iraqis at Nisour Square, that gave ClearAire an opening and they took it. They're trying to conduct business in a more discreet fashion. They've remained under the radar as far as political contributions are concerned.

"Tuck, it's pretty obvious they're zeroing in on us. I'm guessing that last night's thug was what is called a 'leaner' in the trade. I learned these terms by reading espionage novels. They weren't trying to kill you. They try very hard not to kill anyone within the US. They leave that for 'war zones' where they can kill with impunity. We must be getting close to something and it's my strong suspicion it involves Chimera, Hydra, and Cerberus.

"All we know is that money, in varying amounts, has been regularly sent from affiliates or customers of ClearAire to these companies in Madeira. In turn, those monies were wired to or deposited in accounts in Spain. That was until two weeks ago. Then these payments stopped for one of the companies, Cerberus. We just found out that all three were represented by the same law firm in the Madeira capital, Funchal. They clammed up when we called them—understandably—and suggested we put the request in writing.

"Frank Mack, by the way, suspects ClearAire is already hacking our personal e-mails. Apparently it's quite simple even though it's quite illegal. So he's issued us new encrypted phones—ICDs—which he claims are almost impossible to hack. Wants us to use them for any stuff we don't want the bad guys to see or hear and use the current ones for chatter so they don't think we are onto them."

"Dixie, to be candid, I'm not sure where we go from here. And we don't have much time. Six days to be precise. I'm going to go see Dorothy as soon as possible. If Nip is OK, I'll leave tomorrow. And I think I'll stop over in Barcelona. Have a hunch that I might learn something from the priest that Ben visited before he died. Hopefully he'll be forthcoming. We'll see. So if I leave tomorrow night, I could drop in on the good friar—unannounced I think would be best. Then I'll take the afternoon plane to Paris. Could you set that up for me?"

"I'll do it via the ICD and let Terry make your reservation under Ben's personal card. That's the least traceable," Dixie suggested.

"Are we getting a bit paranoid?"

"Maybe, but sometimes I like to go into that world. They know me there."

38

This was more than I had bargained for.

The siren's call of Big Law had lured me back to a life I thought I'd left behind, and I'd deluded myself into thinking that this discrete assignment would be a harmless divergence from a walk in the woods. Yet all it had produced was unanticipated anxiety and painful memories.

The thought of losing Nip is incomprehensible.

I feared losing sight of Alice and the kids. Nip, in her wonderful way, was my guide dog. She led me to my memories. Touching her was like touching them. And when she went down, all of the quality left in my life slipped away. I knew she couldn't be with me forever, but for now she was my lifeline.

The Ambien was working. I sensed my anxieties ebbing. A gentle touch from a smiling steward brought me back to consciousness six hours later.

Barcelona lay below me. Today the sky wore gray. It wasn't like that when Alice and I came here. There's a lot that brings one here, even in bad weather. We'd walk the promenade at night, seduced by mournful strains of fado and the proud theatrics of flamenco, while warding off an annoyance of peddlers and a jam of tarts in order to hustle back and seduce each other.

Maybe it wouldn't be too difficult to be here.

A city that treasures fado must be a good place to be sad in, but I wouldn't have time to listen, weep, and drink brandy.

Terry had arranged for a car to pick me up and take me straight to Montserrat. I had but four hours to visit the mysterious Father Jeronimo, to whom Luc and Ben had paid their respects. My antenna was telling me the connection was more than just spiritual.

Fortunately the driver respected my privacy. Within an hour we began the extraordinary ascent up this astonishing mountain. It was like no other mountain I had ever seen. Montserrat is in the very center of Catalonia, rising almost perpendicularly 4,000 feet out of the rather uninteresting and commercially blighted plains. I was reading a guidebook on the mountain, monastery, and sanctuary that I'd found in the back of the car with one eye, while the other was riveted on this natural phenomenon.

It was otherworldly, as if carved by Gaudi's ancient ancestors. Romantics got carried away by it. Schiller believed that the mountain sucked a man from the outer to the inner world and Goethe went one better, professing that nowhere but in one's own Montserrat would one find happiness and peace. Maybe this was Ben's Lonely Mountain, where Smaug or some evil force ruled over his gold.

The mountain itself certainly has a rich history, but its fame is anchored by a Romanesque sculpture of the Blessed Virgin and Child, believed to be hidden there in a cave in 800 AD and rediscovered centuries later. It's called La

Moreneta—the Black Madonna—or, more literally, the "dark little one." Could that be the "Dark Lady" in Ben's letter? He had come here twice recently according to Terry's travel records. Once four months ago and the other time the morning before he died. Why? Perhaps Father Jeronimo would shed some light on that.

Our ascent finally came to an end as the driver pulled next to a livery of limos. He opened my door and pointed to a nondescript orange-tan two-story building adjacent to a large aggregation of similar buildings that grew progressively taller. At its apex was the basilica. The driver told me to return to the car when I wanted to leave.

The plaza was filled with life.

A flock of tourists, a scurry of nuns, and a cloister of monks all scampered about while blackbirds kept busy marshaling troves of discarded tidbits. The blackbirds of Montserrat are quite large. They were made famous by Picasso when he painted one in a woman's arms.

I was greeted upon entering the foyer of the building by a nun receptionist. When I asked for Father Jeronimo, she told me to wait and hurried away, returning with a more imposing nun, whom she introduced as Hermana Clavel. I remembered that Hermana was Spanish for Sister. The new nun politely ushered me into an anteroom.

"I'm saddened to tell you that the good father passed away a short while ago," she said in perfect English. "Perhaps I can help you in some way?"

I tried not to show my disappointment.

"How sad. Was he ill a long time?"

"No, not at all. It was quite sudden. I went in to clean his bedroom and there he was—dead. May God be kind to him," she whispered as she crossed herself.

"If it's not too personal, do you know what he died from? Did the doctors know? Did they do an au . . ." I stopped, perhaps too late.

"Heavens, no, Mr. Tucker. Death here is not dreaded; it's welcomed, for it brings you to the Kingdom of God. I suspect, though, that it was his heart."

"When did he die?"

"I believe it was a month ago next Tuesday." She blessed herself again, her countenance softening.

"Mr. Tucker, tell me about yourself and why you are here. Unless you are in a hurry to leave."

"No, I have some time."

I told her that I was a lawyer who represented a company called Ozone that did some business with the late padre.

"Do you have family?" she asked.

"I had a wife and two children, but they died in a car accident. That was more than three years ago . . ."

She blessed herself yet again, as she murmured something in Spanish.

"I know a little of your grief. My husband and child also died in a car accident. It was in Monaco. Oh . . . they were so young."

She must have seen my eyes widen.

"I am not a nun. I'm a lay sister—an avocation often sought by widows. I basically attend to a number of retired priests, helping them in many ways—their food, their rooms, their hygiene. Easier for a woman who has had a husband or a son. I am sure you know what I mean," she smiled.

"Sister, your English is excellent."

"Thank you. Actually I speak five languages. It comes in handy here. French is my mother tongue. You see, a long time ago I was a student at a little private school in Paris," she said, tucking a snippet of red hair under her veil. "I still remember the old schoolhouse, covered with vines. Miss Clavel was our teacher. I took her name when I took my vows, though most people here call me 'Hermana Maddy.' Madeline was my given name. I was the smallest girl in the class, but the most curious.

"It was in Paris I met my husband," she said with a smile. "I fancied him from the start. We married as soon as we turned of age—eighteen. We had a son who grew up handsome and tall. Just like his father. We were well off. My father-in-law was a Spanish diplomat. When my boys died, there was no world for me in Madrid. So the ambassador, my father-in-law, arranged for my placement here. He had a lot of influence," she smiled again.

"You and I have a great deal in common, you are right. I left my law firm after the accident and cloistered myself in the country, alone with my memories and my dog, who, you might be amused to know, was named after Junipero Serra."

"I had a dog too, when I was in school. Her name was Genevieve. She was my first stray. I still miss her. One of my responsibilities here is to care for the abandoned dogs. People who can't keep their pets will bring them up here and leave them, feeling less guilty in the hope that God will attend to them. God is too busy so I now have six."

"Sister, I came hoping to ask Father Jeronimo about some accounts that may be relevant to completing the probate of my client, Benjamin Baum. That means the filing of his Will. Mr. Baum may have had an interest in three companies, all incorporated in Portugal, Madeira to be precise. I had hoped Father Jeronimo might be able to provide me with some documentation on them. I understand that Mr. Grogaman and Mr. Baum visited here recently."

"Well, I'm not sure what I can tell you that might be helpful. I met those gentlemen when they came here. Mr. Grogaman I know little about. Mr. Baum, however, I spent time with. After his last visit with Fra Jero—that's what we called Father Jeronimo—I took Mr. Baum for a long tour. He was keenly interested—very inquisitive and quite charming. And very generous. After visiting La Moreneta, he gave me 1,000 US dollars to help with our dogs! That was the biggest gift we ever got.

"What else? Let me think. Oh, I believe I heard that Mr. Grogaman and Fra Jero were distantly related. Their families were both from Madeira. You have to understand a little background on Fra Jero. He was more a patriot than a priest—at least late in his life. He no longer performed his priestly obligations—Mass, confession, and Communion—but I'm told he was very good at finance. He handled all the monastery's investments as well as others—including some of the Catalan separatist groups.

"Mr. Tucker, don't misunderstand. I have the greatest respect for our priests. Some of them are truly saints. You mentioned Fra Junipero Serra—the one you named your dog after. Did you know he was Catalan? In fact, he's a follower of our revered Saint Francis of Assisi. You know of Capistrano?"

"Of course, a meiny of sparrows return every year. One of my favorite happenings," I responded.

"Aha, so you also enjoy the passion of venery. We sisters often indulge. In fact, the first compilation of venery terms was done by a nun in the fifteenth century. It's quite entertaining and we have plenty of time on our hands.

"Well, back to your inquiry. Fra Jero traveled on business constantly—Funchal, Geneva, Zurich—almost weekly. I thought it exciting, but he seemed to trudge through it with a guilty soul. His eyes were always gray and never hinted of contrition.

"Something bothered me about his death. After he died, I went back to his office. It was apparent that some of his files had been removed. I've always suspected Mr. Grogaman may have taken them. Fra Jero saw him the day he died. Perhaps they were his and he took them. I don't know. All the remaining files seem to relate to the Catalan independents or the monastery as far as I could determine, although I've not yet finished sorting through them."

"Do you remember any that were entitled Cerberus, Chimera, Hydra, or Typhon?" I asked. "Those would be helpful to Mr. Baum's estate. We need them to complete those filings I mentioned. That's part of my job."

"No. Not that I can recall," she said. "But I will look at what's left. There are some folders I have not gotten to. Those are the ones that he kept in his bedroom. As I said, Mr. Grogaman, I believe, may have taken some of the others."

"Sister, I appreciate your taking time to help. I think I might visit the basilica now and perhaps I could see you a little later."

She said, holding my hand, "I sense that you are troubled. As my beloved teacher, Miss Clavel, often said, 'Something is not right, something is quite wrong!' I sense that may be the case here.

"Yes, go visit La Moreneta. Perhaps she will calm your worries."

39

It's not like me to show emotions, particularly in the presence of strangers. Must have been the Ambien. More likely the aftershock of the Nip attack. Maybe it was the place. Perhaps Barcelona is the city of the damned. I needed some space to think. Obviously too many coincidences. Ben and Fra Jero die the same day. Luc and the good padre related. Both families from Madeira. A priest who spent most of his time in the vaults of Switzerland. Was he an alms dealer, an arms dealer, or just the proprietor of a financial Laundromat?

A saint or a sinner?

I wandered into the basilica. It was the most luminously beautiful room I had ever seen. Saint Peter's pales in comparison. Dynamic and graceful all at once, the ornate nave with candles flickering, the Madonna cradling the Infant, the glitter of gold-leafed mosaics radiating around the room. A score of pillars with gold inlays of liturgical icons supported the dome. Above the altar, a larger-than-life crucifix floated, suspended by barely visible wires.

I decided to follow Sister Maddy's advice. It required falling in line with a flock of the faithful slowly making their way up a small stone stairway embedded in the rear side of the dome, rising at least one hundred feet to its peak. I joined the suppliants holding on to the well-worn iron banisters, polished clean by the clenching hands of those who awaited their turn to pay homage to, or gain forgiveness or at least comfort from, the Black Madonna. Ben had been one of them.

Apparently it didn't work for him. That must be the meaning of his comment in his prec letter. *"Evil may be coming my way and even the Dark Lady cannot protect me."*

The satisfaction of that epiphany was suddenly replaced with unease. I had the sense I was being followed. Perhaps it was just my now quite robust paranoia. I was out of my element. I was a paper warrior, a brute in the boardroom. Atticus, not Bond, was my idol. As if to underscore that, a hand on my back gave me a violent shove. My knees buckled but my hand braced me, preventing a nasty fall. Fully expecting a helping hand from a sympathetic stranger, or a brush-off from a maniacal fanatic rushing ahead to heal his sins, I saw only an older couple, in matching hiking coats, apologetically nodding as they advanced up the stairs. I followed suit with a certain chagrin. I was hell-bent—probably again not the right term—on seeing the orb. Arriving at the peak, I crossed a tight parapet and walkway to the statue, which was housed behind a sheet of glass. One of the Virgin's hands was not shielded. It held an orb. The tradition is to kiss the orb while raising your other hand to Jesus. I demurred and just closed my eyes and thought about Alice.

Downhill was easier and, upon reaching the altar level, I saw Sister Maddy, who was kneeling at a stand of votive candles.

"Kneel down and don't engage me," she whispered. "Just listen as you light a candle. You're being followed. Your driver is keenly interested in your whereabouts. I want you to get up and go to the gift shop. Buy enough books and things to fill a gift bag. Come back here. If you look to your left you will see a confessional. Step into it if the red light is on. If not, kneel here again and enter when the light does go on. Sorry for the intrigue. I'll explain later. Be sure to bring your bag of goodies."

With that she blessed herself and scurried away without a word—the way only nuns can do.

I followed her instructions faithfully. It took me a good half hour to work my way through the crush of shoppers. And as I returned to the confessional booth, gift bag in hand, I saw the little red light was on and dipped behind the curtain.

"Bless me father . . ." I halted. Pavlov was right. Conditioned reflexes never die, but in this case it was habit, not hunger, that triggered them.

"No," she laughed. "The Church hasn't come that far and I'm way out of line being in here. But I sense that something is very wrong. As I said before, when I found Fra Jero dead, it was clear that some of his files had been removed. When I checked his bedroom, I found several folders filled with receipts and some other documents in Portuguese. I just now quickly perused them. Most have markings in Fra Jero's hand with the names of those companies you mentioned."

She opened the latticed partition that was intended to provide anonymity and separation between the priest and the penitent and we exchanged identical Montserrat shopping bags.

"You must understand. I love the Church, but I don't always love some of its members. Some have guilty souls. You can see it in their eyes, as I did in Fra Jero's and in Mr. Grogaman's. I did not see it in the eyes of Mr. Baum and I do not see it in yours. Now go. And may God be kind to you. You will see a neon exit sign when you go toward the main altar. Take that door and just outside there is a line of cabs. There you will see another nun with your suitcase. Luckily it was on the backseat of your limousine, which wasn't locked. I took the liberty of removing it. Take any cab, give the driver fifty euros, and you will make it to the airport in record time. I have made sure your old driver will be distracted. I have some pull with the basilica guards. Now go . . . go! And may God be with you."

With a broad smile, she added, "And thank you for the lovely gifts."

40

Luck was with me. Sister Maddy must have lit more candles.

A flight to Paris took off shortly after I arrived at the airport. I stuffed the contents of the shopping bag into my carry-on and stowed it overhead, spending the entire flight eyeing every passenger for any sign of a tail.

On arrival, I took a cab to the Plaza Athénée, paid the driver in cash and hurriedly entered the lobby, and proceeded directly out the side entrance, where I hailed another cab to take me to my destination—The Ritz.

James Bond I am not, but careful I am.

My phone beeped with the acronyms CM BGLOS DTB. I've had to learn a whole new way of communicating—texting acronyms, annoying but amusing shorthand. In this case, not so amusing. "Call Me. Bad Guys Looking Over Shoulder. Don't Text Back." I quickly grabbed my new secure phone and dialed Drew.

"Hi, it's me. How's my girl doing?"

"You mean the Divine Miss Nip? The lady is fine."

"Great, but really, how is she?"

"She's fully recovered, according to the vet, who made a house call. Can you believe it? She's one special dog."

Drew paused. "There's lots to tell you, but we're concerned about security. The people Terry hired to watch our perimeters here believe we are in fact under surveillance. Same people parking different cars every day and just hanging out in their vehicles. Not very sophisticated, but effective in letting us know they're watching. Dixie thinks you should continue to use your personal phone for harmless chatter and the secure phone for sensitive stuff. OK?

"And you were right on about circling back to Pervy and Kati. Struck out with Peter, though. Seems he's tied up with foundation issues and is unavailable. Tremaine's lawyers are pushing their motion to remove Evan as a director of the foundation and replace him with their—or the court's—designee. Abelard continues to function as executive director.

"I did some research and found out that Tremaine's father was in fact buried in a cemetery just outside of London—not at sea. I asked an associate from the London office to check it out. According to the obit, he was buried at Abney Park in Stoke Newington. It was on her way home so she stopped by. She befriended a groundskeeper and asked if the deceased's body was buried there or just his ashes. He said he didn't have to check. 'Ashes are for Mum's mantel; this is a proper cemetery. We only bury bodies!' Curious, isn't it?

"And some good stuff on the other front! First, I reached Pervy at home after work. Sounded like she'd already had a bit of bitters. I'll read you her response: 'Allo, o ar yu. You callin bout the afloat. You know, I'm no twocker and I'm no tea-leaf.' Translated from her cockney—'Hello, how are you? You calling about the overcoat? Please understand I don't take things without consent and I'm no thief.'

"Pervy went on to explain that after everyone left the day Ben died, she went into the closet of the suite for a final clean-up and found Ben's overcoat. Apparently Abelard missed it. Assuming that no one would want it, she took it for her husband. He's about Ben's size and could use a good coat. They put it away during the warm spell and just this week pulled it out. Her husband found in the upper pocket an envelope with a handwritten letter addressed to Dorothy. She was going to call me, but hadn't gotten a chance. She didn't think Ben would have minded. I assured her she was right and we all knew how fond of her Ben was. I asked if she could bring the letter to work and I would have someone pick it up. The London office handled that and I had them send it straight to you by office courier. His name's James, and he's on his way by train to the Ritz to hand deliver it. He should be there, I suspect, very soon. Told him to personally give it to you and no one else."

"Great, what does it say?"

"I had him fax me a copy, mostly personal stuff. I'm not really sure what it all means. Hopefully you and Dorothy can sort it out."

"Well, I'm stuck in Paris traffic so it will be awhile. What else did you learn?"

"Oh, yes, on another matter. Pervy told me she called up to the suite on the night before Ben died to witness a letter Ben signed. It was also witnessed by a 'dandy gezza.' I think she was referring to Mr. Amaroso. Ben gave her three hundred euros for witnessing his signature. That pleased her.

"And Kati was much more forthcoming too. She admitted that she was not so before. She didn't want to get involved in a public fight or a lawsuit. Her visa status is shaky. She came to London on a compassionate visa revocable if her conduct is considered inappropriate. She's already on thin ice due to her 'profession' and her brother's suspected activities. She then volunteered that after Ben's death, Dorothy had sought her out and befriended her. She is covering all her pregnancy expenses and found her an excellent obstetrician. Dorothy even told her of her plans to have a child with her mate and promised to continue to help her. Kati feels like she has a new Baum benefactor.

"I probed her more about the night Ben died. Oh, by the way, she did not see him the night before so no help there. He told her he was going to be busy with his daughter and his banker. What she did tell me was that Ben, Luc, and 'the lawyer'—Evan, I assume—had a very big row. Ben talked about something he learned in Spain, she thought. Ben and Luc, whom she referred to as the 'soldier-man,' were yelling at each other. She remembers hearing Ben scream, 'I'll sell the fucking thing! Never liked it. The devil's business.' The 'soldier-man' yelled back, 'That's suicide.' He then left and slammed the door. The 'lawyer'—Evan—kept promising Ben he could make it all go away, but Ben wasn't buying it and just kept asking for another drink. Kati tried to calm him down. She had never seen him so upset. He started to sweat; his speech got slurred. He kept talking to himself. That's when she left.

"Well, that about covers it."

"Thanks, Drew. Very interesting. I'm seeing Dorothy early tomorrow and I'll let you know what transpires. Is Dixie there?"

"No, he'll be back in a few minutes. He's back in the stable."

"OK, I'll get him later."

Interesting. Everything pointed back to Barcelona. Ben may well have figured out what the good friar was doing. But I wasn't sure I had. He was an obvious cash courier. That is not unusual for Spain. Even the royalty and the government leaders seem to have monies slide off into Swiss accounts. And he would be a perfect agent. Every Swiss bank knew that Montserrat was a cash cow. Millions of visitors, making donations and buying souvenirs, make it the "religious Disneyland" of Spain. And the money was all in cash or credit cards. A few million more from Luc's operations added to the Basque insurgency funds wouldn't cause suspicion or concern. Especially since Fra Jero had no doubt been depositing the monastery's cash receipts in Switzerland for decades.

The day turned gray, blending in with the buildings, all motley from centuries of smoke and fumes. I think all I really miss about Paris is Alice. She made it special for me—not the nightlife or the bistros, the ungodly traffic, the horrid pollution, the leaky autumns, the frigid winters, and certainly not its annoying love of self.

The driver announced our arrival. The Ritz hadn't lost its luster. It was still radiant, a small gem nestled near the Place Vendôme. Dorothy had said to ask for Frederick. I did and he was very solicitous. The suite was under Mademoiselle Baum's name. He never asked for my passport and refused my offered gratuity.

Dorothy, obviously, had real pull here.

It's true the Ritz never changes. The service remains legendary, the place immaculate. The *femmes de chambre*, wrapped in their crisp white aprons and armed with feather dusters, kept the Oriental rugs and Louis XV furniture looking new. But what elevated it above all other hotels was its history. Chanel

and Hemingway lived there; Diana and Dodi dined there
before their demise.

Once in my suite, which could only be described as a
period piece, I finally exhaled. As if on cue the phone rang.
They were sending up a young man from the London office
with a letter. He arrived. I thanked him and sent him on
his way.

What to open first? I opted for the stuff Sister Maddy
had appropriated for me—the contents of the gift bag we
exchanged. It consisted of three groups of deposit slips, each
held together by a heavy-duty rubber band. Each stack was
about five inches high. There must have been more than one
hundred deposit slips in each pile, and I noticed that they
were in reverse chronological order—the last being about a
month ago and the first five years earlier. The first pile contained deposit slips for Zingg & Co., Cie, Geneva, each
with the same numeric identification number. The only writing on them was the amount—usually in denominations of
100,000 Swiss francs and an initial I couldn't decipher—Fra
Jero's, I presumed. A square date stamp with the word "reco"
was pressed onto each deposit slip, with what appeared to be
a hand-signed initial evidencing acceptance. The other two
piles were similar. Only the bank name was different. One
was for East West Bank, Zurich, the other Barquet S.A.,
Banque Privée. It wasn't until I turned them over that I saw
the names of the accounts—Cerberus S.A., Chimera S.A., and
Hydra S.A.

I stopped totaling the amount when I got to two mil-
lion US dollars in each pile. This was where the money that
Dixie and Frank Mack had unearthed had gone. Monies from
ClearAire affiliates, clients, finders, or middlemen, I suspected.
Payoffs? Kickbacks? I couldn't tell.

The time difference and the drama of Barcelona had finally drained me. I couldn't function; I couldn't calculate. I couldn't even begin to decipher the letter that was delivered. It appeared to be a poem of sorts to Dorothy, written by Ben— Pervy's purloined letter. I dropped my clothes on the edge of the bed, hit the lights, and remember nothing but awaking the next morning.

41

We met at L'Espadon, one of the Ritz's epicurean pleasure palaces. I would have been more gastronomically involved had circumstances been different.

"Dorothy, it's great to see you again. It's been quite a month—for both of us."

"You're so right," she said ruefully.

She was as attractive as I remembered, exuding a classic elegance—appropriate for the Ritz. Yet there was nothing porcelain or patrician about her. Her countenance was more complicated. A mix of irony, intelligence, melancholy, and contentment made her all the more mysterious.

"Café au lait, skim milk, decaf, heavy on the milk," I said and she echoed ditto. The waiter took our order with expected deference, but with a hint of condescension that he couldn't quite tamp down.

"*Oui, mademoiselle, monsieur.*" I thought I heard him mutter, "*Pourquoi s'embêter.*" To a connoisseur, I suppose, without the whole bean and but a touch of cream, it really wasn't worth it.

"There is quite a lot we have to talk about, but I suspect the subject you are most interested in, understandably, is your father's involvement with the pregnancy." I smiled.

"Yes, of course. Do you have news on that? I gather you know we had a terrible fight with Dad just before he died. It was awful, especially with Leo and Eloise being there. He was in a very bad mood and had been drinking heavily before we arrived. He announced a new condition before he would give us the release letter for the sperm bank. He wanted us to agree to abort if the child was female. Even though that would probably be unenforceable, it put an ugly pall on the whole thing. I was hoping he would relent when he sobered up, but he died not long afterward."

"Well, I may have some good news on that front."

I told her about Pervy and the coat. Her eyes seemed to double in size.

"Please let me see the letter . . . please."

She devoured it. Smiles, frowns, and every other expression crossed her face. She was taking her time. In that prolonged silence, the only thing I sensed was a faint odor of French milled soap that emanated from her. I saw tears form in her eyes.

She proclaimed, "Yes, yes, yes!" as she leaned over to embrace me.

Her public display of emotion caught the attention of the surrounding diners, who responded with grins and thumbs-up.

I whispered, "They all think we just got engaged!"

She blushingly smiled and took my hand. Our coffee depleted, we awkwardly retreated from the restaurant to an anteroom across the hall. Dorothy immediately took leave and called Eloise to share the news.

With nothing else to do but await her return, I sat there and soaked up the Ritz's ambience—the gold-leafed settee with puffed pillows had a matching coffee table (not meant for decaf, I suspect). Classical music played softly, seemingly syncopated with the tinkle of the crystal chandeliers. Duc de Longueville, a seventeenth-century prince, looked benignly down on me, or at least his portrait did. He seemed like a friendly sort. Below the duke, a marble mantel surrounded a faux fireplace with matching bronze dogs at play on the hearth.

Those I liked.

The ghosts of this hotel were never far away—Hemingway downing Bloody Marys, Coco cuddling with the Krauts, Hepburn making love in the afternoon, and Barbara Hutton taking a razor to her wrist, while the staff saw it all without looking and heard it all without listening. It was César Ritz who coined the phrase, "The client is always right!"

Dorothy returned and handed me the letter.

My Dorothy,

Look beyond the rainbow, for there where the Höcker-schwanns hover, you can obtain what you seek. There, in that other Emerald City, you will find entrance in the signs of the Zodiac, the months of the year, the tribes of Israel, the stones on the pectoral, and the birds of Christmas.

The aegis holds the key; the kiste holds the future.

It is to you and my grandchild that I look for the future—one that will be bright. I am not blind to the problems ahead for they are largely of my doing. You are lucky to have a mate, one you can rely on. As blind as I have been to your extraordinary success, grace, and judgment, they have always been your strengths. New beginnings are here; perhaps it is time to go.

Ever drifting down the stream. Living in the golden gleam. Life, is it but a dream?

With all my love,

Dad

42

"Dorothy, I need help with this. I think this is the consent you were seeking! I generally get its drift, but I'm not sure what this letter is all about."

"Ah . . . well, Tuck, one thing troubles me for starters. Will this satisfy the sperm bank?"

"No. I'm sure they will need a much more formal and notarized or witnessed permission document, but don't despair. The maid also told my associate that she witnessed your father's signature on another letter, along with Mr. Amaroso's. She described him as your father's 'dandy Italian friend.' Your father tipped her a goodly number of pounds so she wouldn't forget the signing. I assume that was actually the consent letter and I expect that Andreas took that letter when he left. The one you just read I suspect was telling you where you would find the formal consent."

"I hope you're right," Dorothy said. "Like all my father's personal letters, it's a bit complicated. Not sure I fully understand it all, but maybe together we can parse it out. The first sentence, *'Look beyond the rainbow, for there where the Höck-erschwanns hover, you can obtain what you seek.'* That's pretty obvious. It refers to Zurich and its lake, which is home to a large overfed swan population. Maybe that means the formal authorization letter is in Zurich at the Sparkasse der Stadt. That's the bank where Dad told me the safe-deposit box is. Both Andreas and I are authorized to access the box.

"The next sentence is a little more complicated. *'There, in that other Emerald City, you will find entrance in the signs of the Zodiac, the months of the year, the tribes of Israel, the stones on the pectoral, and the birds of Christmas.'* I'm a bit lost. I know they all have the number twelve in them, except I don't know about the last one. Dad loved duodecads—groupings of twelve. He felt that twelve was his lucky number—'Benjamin Baum' has twelve letters. He once told me that the number twelve in biblical numerology signifies that which will finish or complete a perfect harmony. I'm presuming that it refers to accessing the sperm deposits. Not sure about what the 'birds of Christmas' has to do with this."

I interjected, "Oh you must know them: one partridge; two turtle doves; three French hens; four calling birds; five golden rings—that's a covey of ring-necked pheasants; six geese a-laying; seven swans a-swimming; eight maids a-milking— a tiding of magpies; nine ladies dancing—female lapwings gyrating during courtship; ten lords a-leaping—an asylum of cuckoo birds; eleven pipers piping—a watch of nightingales trilling at night; and twelve drummers drumming—a wisp of snipes, whose call sounds like drumming. Collectively a group of twelve birds. It's a Christmas song."

"You're a bird person."

"Yes, kind of. Alice and I used to sing that song to the kids every Christmas."

"Well, if this all works out, Eloise and I will too and we'll invite you to lead the chorus."

"OK. Now we know that the number twelve has something to do with the riddle he embedded in the letter."

"I've got it! Twelve numbers! So obvious!" she screamed. Grabbing the letter back, she took out a pencil and began to mark it up.

"Bingo," she proclaimed, handing me the letter.

"Dad was into what are called acrostic codes. They are like crossword puzzles. The word in Greek means 'covered writing.' It's the art of writing hidden messages in such a way that no one apart from the sender and the intended recipient can easily decipher the message. Dad loved them. This particular puzzle he shared only with me. When a number reference was included in one of his letters, such as the number twelve was in this letter, all I had to do was convert the words that also connoted numbers in the letter but disregard the last one. That would give me the coded numbers. He always added an extra number. If a person stole this letter, he could without much difficulty figure out that the code had twelve numbers. And he might even discern that words like 'to,' 'two' and 'for' stand for numbers. He could steal the key from Andreas or Dad, but he still wouldn't have the safe-deposit account number, since only I would know to delete the last number.

"Let me show you how it works. The words 'I' and 'one' denote the number one, 'to,' 'too,' and 'two' all convert into the number two, and 'for' is the number four. It can get much more complicated. Here he's made it quite simple. So the code we are looking for is 421411242112. Twelve numbers. The same as the total number of letters in his name— 'Benjamin Baum.' That must be the numeric account number for the safe-deposit box!

"When he told me about this account, he said someday he'd give me the number and the key, but if I ever needed immediate access I was to call Andreas. I've been trying for weeks. He's not answering my calls. His office said he's on holiday. The last time I saw him was at the funeral. He was very solicitous but now nothing. Strange. I hope nothing bad has happened to him. He was my father's best friend."

"I agree. I've also tried. In fact, I asked your dad's chauffeur to contact his relatives in Italy. Apparently they haven't heard from him either."

"Returning to the code. What tipped me off was the last three sentences. Dad lifted them directly from Lewis Carroll's acrostic poem at the end of *Through the Looking-Glass*. Carroll used the first letter of every line to spell out the name of his secret muse—Alice Pleasance Liddell. The last three sentences of Dad's letter start with the letter E, L, and L like at the end of Liddell. That's how I got it. Liddell is my middle name.

"The last sentence of the first paragraph of Dad's letter is the one I don't yet get. *'The aegis holds the key; the kiste holds the future.'*"

"I can help you a little there," I said. "I was a Latin and Greek major in college. It sometimes comes in handy. A *'kiste'* is a box. The safe-deposit box perhaps? *'Aegis,'* at least in classical Greek, meant the breastplate of Athena, with a gorgon embossed on it. Now it refers to a place of protection. I'm guessing that's where your father's key is . . ."

"Oh, my God, right under my nose," I shouted. "It's in the study in his downtown brownstone—our office for this investigation. There's a replica of a Greek warrior's breastplate hanging on the wall in the space between the bookcases . . ."

"Wait, I'm calling your father's house," I explained as I dialed.

"Dixie? Hi! Go into the study. You're there? Great, now take that breastplate off the wall. Is there anything taped on the inside?"

The wait was excruciating.

"Tuck, there are two keys taped . . ."

Hoorahs drowned him out, as Dorothy and I embraced.

"Are you there? Tuck?"

"Oh, sorry. Guard them with your life and get on a flight tonight that will get you to Zurich tomorrow morning. Meet us . . . hold on—" I held the phone toward Dorothy.

"The Baur au Lac Hotel," Dorothy shouted out. "Every cabbie will know it. Wait for us in the courtyard off the reception area. If they ask what you're doing, say you're waiting for me. They all know me there. See you soon and thanks."

I took my phone back.

"Dorothy, this is all very exciting, but we have to be more vigilant than ever. We can't let our guard down. Too much is not adding up. Amaroso's absence is very disturbing."

"I'm not going to exhale 'til we gain access to the box."

"Me neither," I concurred. "I'm paranoid by nature. It's an occupational hazard when you practice in a Wall Street firm."

"Truth is, so am I. It's also a common malady among women executives."

"OK, then it's agreed. Be careful. Just because we're both charter members of Club Paranoia, doesn't mean we're not being followed."

"A few more things about the letter. Dad copied the masthead from a Tolkien drawing. The runes underneath it translate as 'the road goes ever on.' And that little scene at the bottom he also copied from a Tolkien drawing. Across to the right the rune means fare well, take care of yourself . . . not really good-bye."

"I noticed he signed the letter 'Dad,' not 'Ben,'" I observed.

She nodded and looked away, too proud, I suspect, to let me see her tears.

43

We both took breaks, each heading to our respective washroom. When we returned, we were no longer alone. An elegant elderly couple had staked out a place across from our encampment. We removed ourselves to another alcove—empty, at least for the moment.

"Let's go back to your father's Precatory Letter and see if we can decipher some of it too. *'People who have no shame'* . . . *'who will go to their graves'* . . . *'a murder most foul.'* That can't be a reference to Fra Jero's death because it postdates your father's death. Perhaps it refers to his own death?"

"Who is Fra Jero?"

I told her about my visit to Montserrat. "Ben's reference to the *'Dark Lady'* must be La Moreneta, the Black Madonna of Montserrat, that he visited.

"He also mentions others *'too close, or too despicable, to mention.'* Any ideas?"

There was silence. I sensed she was processing this new information and crafting her response. A lawyer always observes the silence that precedes a witness's response. The shorter the silence, the more candid and less calculated and, in many cases, the more incriminating the answer. That is why a good litigator always tells his client to take time before responding.

"Dad rarely used the word 'despicable' in my presence, and when he did he was usually referring to Peter Abelard. I was always puzzled by the depth of his disdain for him, even if he suspected that Peter's closeness to Tremaine had become physical. Since he was no longer intimate with her, I couldn't understand his anger. Well, maybe I could. Dad was possessive to a fault."

She paused to grab hold of her emotions. "This is so difficult to discuss. The real reason Eloise and I removed Leo from Dad's presence was the fear that he would do him harm. Leo—as truly lovable as he can be—has developed real anger issues. He wants to be an adult. He wants to be free to live and love and make a family and get a job. All impossible dreams—at least for now. Yet not to Leo. So he viewed Dad as his jailer. As you know, on the day Dad died, Leo violently assaulted him. Dad wanted to spend some private time with Leo, so they went into Evan's room. Kati was in Ben's room. I have no idea what happened, but you know about Leo's Merlin obsession. The truth is I've always feared Leo might lethally spike Dad's drink. He prided himself on being Dad's favorite bartender. Dad always said Leo made the best Hemingway Highballs. It's too horrible to think about."

I changed the subject.

"Those Tolkien runes, I believe, relate to Terry, thanking her for her support over the years."

"Tuck, I know all about Tereza's relationship with my father and the fatal effect it may have had on my mother. I'm not blind and deaf. He thought it was a secret, known only to him and Terry. Dad willed himself to believe I was oblivious, and if he suffered because of that he deserved to. In some ways, he was truly a bastard."

"As to '*Namárië,*' I believe it means good-bye. I wonder if that was Ben's formal farewell?"

"No, I don't think so. That word is in Quenya, an Elvish language Tolkien created. Sometimes I say I'm fluent in six languages but speak only four. The other two aren't really spoken—Cirth, the proper name for Runes, is a dwarf language, and Quenya is the Elves' language. It appears only in *The Lord of the Rings* and the *Song Cycle*, Tolkien's musical collaboration. The music is quite good. One could sing along with Frodo and Sam journeying to Mount Doom—and with Bilbo as 'the road goes ever on.' *Namárië* is not 'good-bye'; it's 'take care' or 'be well.' I think it's Ben's warning to those of us who remain."

"Tell me more about your life with your dad. It might help me understand."

"Most of my education came from my father—sort of like homeschooling—although he did not call it that. I also went to the local private school, like all the other children of the well-to-do. It was Dad's obsession with children's literature that gave me my role models, though. The White Knight, the White Queen—they were my elders. I found the males know-it-alls and the females immature and haughty. Not too much to emulate.

"Terry remained my father's paramour and my mother surrogate—mistress and mother. And I had a brother who couldn't protect me. There it was a role reversal. I became the macho protector, Leo the needy dependent. Such was the chessboard of my life.

"Dad introduced me to 'his bible,' as he called it—the gospels according to Frank, Lewis, and JRR. Dad disliked organized religion. It was in the children's literature of Baum, Carroll, and Tolkien that he found his scriptures.

"The role he played as a father was different from the man he was. It's hard to articulate. You have to look at him as a hero in a fairy tale. It's the only way to understand his actions. He was unaffected by the more violent forms of megalomania that you find in big business. Yet he viewed all of his problems from an epic standpoint. He merged his fantasy world with his real world and he believed his enemies were monsters."

"What about the diaries?"

"He kept preaching his beliefs to me through them and his letters. I've always been puzzled about why he communicated in writing rather than engaging me in conversation, but I must admit for me to be the only recipient of his diaries was thrilling. It was like growing up with a secret. I think that writing diaries was his way of creating his own fairy tale.

"Unfortunately, overriding all of this was his obsession— his need for a male heir. He wanted his very own Bilbo. He was desperate. He was like Henry VIII. I was neuter as far as he was concerned—unwilling and hence unable to bear him his male heir. Ben wasn't quite sure that a woman would be up to the task of captaining his kingdom. That, I suspect, is why he was so anxious to use Eloise to produce Ben II and so willing to let me be the regent. Like Baum's Dorothy, I finally left home and moved to the magical land of Paris. It was there that I found my silver slipper."

"Quite a story!" I interjected, giving her a chance to exhale.

"Now let me bring you up to date on our investigation," I continued. "There are things you have to know. I became your fiduciary when I agreed to that role the first time we met here in Paris. A short while later, I undertook this investigation. I advised the firm of my relationship with you. They had no problem and you had no problem. Nevertheless, I've had to walk between a number of ethical raindrops.

"I've decided in this case to err on the side of overdisclosure. I feel in my gut that it will be best for you—and best for this investigation. I think for once the interests of my clients—you and the Firm—are aligned."

Again we were forced to relocate. The hotel was getting crowded. We finally settled in the Bar Vendôme. It was lush and intimate, made even more so by dark mahogany and inviting velvet. It suited our purpose. It was empty. We ordered their famous club sandwiches. Dorothy ordered Bloody Marys to accompany them.

She took pleasure in explaining the derivation of the name. Hemingway drank prodigiously. As the story goes, his doctors had forbidden him to drink and his wife Mary was holding him to it. A bartender at the Ritz conspired with him and created a vodka drink, filled with tomato juice and other ingredients to prevent the detection of alcohol. Having gotten the better of his bloody wife, he christened the drink after her.

Amusing, but probably not true.

So with our stomachs filled and our spirits lubricated, I proceeded to fill Dorothy in. I told her about the three Swiss accounts and my growing suspicion that they were evidence of illicit transactions at ClearAire. That did not surprise her. Like the rest of us, she was not a Grogaman fan. Then I recounted the Barcelona adventure and took her through my pilgrimage to Montserrat, the curious death of Fra Jero, and the revelation of Sister Madeline. I told her that the documents the good sister gave me might shed some light, but how much I still didn't know.

They are, I suspect, Sister Maddy's personal recompense for the sins of the not-so-good father.

I then told her the details of my concerns about being shadowed and worse—the Nip attack, my Barcelona chauffeur, and the thugs around Ben's place in Manhattan. Her attention turned to consternation.

"Do you think you'll be able to find out if my father was murdered and who is responsible? Eloise and I worry that if you don't, we will spend the rest of our lives in fear of Leo's being around our child, especially if it's a boy."

"I cannot assure you of that but we are trying. As of now we have suspects, but nothing more and time is running out. The board and the Firm's Executive Committee meetings are in four days. You'll be there, I assume."

"Yes, of course. There's a lot going on. I leave the day after tomorrow."

"Dorothy," I whispered, trying not to sound alarmist, "it's time to be prudent, even perhaps to overdo it. Here, this phone is encrypted. It's secure. Call Eloise. Have her book us flights using someone else's phone. We should try to get out early. There's an eight o'clock Swissair flight to Zurich. We should be in by nine thirty. Dixie won't get to Zurich 'til around ten, so we'll have to find a place to wait. I'll meet you at the airport at sevenish. No need to call me back."

"I've no problem with that. Your associate is going directly to the Baur au Lac. We'll go straight there too. I'll alert them of our arrival."

"Perhaps it would be best if you didn't."

44

As the plane gained altitude, our spirits rose too. Earlier that morning, I'd Googled the bank. Its web page was simple, discreet, and uninformative. It described the bank as a cantonal private bank serving individual and institutional accounts. Amaroso had told Dorothy that her father had his principal accounts at UBS in Zurich, but had a safe-deposit box at Sparkasse der Stadt.

He never gave her a reason.

I had learned the previous week from Terry that Ben's Swiss account at UBS had a little less than three million in it, which, upon his death, was to pass to Dorothy and Leo, in equal shares, and that he'd always included the income from that account in his US taxes.

Ben's annual interest was only a little more than thirty thousand. Not surprising—the Swiss sell safety, not return. Ben was not looking to Andreas for capital enhancement. I suspect that Andreas was more than a banker, rather what Europeans call a *'treuhänder'*—a confidant whom you can trust to handle your most discreet affairs, including facilitating private matters that the principal would prefer not to leave his fingerprints on. Kati was not, I'm sure, Ben's first special friend. He could not delegate those kinds of matters to Terry. That would be asking too much—even for him.

Dorothy, having finished reading materials she extracted from her attaché case, turned to me after we leveled off. She was radiant this morning, dressed very smartly, but not so as to draw attention. I cannot say the same for her stockings. They were almost luminescent, covering but not disguising her stunning legs. A string of pearls rested unobtrusively on her collarbones.

"Tuck, tell me more about Swiss banks. They've always been a mystery to me."

"Dorothy," I answered, "as you know, until recently, secrecy was Switzerland's most lucrative export. And most of the smaller banks are surprisingly low-tech. Unfortunately there is a James Bond 'vision' when you mention 'Swiss banks'— shady dealings, international bands of bad guys, secret agents, and tax dodgers one step ahead of the law, at state-of-the-art financial citadels with bankers who greet you with the perfect dry martini. The truth is that small Swiss banks offer nothing more than confidentiality and safety. It is unthinkable that the Swiss government would fail—it's too small—and as a consequence depositors feel confident that their assets will never be frozen. The Swiss are very righteous people. They are not unscrupulous. In fact, they are very proper. The big philosophical difference between the Americans and the Swiss was never over tax avoidance—everyone preaches that—but rather tax evasion. The Swiss for a long time just didn't view that as sinful. Of late, with some strong prodding from the Germans, the English, and the Americans, they have found religion on that score."

"Let's go over what you expect to happen at the bank," she said. "I hate the unknown. I worry I won't be at my best."

"OK, but remember, this is my first time too," I whispered. "You simply identify yourself as Ms. Dorothy Baum, have your passport ready, and advise them you are seeking access to your father's safe-deposit box. Do not volunteer that he is deceased. If they mention it, simply thank them for their condolences. Introduce me as your attorney and reiterate that you are here to access the deposit box. No more, and don't let them put you on the defensive. Act polite, but a bit haute."

"That won't be hard," she smiled.

"If they ask about your father, deflect the inquiry. If they ask about Andreas, say that he's on holiday. Don't offer your identification number unless it's absolutely necessary. They will know this is your first visit. I'm assuming that they keep a precise log of visitors. And as I said, just try to relax. Don't expect any small talk or banter. That's not in the Swiss DNA."

The plane arrived and we exited quickly with our luggage in hand. Dorothy had some type of card that got us VIP treatment and within minutes we were in a cab. After a quick exchange with the driver in what I assumed was Swiss German, she advised that the trip would be slow and tedious—rush hour and some very early snow had reduced travel to a crawl.

"OK. Then we have time. Tell me what's going on at Ozone." I thought it best to divert her attention for a while.

"The board, the proxy fight, the foundation, the Trust. Quite a scene, I suspect."

"You're right about that," she agreed. "I'll start with the board. Utter chaos. It's divided into camps, as you would expect. The outside directors are in thrall to their special counsel, Jack Newsome. Do you know him?"

"Only by reputation. He's supposed to be the best at that."

"Then there are the insiders—Luc, myself, Jeff Donaldson, our CFO, Patricia Sampler, my acting division chief. I've been elevated to president at Ozone. Doesn't mean very much, since the board designated Luc as the CEO. They are terrified of him. He sits over Ozone's most profitable division. They're coining money right now and he's not bashful about saying so. He does, however, stay clear of me. The remaining board members are all just numb. They know a Russett takeover means they're gone. And they know that even if we deflect Russett, the battle for control between Luc and me is bound to be nasty. There will be blood. Poor Evan—he's trying to keep his toes in each camp. He's stressed. You can see it in his face.

"It may be that we can convince Tremaine to vote along with management. It should be in her best interests financially—unless she is hoping that Russett's impending offer will be too sweet to reject," Dorothy said.

"What about the possibility of Russett's offering her a special sweetheart deal, although I'm not sure he would do that. Wasn't he a very good friend of your father's?"

"Yes, he was, but he's also a tough guy and apparently really wants Ozone. Remember, he waited until my father died. He would never have done this when he was alive. And I'm told he doesn't want Luc at the helm. So there's no alliance there."

"How are you holding up in all this career-wise?"

"Fine. Obviously, I'll miss having Dad at my back. For all the things he did and did not do as a father, he was super as a boss, booster, and benefactor. He gave me a long leash to run my division—and I took it. We're on the cusp of some great things.

"We're about to announce a blockbuster deal—a joint venture with Paramount to bring out the ultimate sequel, *Back to*

Oz. Paramount hasn't signed off yet, but we're close. It could be a megafilm—an updated version of Dorothy's daughter's return to Oz. We call her Ozma. In our version, the world of Oz is dominated by annoyingly condescending Wizards— Johnny Depp, Kevin Kline, and John Cleese being the most annoying of them. And, as always, there's a Good Witch, Glinda—played by Tina Fey—to save the day.

"It takes place forty years after the original. Ozma returns to Oz to try to right things. Seems the Munchkins are growing sad and restless. Ozma is everything her mother was and more. But we can't use the ruby slippers. Warner owns them and they're aggressively protective. This time Ozma wears silver slippers like Dorothy did in the book, but updated with thick higher heels and bright yellow soles. Hopefully we'll have a great movie and it will make us a player."

"Heady stuff!" I conceded.

"Yes, but all this pales next to getting Dad's consent letter. I'm so anxious . . . Ah, we are here!"

The cab had wound its way through the back of the city and come upon the Zürichsee—the vast lake that anchors this Emerald City.

And yes, the Höckerschwanns were indeed hovering.

45

We finally arrived at the Baur au Lac.

Traffic at rush hour had indeed been very bad. Dixie was sitting on a bench in the courtyard inhaling the crisp air and soaking up some sun. After eight hours in flight, I'm sure the fresh air was invigorating. He quickly rose and produced the keys. We then moved into the lobby lounge and ordered coffee.

No decaf this time.

One key was rather large and intricate, the other small and undistinguished. They had been taped to the back of the ornate breastplate that hung on the wall behind Ben's desk. The larger one had an oval end with the number 2424 stamped on it. The insertion end was two-sided, with distinct denticulations on each side. It was slightly tarnished and appeared to be silver. With great care, Dorothy placed the keys in her handbag and secured the strap across her chest and the bag under her arm. Only then, as she patted her bag, did she smile. With profuse thanks, we told Dixie to go unpack and we left.

It was a nice, brisk day.

The sky was a brilliant blue and the white-capped mountains that ringed the city sparkled. There was a flotilla of Höckerschwanns, hundreds of them, plying the waterway that connected the city with the lake and accepting their daily rations.

It was a handsome backdrop to this very proper Swiss city.

A modest polished gold plate affixed to a century-old undistinguished building on the Stadhaus Quai identified the entrance to Sparkasse der Stadt, Zurich. Inside the foyer a buzzer system unlocked the exterior door. We depressed the button next to the bank's name and a glass door to the left opened.

We approached the receptionist, advising her of our wish to access a safe-deposit box. She nodded with a smile, gesturing to the reception area chairs while she dialed for assistance. Shortly thereafter, a small, very neatly dressed man approached, introducing himself as Herr Roald Dahlgrens.

He resembled a short peach of a man with a Tweedledee physique. Not your stereotypical banker. But then again, he was a safe-deposit box escort—there to match only keys, not wits; he didn't handle any investment or financial matters.

"Grüezi Mitenand," he uttered as he bowed his head ever so slightly.

"Grüezi," Dorothy replied.

They spoke a few sentences in Swiss German, and then she nodded toward me. They switched over to English.

"Welcome, Mr. Tucker. Is this your first visit to Zurich?"

"No, I've been here several times . . . on business. A lovely city. I compliment you."

He beamed. Turning to Dorothy, he asked for her passport, which she produced. He then took out a little notebook and very carefully made notations, continuously glancing at the passport. When he was finished, he returned it to Dorothy.

"And how is Mr. Baum these days?"

Without flinching, she answered, "Peaceful."

"*Wunderbar* . . . And Herr Amaroso?"

"He's on holiday."

A smile crossed his face, as he extended his hand and led us to an elevator.

The vault rooms occupied the third-level basement. There was a square center foyer that led to steel-framed glass doors, which in turn gave access to seven rooms, each with a rectangular table and chairs. Herr Dahlgrens took us into one of them. After locking the door from the inside, he led us to one of the identical drawers that rose from about three feet off the floor to about six feet high. Rechecking the number on his manifest, he asked, "Fraulein Baum, do you have your box number handy? Just for protocol's sake."

Dorothy smiled, taking out her wallet and extracting a card. "421411242112." Her recitation was clear, her voice unwavering.

The silence that followed seemed forever. The good Herr Dahlgrens finally looked up and smiled.

"All set, as you say. You know the number isn't really necessary. It's only for our internal purposes. The key is what matters. If you notice, there are four numbers engraved on your key. That's what's important—and your identity, of course.

"We are a small bank here in Zurich and we get to know our customers very well. We are all very fond of Mr. Amaroso . . . and your father, whom I have not yet had the pleasure of meeting."

He extracted a key from his vest pocket and inserted it in one of the holes, and then nodded to Dorothy. Without any change in her countenance and without any hesitation, she slipped her key into the box's other keyhole.

"May I?" the good banker asked.

Acknowledging Dorothy's nod, he proceeded with two hands to open the drawer and lifted out a large back-hinged rectangular metal box and with practiced ease placed it on the table. He removed his key and motioned to Dorothy to do likewise. He then invited her to access the box.

Dorothy very slowly and methodically removed the contents—except for four stacks of euros that must have each measured four inches high. I noticed a thousand-euro note on the top of each pile. Assuming they weren't Texas rolls, we're talking beaucoup bucks.

They were of no interest to Dorothy.

There was a series of folders of various sizes. Without looking at them, she removed a small interior metal box, which had its own lock. Assuming that the smaller key was meant for that box, she took it out and gave our officious host a commanding glare. He nodded, retreating to the far corner of the room, his little notebook in hand. After a brief moment of hesitation, she opened the box and immediately saw a Lyceum Hotel envelope. Without a trace of emotion, she opened it, read the letter, and with an imperceptible nod to me, returned it to the envelope and placed it in her purse.

Herr Dahlgrens made another notation in his pad. Yet Dorothy remained imperviously calm—steel tough.

In a heist, I want her on my side.

She then motioned me to join her at the table and began to hand me the assorted folders. One contained an old copy of Ben's Will—outdated, I suspected. Another contained bank statements relating to his checking account. I put those aside.

The last one was larger. It contained a series of documents in what I thought was Spanish. It didn't take me long to realize that they were the certificates of incorporation for the three Madeira companies—Cerberus S.A., Chimera S.A., and Hydra S.A., along with the bearer share for each.

Directing my conversation to Dorothy, I said, "I think these could be of some use, Ms. Baum. May I take them?"

She nodded affirmatively. I placed them in my attaché case. She signaled that we were done and thanked Herr Dahlgrens matter-of-factly.

"Is there anything else I can help you with?" he inquired.

And for no good reason, I asked, "Can you direct me to a good chocolate shop in town? I've got a yearning for some of your best."

"Of course, Herr Tucker, Sprüngli, Lindt, and Teuscher are the best. They're all along the Bahnhofstrasse. And if you have time, there is a Lindt factory in Kilchoerg—not too far away—that's fun to visit. I have always wanted to own a chocolate factory but it was not to be. I am quite happy as a 'keeper of the keys.'"

We quickly exited the bank, advising our host that we might have to return.

Once on the street, we strained to keep our pact. No show of emotion until safely out of sight. Since the walk to the Baur au Lac was only a few hundred yards, we were able to keep our decorum.

Once inside the hotel, we hugged each other and Dorothy let out, for everyone to hear, a very unladylike, "Yes!"

She quickly regathered her reserve and added, "And, on a small note, I don't think it was a coincidence that the safe-deposit key number—2424—adds up to twelve. Dad knew that and that must be why he chose a duodecad puzzle.

"A game within a game. Just like him!"

46

Somewhere close, a clock bell tolled.

My anxiety began to abate even though these revelations brought on shudders of excitement. Dorothy had left for Paris, future hopefully in hand. Dixie and I ambled up the Bahnhofstrasse, Zurich's opulent main drag lined with the likes of Breguet, Bulgari, Cartier, Chanel, Armani, Hermès, as well as the obligatory Apple store and H&M.

It was lunchtime. Loden-clad bankers shopped for something to buy for their wife's affection or their mistress's attention—assuaging their guilt in one case and fanning their passion in the other. They all proceeded in measured strides. Zurich does a good job of hiding its innate detachment and rigidity. Its devotion to finance and adoration of self bordered on pious zealotry.

So, as the saying goes, when in Rome, we joined in as we made a beeline to Paradeplatz, which is home to three of Zurich's commercial titans—UBS, Credit Suisse, and Confiserie Sprungli. Herr Dahlgrens had directed me there, allowing that all proper Zurichoise went there to pleasure themselves on the world's best chocolate.

In truth, it was as advertised—sheer ambrosia, sustenance for the gods. After we satiated ourselves, we settled in and topped it off with equally delectable coffee.

"Tuck, since we've got the time and there's no one nearby, let me start to tell you what I found and what we know. Our flight isn't 'til tomorrow morning. We're making headway with the three foreign accounts. Uncovered a whole lot of transactions—both inflow and outflow. Only wire transfers so far. We can't capture nonwire transfers such as personal deposits. Those don't track back on our system.

"We knew that substantial payments were made to Cerberus, Chimera, and Hydra, the three Madeira companies. Now we know, thanks to a quick perusal of the documents Dorothy picked up at the bank, that the priest in Montserrat transferred most of that money into those three Swiss banks.

"One account is in Barquet S.A., Banque Privée Gèneve. From the notation 'LG'—written, I presume, by the priest—on that batch of deposit slips provided by the sister in Montserrat, I'm assuming it's Luc Grogaman's account. It's the largest of the three. My quick tally indicates about six million, and that's just from these deposit slips. It's distinctly possible that there were other deposits that we are not aware of.

"The second packet showed deposits in the East West Bank, Zurich. Those receipts have a 'BB' on them and I'm assuming that's an account for Ben's benefit. That has, according to those deposit slips, about two and a half million in it.

"The deposit slips in the final packet total a little less than four million and have the initials 'ET' on them. He paused, clearly uncomfortable. I'm guessing that's 'Evan Trombley.' They were deposited in the third Zurich bank, Zingg & Co., Cie. The deposits in all but the one attributed to Luc ceased a few days before Ben and the priest died. And those three sets of initials are consistent with the names on the Madeira incorporation documents you just got from the safe-deposit box.

"So summing it up, what we have, I think, is a rogue priest who was in fact a cash courier who made many trips from Barcelona to Switzerland and muled substantial cash deposits to at least three Swiss accounts. Tinker to Evers to Chance. A sweet play! Luc directed monies to be put into Ben's and Evan's accounts, most likely without their knowledge. It would serve as insurance in case either or both started to give him trouble about his activities at ClearAire.

"Quite ingenious. Ben and Evan would be outraged and would, of course, deny any knowledge of the accounts, but the burden of proving that they didn't know would be difficult. And just the adverse press about it would be devastating to both their careers and their legacies. Blackmail insurance!"

"That's a lot to digest and I think you're right, Dixie. Fra Jero was a fence, a common moola mule. I assume he took a fair percent for his efforts. All for the greater glory of God and an independent Catalonia and not necessarily in that order. He would have made Machiavelli proud."

Sister Maddy was also right. Fra Jero had a dark heart and Luc took advantage of that.

"I suspect," Dixie added, "Luc decided to kill the priest once he told Ben about what he had done."

"Dixie, you have to hand it to Ben, he was a Wiz. We'll never know how he pried the info and the certificates of incorporation out of Fra Jero. My guess? Ben was a great manipulator and he conned the old priest into assuming he was privy to the whole operation. After all, his name was on one of the certificates. As far as our priest knew, Ben, Evan, and Luc were all one happy family—of thieves!

"One thing, though, why would Fra Jero need to have the certificates of incorporation in his possession? I can't figure that out."

"I think I can explain that," Dixie volunteered. "Money laundering is really a misnomer. Should be called 'money soiling.' In the late eighties, it got to be an epidemic. Narcotraficantes had tons of dollars, francs, marks, and pesetas, duffel bags full, ready for deposit. Fear of being tagged complicit with these dirtbags, the Swiss and other European countries passed legislation that required proof of the account holder's identity. That's why the good padre needed impeccable proof of ownership—namely, the three certificates of incorporation. Fra Jero, I suspect, was the perfect—what did you call it— *treuhänder*, a trusted messenger beyond reproach."

"Poor Evan. If this has to go into our report, he'll be mortified. It could sink his bid for Executive Committee chairman. Most won't believe it, but others will speculate that he just might be complicit."

"Well . . . Tuck, one could argue that it's not germane to our specific undertaking and doesn't necessarily advance our inquiry into 'who done it.'"

"Good try, Watson, but I'm not sure about that. Although we don't have a scintilla of admissible evidence, I'd lay odds that Luc did it—motive plus opportunity. I'm betting that Luc killed Ben, Fra Jero, and, I fear, Andreas Amaroso. Ben wouldn't succumb to Luc's bribe. This was his *'private purgatory.'* I think he feared that Luc would kill him. He sensed *'an unkindness—a murder most foul.'* And he knew that La Moreneta—the Dark Lady—*'could not protect'* him from that."

"Tuck, you're good. Have you memorized the prec letter?"

I smiled. "I can recite it in my sleep.

"When Ben didn't blink, I suspect that Luc had no choice—kill him, kill the delivery boy, and kill Andreas, for good measure."

47

Viggie, with Drew and Nip, picked us up at Newark. Nip looked great, though she could have been a bit more animated to see me. Perhaps they were spoiling her. After obligatory rubs and licks, she settled in the back between Dixie and me. The trip to Mohonk Mountain House for the Executive Committee meeting would take a little more than two hours. The flight from Zurich was long. Fortunately Dixie and I had slept most of the way. Drew brought copies of our report along with her laptop and printer so she could quickly make changes. She had found a nearby bed-and-breakfast for the four of us. Mohonk Mountain House was not dog-friendly and definitely not associate-friendly, at least not that weekend, with a huddle of partners and a choke of clients present.

Not a day in the park for Dixie and Drew. Their professional lives might well have been compromised by this assignment. I would have to address that soon.

It seemed colder than it should be. It was still early November. Until now, autumn had been quite mellow and

soft. At least the foliage was cooperating. Its plumage was
dappled by the sunlight. The leaves remained firmly on the
trees, golden yellow with flashes of crimson and bronze, while
the undergrowth was still stubbornly green.

I remembered why I liked this place—the birds. Autumn
is the best time for watching them and the Mohonk Preserve
is perfect for that. Alice, the kids, and I would come here
once a year in the fall. We too had to settle for one of the
bed-and-breakfasts. Nip was always with us. The rooms were
quaint, a bit corny, and a little crowded for intimacy, but at
least four of the five of us loved it.

Fall was harvest time and the birds knew it.

Winter was coming. The rhythm and ritual of a bird's
life brook no delay. The jackdaws and herring gulls skittered
about without much purpose while the hawks, kestrels, and
crows were dogged in their efforts to take advantage of the
harvest. They were the smart ones.

Particularly the crows.

The air was bracing. The road was moist. There were snow
flurries dancing around, yet the sky was filled with birds. The
whir of their wings grew increasingly loud. Clearly they were
preparing to roost. Already hundreds had settled on the treetops. Their caws magnified their number. Frantic noisy dis-
plays like this are the hallmark of a crow gathering. Roosting
is not their normal daytime activity. They prefer to spend
most of their time at their home base sunbathing.

It's likely that the local farmers had turned over their fields
and unearthed a treasure trove of edible delights. A large con-
gregation would give them mutual protection from the night.

Tomorrow, quite likely, they would feast.

I was not looking forward to socializing with a squabble
of partners. This kind of event was difficult to take, even in
good times. And all eyes would be on me. What happens to

their largest client—their biggest feedbag? And how will it affect the upcoming Executive Committee succession election? Will Evan be advantaged or disadvantaged? The intrigue that plays out at these infrequent events rivals that attending the election of a new Pope.

And no divine intervention could be expected.

I fear God looks the other way when it comes to lawyers.

Dixie left me at the front entrance to the Mohonk Mountain House, promising to return in two hours with Drew to shuttle me down to the hotel in New Paltz where the annual meeting of Ozone's shareholders would be convened and where the Firm's Executive Committee would hear our report tonight. Drew would make the changes I penciled in and have copies ready for the Committee.

The sheer magic of the Mohonk Preserve always awes me. A tranquil and mysterious lake abuts a massive hodgepodge of architectural styles as ungainly as its Indian name. It is the culmination of the dream of Quaker twins, Albert and Alfred Smiley, who purchased the several hundred acres in the late nineteenth century. The hotel is an uncomfortable pairing of Victorian and Edwardian marvels intended to be reminiscent of the grand castles and chalets of Europe.

It was no Montserrat.

Its founders hoped it would become a sanctuary for those who shared the Quaker compassion for nature and Native Americans. Unfortunately today the mood of its guests, who come mostly from New York, is starkly opposite to the tranquility Mohonk aspired to.

Nevertheless even the stubborn eventually succumb to its spectacular solemnity.

I entered the main building, sucking up as much mountain air as I could, and made my way to the partners' welcome gathering in the Grand Hall, a high, wood-paneled room with a panoramic view of the lake and the comfort of a gigantic roaring fireplace. Big Law partners were at their worst at events like this. These partner gatherings were never relaxed. One did not come to blow off steam. Everything was moderated and manicured. No mojitos or champagne flutes. German beers acceptable. Good but not great wines were the drink of choice. A quick reflection on Woolly's warnings was advisable. Try not to laugh too loud at silly jokes; keep in your comfort zone or at least outside your paranoia zone. It was fine to dress to the manner born, but one had to be careful—not too-hip styling, no edgy fits, or British flair. If in doubt, fall back on your baggy blue blazer, a button-down shirt, and a rep tie.

The partners all seemed to have aged and enlarged in the three years since I'd seen most of them last. Success was settling in. Less hair, larger waistlines, and less interesting repartee were evident. I was sure that most had larger mortgages and bigger overdrafts, having moved on from their starter wives. They all, I'm also sure, had given up the weed and limited themselves to wine to stanch the constant stress of maintaining their billings. For many, these weekend retreats were welcomed in only one respect. No spouses invited, saving many from the harassment of husbands or the whine of wives.

Everything in moderation, except in the parking lot. Most of the partners are hooked on German metal.

Unfortunately my presence didn't go unnoticed for long. Lots of backslaps, knuckle-crushing handshakes, and shoulder rubs. No embraces. That would only bring unwanted attention. "How are you!" "How ya doing?" "Been too long!" "Hope to see more of you!" . . . the last being a recurring theme.

It was evident that I would be heartily welcomed back into the fold as a counterbalance to Evan. I would be a perfect candidate to take over the Ozone account. It was known that I was close to Dorothy, who many suspected didn't cotton to Evan. I looked for Evan, but he was nowhere to be seen. He was likely meeting with Luc and others, prepping for the board meeting.

Luc's vile plan to keep Ben from going off the reservation and Evan from freaking out might have backfired on him. Vile is not a strong enough word for a serial murderer of friends. I wonder how he treats his enemies. Ben's legacy in shambles; Evan's elevation to chairman about to collapse—the consequences of not-so-perfect blackmail.

Charlotte tapped my shoulder, ending my dark musing.

Ms. Williams—Charlotte to most of us—was her radiant, if not assured, self. Unlike most women partners, she made little attempt at neutering herself. No pantsuits or formless smocks to mute her gender. She was, as usual, the bright light in the room.

She had two new partners in tow. I recognized their names from the Firm's announcement of their elevation. Ex-partners remained on the Firm's mailing list for life. I extended congratulations. They feigned humility and wandered off.

"Tuck, how are you?" Charlotte inquired. "You look a bit tired. You OK?"

"Yes, just off the plane from Europe. I'm getting a little long in the tooth for all-nighters."

"Sorry to hear that!" she whispered with a wry smile, her double entendre not lost on me.

"You're reporting tonight. Right? How 'bout a little scoop?" she begged with a smile. "Tuck, the Firm is as tight as a drum. I fear that the tide is turning on Evan. He's proposed lots of changes that some of the partners find difficult. His arrogance continues to bug some partners. I'm afraid his lead is dwindling."

"Where is Evan, by the way?"

"Have you forgotten?" she smiled. "The election of a chairman is like a beauty contest. At the end you stop strutting your stuff. No late-game advantage can be gained by mingling with inebriates. I think Evan expects your report to give him the boost he needs."

"Well, he's going to be disappointed, sorry to say," I allowed. "We're coming up with a big 'beats us' when it comes to how Ben died. I better go. I have a car outside."

Dixie was standing at the door, clearly very agitated, frantically motioning me to his side. It must be very important. It was a cardinal sin for an associate to intrude into this conclave and Dixie knew better.

I ushered him into an anteroom, hoping his transgression had gone unnoticed.

"Sorry, Tuck, but you need to know this now. Frank Mack was able to cross-check our info with his existing files. Seems that members of Ozone's Executive Committee are required to list their banking references and accounts with the company and periodically update them. Frank ran them all down. What he came up with will floor you. Trombley has wired more than a million and a half dollars out of his supposed 'unknown blackmail account' in Zurich over the last three years."

Pausing to catch his breath, he said, "That can mean only one thing. Trombley is complicit. He's an accomplice of Luc's, not a victim!"

48

Dixie and I hastily returned to Ben's car, where Drew and Nip were waiting. Luc's gray SUV with black-tinted windows and no hint of dust or ding pulled up beside us. The window came down and Evan peered out. "Jonathan . . ."

An uncontrollable eruption of indignation over his larceny rose in my stomach. He'd violated every tenet of every oath that lawyers are bound by when he succumbed to Luc's rank payola. Evan had breached his allegiance to Ben, his oath to the Bar, and his obligation to the Firm.

I was unable to contain myself.

"We know about your Swiss account. That will be in our report."

"Jonathan, you're way off base. My accounts—wherever located—are all aboveboard and completely legal. I'm surprised you would suspect otherwise. I'm disappointed in you. For your information, that account represents the after-tax dollars from profitable investments. If you had concerns, you should have told me so in confidence, not blurted them out in public . . ."

Luc interrupted from the backseat. "Evan! This is a private matter. I told you Tucker and his asshole assistants were out of bounds again. I told you to remove them. You ignored that. Now I suggest you SHUT THE FUCK UP! Sandy, move out!"

As Luc's SUV drove off, everyone fell silent, lost in their respective self-doubts and recriminations. For Dixie and Drew, this was deeply embarrassing. Partners rarely argue in the presence of associates. Did I leap to the wrong conclusion? Did I not owe Evan at least a chance to explain? Wasn't that what I was just doing? Not really. I was accusing.

This was going to get messy.

I rolled my window down. The air was crisp; the sky was cloudless. The moon had not yet risen but served as a back light that made the night creatures more visible. I noticed the crows roosting on the treetops and outer branches. My hunch was right—a harvest roost.

"Everyone, look up. The crows are roosting. This is going to be a big one."

We all watched in awe.

Dixie attempted to break the uneasiness that embarrassed silence brings.

"Maybe they're having their annual meeting up here too."

"Personally, I find it a bit creepy!" Drew shuddered, hugging Nip tighter. "It's not like that Hitchcock movie, is it?"

"You're not going to go Tippi on us, are you?" Dixie added with a smirk.

We calmed our nerves with small talk and inanities. We were collectively giving our anxiety a time-out, but not for long.

"Oh, my God! What about our report? Do you want me to take out the info on Trombley?" Drew asked.

"No, don't redo it," I replied. "We just won't submit a written report. I'll wing it and let it all hang out. I'll drop this load of dung right on their table—including Trombley's accounts. Let the Executive Committee deal with it. Let them explain it to the SEC, the IRS, Justice, and the Bar Association. But first, I'd like you both to stall them. Tell them I'm tied up with Trombley. Serve them some factual hors d'oeuvres. Summarize the results of the interviews with the maid, the doctors, and the coroner. Feed them Abelard tidbits. Go easy on Kati, though; she's gotten close to Dorothy. I'll go see Trombley. I probably do owe him that. If he has a valid explanation for his Swiss cash account, I'll apologize."

What I really wanted to know was more about Alice's accident. I've never fully bought into the official version. She was too good a driver. I have tried to submerge that feeling, but it keeps bubbling up to the surface. If he told me more about how my family died, I would agree to omit his Swiss account from our report—a devil's pact, which later I would break. Fuck him! I didn't owe him anything. He might not have been the cause of their deaths, but he might well know something about what had happened. If he did, I'd destroy him.

49

As we began our descent into town, I noticed that the crows were surprisingly quiet.

From a roundabout on the edge of the road, Luc's car reemerged and drew menacingly up close behind us. Viggie stayed calm. He directed us to keep low and not to open the windows. As Luc's car drew abreast of us, it became clear that Sandino was intent on driving us off the road, sending us down the side of the mountain.

I tensed. Drew screamed. Dixie went white. Viggie went into action.

"*Bastardo,*" Viggie shouted as he turned our car into the side of Luc's. We traded glancing blows but the road favored Sandino. On their side the land was elevated; on ours there was a steep decline.

A brace of deer darted across the road. At the same time we heard an awesome clamour. The crows had taken flight and attacked Luc's car, pecking at its windows in a nightmar-ish frenzy. Drew hugged Nip hard. Viggie remained alert. His eyes were fixed on Sandino. His hands never left the steering wheel as he brought the car to an abrupt stop.

Sandino was no match. Startled by Viggie's maneuver, Luc's car pitched sharply, narrowly missing us, and slid down the mountain's side until it hit a granite mass.

The crash was deafening.

Viggie, Dixie, and I piled out of the car and ran down toward the wreck. We were stopped by Viggie's command. Drew had remained in the car with Nip. Viggie motioned Dixie and me to crouch down, as he unholstered a pistol he had carried under his sweater.

A body lay a few yards from the car. The passenger appeared to have jumped out as the car slid down. His eyes, rimmed with blood, were wide open, vacant—no trace of fear, remorse, or life. Farther down was Sandino—or, rather, part of him. His side window had shattered. His severed head landed on a bed of thistle. The rest of his body was a few feet away.

Viggie shouted, *"Pezzo di merda. Si bruciano all'inferno. Hai ucciso i miei padri!"* Roughly translated: "You piece of shit. May you go to hell . . . you killed my fathers."

I understood. The others did not. Sandino's clan had murdered Viggie's family. Then killing Ben took away his surrogate father. He spit at Sandino's corpse and silently crouched near the smoldering car. He shouted to us, "Stay down. Grogaman. He's not here. Others dead. He got away. Dixie, maybe you come with me. Mr. T, you stay with Drew and Nip. You know guns, yes?"

I nodded, confirming what he already knew. We had had many conversations about my four years in the marines.

"Under my seat, you find a pistol and bullets. Watch for Grogaman 'til we get back."

Dixie interrupted. "Hold on. Let me call Frank. If Grogaman has his phone on we'll be able to track him." He turned away, cupping his phone. Within a few minutes, he turned back.

"OK, we're in luck. Frank has tracked Grogaman's phone with his GPS app and he's also tracking my phone. Luc is moving north-northwest. He's about a quarter of a mile from here. One of Frank's people will call Drew so you guys can follow our search."

"OK, Viggie, we're off. Stay low and follow me." Dixie was taking command. Viggie did not resist.

I returned to the car and retrieved the pistol. Drew had already called 911. We sat and waited. Drew was ministering to Nip, who seemed to have recovered. Our wait was short. Drew's phone rang. It was Dixie.

They'd found Luc. He was dead. They suspect he fell off a ledge. Viggie would remain with the body. He had retrieved Luc's gun and phone and had given them to Dixie. Dixie arrived within a few minutes and put the guns and Luc's phone in Ben's car. Then we returned to inspect Luc's car.

Evan's body was there, his belt still secure. We had seen him before, and assumed he was dead. To our utter surprise, he was not. Blood had crusted on the side of his mouth and as I approached he began to speak, his voice a faint whisper. I leaned close.

"Ben was not supposed to die. I . . . only wanted to make him sick. He was going to ruin everything . . . Jonathan, I had nothing to do with your family's death. I swear . . . nothing to do with killing your family . . ."

He said no more. His head tilted; his eyes became opaque. He was dead.

Evan had killed Ben. An accident, he claimed. Alice, Lilli, and JJ's deaths NOT an accident. They were murdered.

I went limp.

I awoke to anxious questions.

"Yes, yes, I'll be OK."

Dixie and Drew didn't believe me.

"You're sure you're OK?" Dixie repeated.

"Really, I'll be fine."

Everybody fell silent again. Finally my breathing regulated, and I uttered, "I think we now know how Ben died."

Everyone then became animated. Nip's tail wagged at full swing. Theories abounded, followed by shock, surprise, and self-recriminations. "We should've known." "How did we miss it?" "Never liked him!" "Hope he burns in hell!"

And in the end we veered back to the mother lode. "Holy shit, wait 'til we tell the Firm!"

Nip turned and walked to the body of the young man whom we'd come across first. She knelt down and emitted a howl I had heard only once before, when my Lilli found Snowdrop dead at Twenty Acres.

It startled all of us.

Nip continued to direct her soulful ire at the corpse.

A solitary crow flew down, landing near her. He stood still, looking at the corpse, then turned toward us. Uttering a mighty caw, he flew away. As if on command, the hundreds of crows roosting in the trees above followed suit and took flight.

Their clamour was deafening.

A grim silence followed. Nip returned to my side and leaned heavily against my leg. It was finally broken by the wail of approaching sirens.

Too late; they were all dead—assassin, accomplice, aider, and abettor.

FOUR KILLED IN CRASH

OZONE INDUSTRIES SUFFERS ANOTHER TRAGIC LOSS

by PAUL J. HENNESSY

A month after the death of Ozone Industries founder L. Benjamin Baum, the firm suffered another major loss when his successor, Luc Grogaman, and two aides were killed last night in a traffic accident while traveling to the company's annual meeting in New Paltz, NY.

Also killed in the accident was Evan Trombley, Ozone's outside counsel and a senior partner of the prestigious New York law firm Winston Barr & Trombley.

Ozone Industries is an international private security, electronics and entertainment conglomerate based in NYC with assets estimated at $6 billion.

The accident reportedly occurred as the entourage was exiting Mohonk Mountain Preserve. Police records indicate the vehicle was traveling at a high rate of speed on wet roads, and apparently lost control after a minor collision with another car carrying additional Ozone advisers.

Another unusual circumstance surrounding the accident was a report by some neighbors that a large and noisy gathering of birds may have contributed to distracting the driver.

The four passengers suffered multiple injuries and were pronounced dead at St. Francis Hospital. The aides were not identified pending notification of relatives. The extent of their injuries led State Police to question whether all passengers were wearing seat belts at the time of the crash.

Grogaman had been honored in 2012 by the National Rifle Association with its Patriot Award.

The first statements by Ozone Industries and Mr. Trombley's law firm said only that funeral and memorial services have yet to be arranged.

50

The police report was somewhat more informative. The deceased were described as male Caucasians. Grogaman was listed as a forty-seven-year-old naturalized American citizen of Portuguese descent, Sandino as a forty-three-year-old Italian, and Trombley as a sixty-seven-year-old US citizen. The fourth was identified as thirty-seven-year-old Anton Berghov, a naturalized American citizen of Russian descent.

None had any known criminal record.

A number of items of interest were listed in the report. The car's trunk held a cache of sophisticated weapons in a retrofitted compartment that usually carried the spare tire, including two fully automatic assault weapons, several twenty-round magazines, and four collapsible steel truncheons. Additional small firearms were found on Messrs. Sandino and Grogaman. Wallets, jewelry, and medicines were being held pending retrieval by family members.

Ozone and the Firm eventually put out statements of bereavement. The Firm promised to keep the deceased in their thoughts and prayers. I couldn't vouch for the latter, but could for the former, especially since that would be billable.

More concrete actions occurred immediately.

The board of Ozone selected Dorothy as CEO the day of the accident. She immediately reduced the size of the board, cutting out the fainthearted and filling their positions with loyalists, at the same time introducing gender, racial, and ethnic diversity. Her biggest coup was inducing Russett to drop his takeover bid and join the board. Additionally she set about dismantling and liquidating ClearAire—not a short-term project and not without risk. The federal and state authorities were anxious to peek under that tent.

At the same time, she cleared up her family's loose ends and cleaned up some of its dirty laundry. Her evil stepmother was banished in style. For one hundred and fifty million dollars, paid in part by Dorothy, the Trust, and the foundation, Tremaine dropped her petition to contest Ben's Will and her efforts to become Ben's executrix and Leo's guardian. She resigned her position in the Family Trust and on the foundation's board, taking Abelard with her. In the process, she admitted under oath that little Bentley was not Ben's offspring. Lady Tremaine also agreed that neither she nor her son would use the Baum name and she released Ben's estate from any claims she had now or in the future. Even after the vile de Vil took his obscene 30 percent, Tremaine still cleared a tidy one hundred million.

Dorothy now stood alone as the CEO of Ozone. And possibly regent, for Eloise announced she was pregnant with twins. They decided to await the birth to learn the gender of the babies but they had already selected names—Benjamin and Andreas for boys, Ozma and Glinda for girls. In all four instances, Thompson would be the middle name.

Leo moved to a communal home in Paris populated with other similarly challenged young adults, where, according to Dorothy, he was the new guy on the block and loving every moment. He'd given up on Merlin; Casanova was his new role model. Eloise and Dorothy had placed him in the care of R. A. Stein, a renowned expert on adult autism who was a close friend of Eloise's when they both lived in London.

Kati's future was also looking up, thanks to Dorothy's largesse. She was living in Paris in an apartment on rue Furstenberg near Eloise and Dorothy. To better ensure that her brutish brother stayed away, Dorothy set up a ten million dollar trust for her, with Eloise as her trustee. Everyone was awaiting the results of Kati's paternity test, Terry having provided ample traces of Ben's DNA. Should it turn out that Ben was the father, Dorothy's new princes or princesses would have a half-sibling or, if you prefer, a half-aunt or half-uncle. Either way, Kati's baby would be a child with a bright future, but with no line to the throne or share of the Baum fortune. Eloise was looking forward to walks and play dates with Kati in the Tuileries, exchanging mommy moments and life experiences.

Meanwhile back at the Hobbit Hole, Dixie and Drew had hung their shingle—Benson & Dixon Associates, Private Investigative Attorneys. Returning to the Firm was not an option for them, and they were offered a deal they couldn't refuse. Terry gave them three years rent-free if they included Frank Mack and his team—a condition they enthusiastically embraced. Terry agreed to be the office housemother—working, however, only four days a week. But first, she wanted to take a quick trip back to high school in Kansas, to the store she and Ben bought and the hills where they first found romance. Then she would head down to Saint John's where the weather and lifestyle were always warm and welcoming.

To try to get away from the bad memories, I suspect, at least for a while.

Clients were no problem for the new firm. Ozone engaged them to help liquidate ClearAire, investigate Luc's transgressions, to put it politely, and just for the pleasure of it, pursue allegations of self-dealing as it related to Abelard. De Vil, not being a good lawyer, had failed to gain Peter a release for the foundation's questionable art purchases—a pawn that would have been easily traded in Dorothy and Tremaine's negotiations. Additionally Drew garnered a raft of assignments from Charlotte, including settling and administering Trombley's and Grogaman's estates. Neither had any heirs, but both had many legal matters to resolve. Luc had no will. Trombley had an elaborate estate plan, leaving his entire estate to Harvard Law School to endow a chair in his name for Professional Ethics and Responsibilities. Harvard declined, but New York State was less reticent, aggressively seeking his fortune by escheat.

Benson & Dixon Associates became so overloaded with work that they hired two associates away from the Firm. And to add a little gray hair, they retained me as senior legal counsel. It would help dress up their masthead, they claimed.

51

I was content to just laze in bed. Nip was sleeping. Heckle was pecking at the window. Nip just rolled over, ignoring him. She wasn't taking orders from a bird—much less a crow. There she was mistaken.

I gave in and grabbed Heckle's saltine fix, putting it out on the porch table. He would never take it from my hand. Rather he swooped down, his dark brown eyes meeting mine, and grabbed his breakfast, flying off to a welcoming branch. I'm convinced that he was the one who came down to us at Mohonk. I'll never share that with anyone, lest they start wondering about me.

The truth is I'm happy with my secret and delighted to feed him.

The ringing phone caught my ear and I scurried back. It was Dixie and he was out of breath too.

"Tuck, late-breaking news on several fronts. Have you had your java yet? This is heady stuff."

He didn't wait for my response.

"Frank Mack just called. He's hit pay dirt. Since we now have unfettered access to ClearAire's files and computers, thanks to Dorothy, it's been clearer sailing. Every expenditure is at our fingertips.

"Let's start with Sandino. He bought a one-way ticket to Orlando the day before your family was killed. The next day he rented a black van from Avis at the airport, dropped it in long-term parking that afternoon, and flew back to Washington that night. The car was retrieved and returned to Avis twenty days later. The checkout receipt indicated a charge for damages to the front right side and bumper. Too many coincidences, Tuck. I believe he is the one who drove your family into the concrete abutment, killing them."

I fell silent.

As did Dixie.

The circle had closed. It all made sense.

Luc, I suspect, had been afraid that I wouldn't relent until I was satisfied that Ben had no interest in the Cerberus account. He must have been nervous I would trip over the truth. It was his way of chasing me off. Didn't matter to him if they were killed or just injured. I would have taken leave from the Firm to tend to them, and by the time I returned, the matter would have been over and Evan would have reassigned me to projects unrelated to ClearAire.

"Should I go on, Tuck?"

"Is there more?"

"Yes, much more.

"The night Nip was hit, Berghov, the Russian, took the shuttle from Washington to New York and shuttled back late the same night. The New Paltz police reports showed an address in Queens. They found it in his wallet. With that, Mack trolled the Net and discovered that Berghov had a motorcycle license. One of our paralegals went out to Queens and peeked in his garage. Sitting there was a shiny black cycle. He e-mailed me the iPhone image and it's like the one that came at us near the UN. Can't be certain, but it sure as hell looks like it. Put that together with the steel truncheons the police found in Luc's car and it adds up to the Nip attack!

"It gets better—or worse, perhaps. I don't mean to be flip. I know this is serious stuff. Charlotte was able to get an interim letter of administration for Trombley's estate. Armed with that, Drew gained entrance to his apartment. She needed ready access to his bank statements, tax files, checkbooks, art inventory, insurance policies, safe-deposit box key, and his Precatory Letter, if one existed—God forbid. All the normal probate stuff. According to Trombley's secretary, he kept all his personal papers at home. After an unsuccessful search, Drew wandered into his dressing room, which, according to her, was 'big enough to live in.' She found a locked door behind the sliding shirt racks. She had a set of his keys, which Evan's secretary had given her. She opened the wardrobe door and found a secret closet that she said would make Victoria jealous. Evan was a closet cross-dresser!

"He's our very own J. Edgar. Go figure.

"And then his closet got really interesting. He was very neat, almost 'anally neat'—Drew's words. There were drawers and drawers of bank statements, bearer shares, gold certificates, zero coupon bonds, cash in three different currencies, even gold bars and what Drew thinks was his high school stamp collection. I'm guessing priceless rare stamps. They're as good as gold and easier to negotiate. She has our associates taking an inventory. So far, it totals fifteen million . . . and they're not even halfway through."

I had no response.

Even Dixie dropped his patented repartee as we each tried to process this discovery.

"Dixie, I'm going to have to get back to you. Where will you be? I need to get some clear air."

Damn, I have to stop using that phrase.

"I understand, Tuck. I'm on my way to join Drew at Trombley's apartment. Call me back on the encoded phone. You still have that?"

"Yes. I suggest that you not share this with the Firm—at least not yet."

"Tuck, you sure you're all right?"

"Yes . . . and no. I've always felt that Alice's crash was not an accident. Now I know and I need some time to process it."

"I understand. Call us if you need anything."

Technically my assignment was over. I'd slid over to another firm—with roles reversed. I was counsel—that's a euphemism for aging associate—and Drew and Dixie were my bosses.

I smiled. They were less toxic than my previous one.

"Nip, out! I need some beach time."

No argument from her, but we didn't make it to the door. My ring tone was starting to really annoy me. I hated that tune. Time for a change. But, of course, I answered it. I thought I was cured. Three years in self-imposed solitary should have broken the habit.

It was Charlotte. Animatedly she fast-forwarded past the "how are yous" and announced triumphantly that she had just become the newest, youngest, first, and only female member of the Firm's Executive Committee. Her first assignment was to invite me back to the partnership in a senior status. I would head Ozone's corporate affairs. She droned on about the opportunities and excitement that lay ahead, pausing only to tell me that the Firm had dropped Trombley's name from the masthead—part of the streamlining and updating of its visuals.

The conversation then turned personal. She suggested that we could now find some quiet time together. Between the lines, she made it clear that she did not want to share her billing as much as she did her bed.

I declined both. I had lost my lust for Big Law, and was never into polyamory. I still have my first love.

Charlotte's will always be the Firm.

52

The holidays were upon us. For the first time in a long time, Nip and I would be celebrating Christmas. We were hosting a lunch the day before at Twenty Acres for our medley of munchkins. Viggie had already left to fetch Drew and her mother. They'd be loaded down with all the traditional goodies. Dixie and his new best friend were also coming, and would be laden with additional holiday cheer.

The only one missing was Terry, who was off on her long-delayed and well-deserved vacation.

And a cornucopia of presents had arrived from Paris. I didn't wait 'til Christmas to open them. Pounds of Swiss chocolates, Lindt and Sprüngli, of course, seventy-eight porcelain ornaments of the birds of Christmas, and four pairs of silver slippers with their patented yellow brick soles. Dorothy also asked me to alert the team that she was going to make an honest woman of Eloise. The wedding would be in March—at the Plaza, of course—and we would all be invited.

"Nip, we have to go into town. The shelter called. Someone dropped off a baby Lab and didn't ask for a receipt. Must have been the Grinch. It's not right to spend Christmas in a crate. Think of all the wrapping paper he could shred. Besides, you could use a little chaos in your life."

One thing was clear. We wouldn't be talking about Ozone at lunch. That assignment was over, all the villains laid bare—and dead. The Russian, I suspect, was an acolyte in evil, cutting his teeth by menacing dogs and harassing innocents. Sandino was a serious step up—a killer of children and women. I had always thought it best not to know the perpetrator of the Orlando incident. No specific person to hate. I was wrong. You end up hating everyone and everything. Luc Grogaman was uncomplicatedly venal, devoid of conscience, contrition, or remorse.

He was the architect of all this evil.

Or so I once thought. I might well have been wrong. That crown may belong to my past mentor and champion—the "venerable" Evan Trombley. With what has been unearthed to date, I'm now betting on him. Grogaman may not have been clever enough. Trombley had it all—the smarts, the cover of respectability, the ear of the Wiz, the keys to Ben's kingdom, and, like Tolkien's greedy and wicked dragon, most of the gold.

Grogaman would have been an easy recruit for Trombley. He had no moral alarm system, no ethical grounding to fend off Trombley's evil offer. Trombley's master plan? Straightforward—knock off Ben, and magnanimously accept the Ozone board's invite to be the interim CEO and regent to Dorothy, who, he would have argued, needed a few more years of seasoning to succeed him. In the meantime, he would continue to hoard his cache of ill-gotten gains and plot his retirement to Zurich, beyond the reach of the US authorities.

Evan's villainy apparently had no limits. I could easily have been in the car with Alice, if I returned to drive my family back as any decent husband and father would have done. He must have factored that in. To him I was expendable. If all he ever intended was to give his best friend Ben serious indigestion, as he alleged, why would he have sat by in the copilot's seat of Grogaman's car hell-bent on sending me and my team to our destruction? Grogaman was simply Trombley's field commander, his CEO—chief execution officer—an equal in wickedness but a subordinate in deviousness.

Ben must have sensed that something was seriously amiss. Fra Jero likely wilted under his persuasive charm during Ben's first visit to Barcelona and he then learned, for the first time, that one of those Swiss accounts was his. The rest—Grogaman's and Trombley's involvement—was most likely revealed by the not-so-good father on Ben's second visit, the day before he died. It was probably only then that Ben learned of Trombley's secret Swiss account. Armed with a handful of damning deposit slips, Ben must have sought Trombley out, thinking that they both were being set up for blackmail by Grogaman. Fearing that Ben would have soon realized that he was not an innocent victim, Trombley simply killed him with his own wizard's brew.

Toxicity reports from the New Paltz police showed traces of marijuana in all the crash passengers except Trombley. His showed more than a trace of nitroglycerin. Drew found Trombley's medical papers and consulted with his doctors. He suffered from severe angina. His doctors said he was managing it well. He had stacks of nitro in his apartment in various forms—pills, vaporizers, and drops.

Ben, it turns out, was taking powerful medicines for his cancer, along with a bundle of thrill pills to complement his regime of Mr. Blues, according to Kati. She confessed that he was having some problems in that regard.

I think Trombley spiked Ben's drink with nitro drops. When you add that to Ben's other pills, you have a helluva lethal cocktail.

Potent enough to make him worse than sick.

If my hypothesis is right, Trombley used me, duped me, and betrayed me, and, in the process, was ultimately responsible for the death of my family and the attempted murder of my dog.

He broke every one of the principles he so sanctimoniously preached. Trombley was my boss, my mentor, my tormentor. Yet, as demanding and supercilious as he could be, he was also my rabbi and my surrogate father—stern and demanding but deep down supportive.

Wrong, so wrong. That was my template, not his.

His betrayal simply to harvest more pieces of gold is the hardest blow to absorb. You finally come to realize who really matters, who never did, and who always will. Trombley may not have been evil in any epic sense. He seemed unquestionably normal to those of us around him, which is why his villainy is so hard to process.

And what about Ben? According to his doctor, he knew he was on a long march to death. Perhaps that excuses his bitter resistance to Dorothy's and Leo's needs. That and his maniacal quest for a male heir. He must have known about or at least suspected Grogaman's depravity and, in the very end, Trombley's complicity. *"Those problems are my private purgatory. I have among me people who have no shame . . . I can taste their disappointments at my impending actions. Yet I have done things, ignored things, and excused things that were wrong."* Was he not telling us as much in his Precatory Letter?

He was, I think, in his heart a good man.

In his soul, he was more complex. Compared to the criminality of the hedgehogs, oiligarchs, media moguls, web manipulators, and brokerage bandits, Ben was a distant poor cousin. Except for Terry and Amaroso, and perhaps Russett, he had no close friends. He was forced to create his own virtual sidekicks and he found them in fantasy literature. And once there, I suspect, he deluded himself. The sad fact is that Ben never got to live a life that resembled the stories he so revered.

There still remain loose ends, questions unanswered, and amends not made. Investigations like this don't get neatly wrapped up. That only happens in network shows and bad novels.

What's next for me? Winston Barr it's not. It's only a matter of time before some government grunt—the SEC, the FBI, the IRS, Justice—realizes something is not kosher and slowly pieces it together. Then all hell will break loose. "Recently deceased Lion of the Bar turns out to be a mega-thief." Once that happens, the scramble to the exit will be immediate. The Firm's heavy billers will scurry off to those competitors whose ports offer safer harbors. Over time, the Firm will sink, drowning in irrelevance and bankruptcy.

I'm not up for that. Twenty Acres is all the fairy tale I need. I'm going to see if I can make a go of it there. And Viggie's moving in—perfect timing with Terry off on her trip. He loves it. It reminds him of his nonno's place in Pescia. He's already converted the kids' playhouse into a working cottage—with a tabletop stove, a small fridge, a pull-down bed, insulation, and a heater just in case. He's even pirated my cable line so he can watch his beloved soccer. He's only there Thursday through Sunday. Monday through Wednesday he's working for Drew and Dixie. I don't charge him rent, but insisted that he take conversational English at the high school every Saturday. He's loving it. He enjoys making new friends, especially the female kind, and, I suspect, he is trying to make our new pup his own Nip.

My position on the ladder of life may go down a few rungs, but I'm kind of looking forward to that. Alice's "accident" tailed me like a faithful dog. I took the Baum assignment to lose that tail as best I could.

Am I happy? Hard to say. Happy endings are often transitory. Forgiveness is supposed to mitigate past pain and unblock the future. I'm not sure I'm there yet. So what do I believe in? For now the company of animals, the earth beneath my feet, and the sand between my toes.

That's all I really want now—and it's definitely what I was yearning for. Sometimes the very best gifts are those you already possess.

For just a moment I felt at peace. Surprising, given what had recently transpired. That's when it came to me: there *was* one other thing I wanted for Christmas—to forget about Evan Trombley and Luc Grogaman, and even Ben Baum, at least for a while. Nip gave me a curious glance as I stood there motionless. A feeling of contentment that I hadn't enjoyed for a long time returned.

53

Christmas Eve lunch was by all objective accounts a success. Everyone was relaxed and friendly, but there remained a sense of unease. I think we all felt the absence of children. The new yet unnamed pup kept everyone amused and a few hours later, the party ended. Nip and I then went for a walk, leaving our new friend asleep in his crate.

The winter afternoon sun cast a different light on the world. With no moisture to diffuse its rays, it penetrated everything in its path. The shells herded together by the tides showed off their deep purple underbellies and the ice-encrusted sea grass appeared bronzed. The sand at water's edge was still brittled by the morning's frost, yet the green water seemed mellow as the moon started to rise.

It was good to be alone again.

Tolkien had it right. My journey has not ended. I'm still following Bilbo's footsteps, trying to walk out of the dark orbit of my past. To do that I need Nip. She is a necessity, not an accessory. She is a proficient griever, always awaiting homecomings that will never be, sniffing for scents that are no longer there. Yet she is healing me.

Whatever happens, in this place of ours, we will always be searching.

Perhaps this sad riddle is best for me.

As I walked along the beach that afternoon, I was trying to roll back the rain-gray curtain of my life. I was starting to see things more clearly.

Our walk ended and we took off for town. We now had one last thing to do. As we drove over the bridge, the sun momentarily darkened as clouds passed and the wind let up. The ships in the harbor, having been washed all day by the sun, were happy, I suspect, to return to the serenity of soft sounds and the medley of smells that a calm sea brings.

The village, hoary with age and heavy with history, was alight for Christmas. Soon the stars would be out and the three lights of Orion's Belt—Alnitak, Alnilam and Mintaka— would shine the brightest. I'd long since renamed them Alice, Lilli, and JJ.

"Nip, we're going to see Alice and the kids."

That she understood, her tail vibrating with anticipation.

"It's time to say good-bye . . . and hello."

EPILOGUE

"How could you! You've done some crazy things over the years, but this tops them all! Do you know how much I grieved for you, the pain I felt . . ." Terry's words dissolved into tears.

"Tereza, I had no choice. I had to protect you. You have always been my love—my much better half," Ben whispered in her ear. "I'm sorry I deceived you, but to do otherwise would have put you at great risk. I can explain it all."

Terry took a deep breath and with a somewhat firmer voice uttered, "This better be good."

"There was no real alternative. Luc was even more rotten than I thought. For the longest time I tried to ignore my concerns, but I finally realized that he was as evil as I feared. That became clear to me on my visits to the Spanish priest. I had befriended him with large contributions to his Basque brotherhood. Independence was the only miracle he prayed for. With that money and plentiful portions of the finest port I could buy, I loosened his reserve. He thought that I was privy to the part he played in helping Luc—as he put it—bury money in the mountains of Switzerland. He presumed I knew the drill: numbered accounts for Luc, myself, and—to my utter shock and disgust—Evan! My two closest allies—men I was dependent on and beholden to—were rank crooks. Luc, I understood. He had no scruples or conscience. Apparently he was able to siphon off millions from ClearAire's clients and suppliers and direct that money through the priest to Swiss accounts in our names. Trombley, I then realized, must be his accomplice. The monies allocated to me were a small price to pay to ensure my silence. They knew I would not destroy Ozone to save my name—even if I could. In fact I was afraid they had already destroyed it. Their larceny would not have remained a secret for long. Somebody or something would crack and the SEC, Interpol, or Justice would eventually figure it out. There seemed to be no way to keep this from being discovered even if I turned them in. Ozone couldn't survive the investigation that would follow. I would have had to spend the rest of my short life in the company of lawyers, accountants, and spin doctors. And you would have been called as a prime witness! You would have no privileges. You would have had to testify against me. It was then that I realized I would have to fake my death, hoping that Grogaman and Trombley could weasel their way out of this without destroying the company."

"But how did you . . . the funeral . . . how did you pull that off?"

"With the help of my London doctor and a large dose of good luck. Over the years I had befriended the hotel's doctor. He turned out to be an interesting character. He had a small clinic in London to minister to the homeless, where he spent his time when he was not at the hotel. What he really dreamed of was to leave his job at the hotel and head off to Tanzania to open a free clinic, where his father had been a missionary.

That, however, required substantial monies—well beyond his reach. So with Andreas's help, I forwarded him three million dollars. Then together we plotted my 'untimely demise.' He came to my room, sedated me on a gurney, pronounced me dead, and personally escorted me to his clinic's ambulance. It was parked in the hotel's garage, where Andreas and the cadaver of one of his recently deceased clinic patients were waiting. I was quickly revived. Andreas had brought appropriate clothes and he and I exited the ambulance a few blocks from the hotel. We then took a cab to Saint Pancras, the Eurostar to Paris, the train to Marseille, and a flight to Saint Thomas, where I took refuge on this boat. Andreas had purchased and outfitted it, and personally picked the crew and captain—all loyal, devoted, and exceptionally well-paid Italians. The boat is registered to a Liechtenstein company whose ownership is impossible to trace. Andreas remained with me most of the time. It seems Luc had put a price on his head.

"Back to my demise, the good doctor—armed with a letter from me requesting cremation, just in case he needed it—had little trouble moving my 'corpse' through the coroner's office and into the funeral home that handled the cremation and 'burial at sea,' which I understand was usually accomplished by flushing the ashes into the Thames. What we weren't counting on was the accident that killed Grogaman, Trombley, and their henchmen. That was a sweet bonus, I must admit, and I'm amazed but not surprised how well Dorothy handled all this and saved the company. I shouldn't be . . . she is, after all, my daughter! And I hear that Leo is doing better and Viggie is too."

"Ben . . . can I still call you that?"

"Yes, but I have a new identity—thanks to Andreas. I'm Benedict Lyman now. Best to keep the same first name, I'm told. And as to the hair—or lack thereof—I decided on a new look."

"I wasn't going to ask. I thought it might be the effects of chemo."

"No, nothing like that! In fact Andreas has found a clinic in Switzerland that is working on new protocols for what I have. I'm waiting my turn for treatment. It's not a cure, but it can extend life significantly."

"That's such wonderful news. I have so many questions, my mind is racing. How did you find me?"

"Andreas called Viggie. He gave him your itinerary. Once Andreas told me Saint John's, I knew where you were. We had some great times at that little hotel. It seems like a century ago.

"So here is my proposal. Stay here with me. You can come and go as you please. The boat will winter down here and summer in Europe. And it comes well-stocked. It has all our favorite books. Are you game?

"And there's one more thing. Will you marry me?"

THE END

ACKNOWLEDGMENTS AND ATTRIBUTIONS

This story is a fictional saga, and as such is indebted to some of the giants of that trade. L. Frank Baum (1856–1919) was the American grand master of children's literature. Best known for *The Wonderful Wizard of Oz,* he wrote fifty-five other works of fantasy literature for children to enjoy. Ben Baum of *Clamour of Crows* is wholly imagined and my hope is that readers understand that this creation was not intended to cast any aspersion on L. Frank Baum's or his family's stellar reputation.

Lewis Carroll (1832–1898) and J.R.R. Tolkien (1892–1973) need no introduction. Carroll was a genius—as a mathematician, photographer and logician—but is probably best remembered as the author of *Alice's Adventures in Wonderland* and its sequels. Tolkien, along with Carroll, is England's greatest fantasy writer. *The Hobbit, The Lord of the Rings,* and *The Silmarillion* are classics.

These three authors are the "happy trinity" of children's fantasy books that served as the "gospels" to the fictional Ben

Baum. As a tribute to them and others that followed, I have used throughout this book references to their stories and the names of their characters, as well as references to other great writers and their works—Carlo Collodi's *Pinocchio*, Roald Dahl (the character Dahlgrens, the Zurich bank's keeper of the keys), Ludwig Bemelmans's *Madeline* (the character Sister Clavel), and Kay Thompson's *Eloise* books (Eloise Thompson). Those characters in *Clamour of Crows* again are wholly imagined and bear no resemblance to any persons, living or dead.

Some other borrowed and appropriated characters' names: Drew is derived from Nancy Drew, the fictional heroine in Edward Stratemeyer's juvenile mystery series. Dixie is derived from Franklin W. Dixon, the pseudonym of the author of *The Hardy Boys*. The names Nip and Tuck come from a 1927 children's book by Muriel Moscrip Mitchell about two beaver kits who lived and played in the woods on their own. Charlotte Williams (née Cavatica) was borrowed from the children's novel *Charlotte's Web*, written by E. B. White and illustrated by Garth Williams. Charlotte A. Cavatica is the name of the spider. Lerot and Lapin, Abelard's friends, refer to the Dormouse and the Mad Hatter, Lewis Carroll's creations. Tremaine's namesake is Lady Tremaine, Cinderella's evil stepmother. Heckle and Jeckle are named after the postwar animated cartoon characters created by Paul Terry. Snowdrop, the slain albino deer, was named after Alice's white kitten in Lewis Carroll's book.

The illustrations in the book deserve acknowledgment. The interior frontis and recto pages are details from an ancient Japanese Edo Period (1615–1665) crow screen owned by the Seattle Art Museum.

My depiction of the Firm's lawyers is purely fictional. In fact, in my personal experiences, lawyers for the most part are a likable lot. In my time as an associate, none caused me serious agita, but many caused me sleep deprivation. And most of the lawyers as well as the clients I worked with exhibited the highest standards of integrity and professionalism. As with all things in life, however, there are exceptions, and the same goes for the clergy.

Many helped enhance *Clamour of Crows*. Special thanks go to Paula Glatzer for her enthusiastic support and her enviable attention to detail, to Marie Lillis for her patience and precision in turning my difficult script into type, to Caleb Cain Marcus who so deftly navigated me through the book's layout and design, to Stephanie Fleetwood for her candor and perception, and to Cathy McCandless and her proofreading team for their extraordinary genius.

I am grateful for the support of all my friends, especially those who read the book in its various drafts and offered perceptive comments and corrections.

And finally, to my wife, Carol, my best friend, my biggest fan and my harshest critic, for her patience, sacrifice, and love. She has always had my back and my love.

RWM